What was it that he wanted from Hazel? Jess asked himself.

It had to be more than her ability to make him see himself in gentler, more accepting ways. More than the knack she had of making him want to smile when she smiled and laugh when she laughed. Damn it, it had to be more complicated than that, he told himself. Nothing could be that simple.

He touched the scarred flesh of his shoulder and side. His body was familiar territory to him now—one side the same as ever, the other irreversibly damaged. Like Jekyll and Hyde, he thought.

He'd heard the words, felt the stares. He'd accepted his ugliness, because he'd had no choice.

But a woman as bright and pretty and sexy as Hazel O'Connor had a world of choices. What on God's green earth made him think she might want *him?*

Dear Reader,

There's lots of exciting stuff for you in the Intimate Moments line this month, starting off with Linda Turner's *Gable's Lady*. This American Hero title is also the first of Linda's new miniseries, The Wild West. Set on a ranch in New Mexico, it's the saga of the Rawlings family, whose children are named after movie stars. It's no secret where Gable got his name—and in the future you can look for *Cooper, Flynn* and sister *Kat*. You'll love them all.

We're starting another miniseries this month, too: Romantic Traditions. Each Romantic Traditions title will be written by a different author and will put an Intimate Moments spin on one of your favorite romance plots. This month Paula Detmer Riggs offers up a marriage of convenience in *Once Upon a Wedding*. In months to come, look for Marilyn Pappano's *Finally a Father* (a secret-baby book), Carla Cassidy's *Try to Remember* (amnesia) and more.

We've also got another new author featured in a reprise of last year's successful "Premiere" promotion. Her name's Kylie Brant, and her irresistible book is called *McLain's Law*. All this, plus new books from Heather Graham Pozzessere, Lindsay Longford and Marilyn Cunningham. It's another don't-miss month from Intimate Moments.

Enjoy!

Yours,

Leslie Wainger
Senior Editor and Editorial Coordinator

ONCE UPON A WEDDING

A WEDDING

Paula Detmer Riggs

Silhouette® INTIMATE MOMENTS®

Published by Silhouette Books New York

America's Publisher of Contemporary Romance

SILHOUETTE BOOKS
300 East 42nd St., New York, N.Y. 10017

ONCE UPON A WEDDING

Copyright © 1993 by Paula Detmer Riggs

ISBN: 0-373-07524-3

First Silhouette Books printing October 1993

PAULA DETMER RIGGS

discovers material for her writing in her varied life experiences. During her first five years of marriage to a naval officer, she lived in nineteen different locations on the West Coast, gaining familiarity with places as diverse as San Diego and Seattle. While working at a historical site in San Diego she wrote, directed and narrated fashion shows and became fascinated with the early history of California.

She writes romances because "I think we all need an escape from the high-tech pressures that face us every day, and I believe in happy endings. Isn't that why we keep trying, in spite of all the roadblocks and disappointments along the way?"

For Barbara and Alfonso Covarrubias—
for the warm hospitality
and affection.

Muchas gracias

Prologue

Indianapolis, Indiana
Memorial Day

Jess Dante figured he was a dead man. He'd hit the wall at 200 mph, and the car was a twisted, crumpled wreck. Jagged metal impaled his shoulder, gouging deeper with every breath he took.

Flames were everywhere, searing his skin through the protective clothing that was now beginning to singe. Men wearing fire-fighting moon suits and drenched in fire-extinguishing foam struggled to tear the mangled wreckage that used to be a multimillion dollar race car away from the Speedway's west wall.

Jess wanted to tell them not to bother. Too many years of living on the edge had finally caught up with him. If he didn't bleed to death, shock would kill him.

He was already shuddering from the cold, and his vision was blurred. The pain in his shoulder and chest was beyond bearing, yet he struggled to remain conscious, desperate to experience the last few seconds of his life.

From somewhere far away he heard sirens wailing and voices screaming. Hands reached into the ruined cockpit, frantic to free him before the fuel tank exploded.

Jess screamed a warning, but it was too late. Something tore in his shoulder. Flesh ripped and bone splintered. By the time he was lifted from the car, he no longer had a right arm.

Chapter 1

Fourteen years later.

Child psychologist Hazel O'Connor was pleased. After six weeks of therapy, five-year-old Jimmy Bryan was finally making progress. Using dolls to represent the members of his family had been the key.

"And who's this, Jimmy?" she asked, holding up a doll clearly representing an adult male.

"Daddy."

Hazel shifted position in the small seat. The playhouse in one corner of her office was an effective aid to play therapy, but it was murder on her back.

"How's Daddy feeling today?" she asked.

"Don't know."

Hazel placed the "Daddy" doll close to Jimmy's hands and plucked another from the table. "Who's this?"

The doll was dressed in jeans and a T-shirt and was designed to represent a boy of five or six.

Jimmy grinned. "That's me. Jimmy!"

"How about if we do some pretending?" Hazel handed Jimmy the "Daddy" doll, then picked up "Jimmy."

"I'll be you, and you be Daddy, okay?"

Jimmy nodded. As he did, his small shoulders seemed to grow tense, and his expression approximated a man's stern scowl.

A colonel in the air force, Jimmy's father demanded spit-and-polish neatness, so for years Jimmy had obediently lined up his toys in the same rigid way every night before going to bed, becoming hysterical if any of them was moved.

His father also demanded military standards of courtesy, so, from the time he'd outgrown the babbling stage, Jimmy rarely spoke unless spoken to by an adult first.

By the time he'd appeared in Hazel's office, referred to her by his pediatrician because of an inexplicable weight loss, the undersize boy had become more robot than child.

After the first few sessions it seemed clear that Jimmy was reacting to his father's obsessive control by refusing to eat—a child's version of passive resistance. The goal now was to break that passive/aggressive cycle.

"Daddy, I would like to give you a hug today," she murmured, her naturally husky voice pitched as high as a child's.

"Hugs are for girls, not men." Jimmy always strained for a deeper voice when he spoke for "Daddy." He also barked out orders to the other dolls like Hazel's idea of a drill sergeant.

"But I like hugs," she protested, holding up the "Jimmy" doll for the boy to see.

"I said no!"

Suddenly Jimmy threw "Daddy" against the wall, where the rag doll lay inert and crumpled. At the same time, Jimmy shot from his chair and stomped on the doll's head.

Hazel spent the next ten minutes discussing Jimmy's feelings about what he'd done. When it was clear Jimmy couldn't handle any more that day, she walked him to the door.

Before she opened it, however, she dropped to her knees, so the two of them were eye to eye.

"How about a hug?"

Jimmy nodded shyly, and she pulled him into her arms for her version of a bear hug. He kept his arms at his sides and his body stiff, but she counted the mere fact that he agreed to the small gesture of affection as progress.

"See you next week," she said as she rose to her feet and opened the door.

In the small, cheerfully appointed waiting room, Jimmy's mother was already on her feet. "Same time next week, Mrs. Bryan?" Hazel asked when their eyes met.

Like most psychologists, she preferred working without a secretary. It seemed more personal, somehow, when she made her own appointments and returned her own calls.

"We'll be here."

Hazel watched mother and son walk out before she allowed her gaze to shift to the clearly adult, clearly masculine and decidedly unexpected visitor sprawling comfortably in one of her chairs reading a *Junior Scholastic*.

Her heart gave an extra beat and refused to settle. She hadn't seen Jess Dante since "their" godson, Jesse Mc-Clane, had celebrated his fourth birthday six months earlier.

Wide of shoulder and long of leg, the rangy defense attorney was dressed in a conservative gray suit instead of his usual jeans and rumpled corduroy jacket, which meant that he'd been in court earlier.

Now, however, his neon tie hung askew, and he'd unbuttoned the collar of his white dress shirt. His rebellious black hair also showed signs of a rough day, plowed into unruly furrows by his strong, clever fingers.

"Can I help you with something, little boy?" she asked in her best prissy therapist's voice.

Dante finished the sentence he'd been reading before he tossed aside the magazine and looked up. It was electric, the invisible shiver that ran under her skin whenever her gaze touched his.

"Yo, O'Connor, how's it going?" Jess had been reared on a cattle ranch near Placerville and had a lazy whiskey-and-honey drawl just right for wooing jurors to his way of thinking. Or women to his bed.

Other women, Hazel reminded herself. She and Jess were friendly acquaintances, nothing more.

"I heard you were in L.A. adding another chapter to your reputation as a legal maverick," she teased.

His mouth took on a half shy, half devilish slant, Dante's version of a smile. His teeth were very white and very straight, except for one crooked eyetooth that gave his smile a certain wicked appeal.

"Hacking off the establishment, you mean."

"Undoubtedly, and something tells me you love it."

He stood and came toward her in one economical movement of muscle and bone. Taller than most, with an extremely well-developed chest and shoulders and the strength to match, Jess was a natural athlete, which had helped him learn to compensate for the loss of his dominant hand.

Emotionally, however, he still carried traces of bitterness that he worked to keep hidden from all but his closest friends.

Hazel had seen the bitterness and flashes of a fierce frustration, as well, mostly when he was faced with the unexpected or untried.

"I tried calling," he said as he brushed her cheek with his mouth in a greeting she'd long ago accepted as completely platonic. His olive skin was rough from a day's growth of beard, shadowing a jaw that was just shy of square. "Your service said you were in session."

"It's been a busy day, and it's not over yet."

"Can you spare a few minutes for Jesse's godfather? It's important," he declared when she hesitated. "Or I wouldn't ask."

"I can spare..." Pausing, she consulted her watch. "Seven and a half minutes, but who's counting, right?"

She led the way into her office, conscious that Jess had never been there before. Nor had she been in his, a former brothel in a historical building in Old Sacramento.

They'd met nearly five years ago outside a hearing room at Children's Protective Services when Jess was trying to secure temporary visitation rights for his client, Dr. Tyler McClane, a prominent pediatric surgeon falsely convicted of molesting his own daughter. Hazel had been representing the emotional interests of her then patient, Tyler's daughter, Kelsey.

She'd noticed the confident set of Jess's big shoulders and the smoldering intelligence in his deep brown eyes before she'd noticed the empty sleeve of his suit coat and the dangerous line of his hard mouth.

The chemistry between them had been instantaneous and volatile—a man for woman and woman for man connection that had literally taken her breath away.

By the time she'd discovered that Jess was exactly the kind of brooding, cynical, emotionally scarred man she'd spent half a lifetime avoiding, she'd been hopelessly smitten.

He, too, had seemed to sense the spark between them—but during the next few weeks, as they'd gotten to know each other better, the slow, mesmerizing burn in his eyes had changed to cool indifference. In fact, he'd worked hard at showing her just how uninterested he was.

Hazel had been mystified and hurt—until her friend and his, Cait McClane, had explained that a messy divorce in his distant past had turned Jess into an avowed bachelor.

The more he was attracted to a woman, the more he avoided her, Cait had insisted. But Hazel suspected her insistence was more to soothe her friend's badly dented ego than because it was true.

"How'd the case go?" she asked as she seated herself behind her less-than-orderly desk.

Tired after a long day that had started at seven with a new and difficult referral from a colleague, she slipped off her Italian flats and dug her toes into the soft nap of the carpet to work out the kinks.

Jess sprawled comfortably in the only other adult-sized chair in the office and loosened his tie another few inches.

"We won," he said.

"Congratulations! What are you doing to celebrate?"

His eyebrows rose, giving her a good look at his deep-set dark eyes and thick black eyelashes. She'd never seen eyes so compelling. Or more shadowed.

"Mostly I've been trying to find my desk under the mess that piled up when I was in L.A."

"Your desk sounds like mine every Saturday when I catch up on my case notes," she said with a sigh. "I'd rather clean bathrooms than do paperwork."

"Me, I'd rather muck out stables," he drawled.

"Hmm, sounds like work."

"Only if you have to do it for a living."

"Ah, so that's why you picked an easy profession like the law. I always wondered."

His grin flashed again, a slow sensual invitation that she knew he didn't expect her to accept.

"Hey, haven't you heard? Those of us who are 'physically challenged' are doing all kinds of politically correct things these days."

Hazel hooted her opinion of "politically correct."

"Bad form, O'Connor. Better not let your fellow shrinks hear about that."

It was common knowledge in Sacramento legal circles that Jess had lost his arm during the Indy 500. According to the stories she'd heard, he'd blown a tire and hit the wall rather than take out the two cars on the other side of him.

Hazel had always wanted to ask him if he ever regretted his generosity, especially when she caught sight of his empty sleeve. On the few occasions when she'd tried to engage him in conversation about anything more personal than the weather, sports and Jesse's latest achievements, however, he'd frozen her with an icy look she didn't care to see again.

"So, what can I do for you today, Counselor?" she asked instead.

"Remember when you were fourteen, O'Connor?"

She frowned, surprised by a question that seemed casual, even trivial. She knew better. An intense man consumed by his work, Jess never wasted words on idle chitchat.

"Not really," she said casually as she kept her hands busy and her mind distracted by tidying the files and papers on her desk.

"Me, I had just won the junior bronc-busting championship for the first time. Had to beat my big brother Garrett to do it, and he was steamed. Had his mind set on winning three years in a row."

Hazel tried not to imagine Jess at fourteen, sinfully handsome, physically superb and full of rampaging hormones.

"I don't mean to rush you, Dante, but I have a patient due in, um . . . six minutes now."

Jess glanced at his watch. He was used to setting limits on people, not the other way around. Which was why he had always considered Hazel O'Connor a challenge.

Nothing seemed to rattle her. Not even a guy who'd been about as nasty as he could be so that he wouldn't be tempted to hustle her into an affair that would hurt them both when it ended.

"Let me tell you a little story, O'Connor. Once there was a young girl named Silvia Gomez who was a migrant farm worker's daughter. When she was fourteen and a virgin, her father sold her to his boss, a valley farmer by the name of Cleve Yoder, in exchange for two thousand dollars and a used pickup."

"Sold?" Hazel asked skeptically.

He dismissed her doubt with a quick wave of his big hand. "Technically, he signed the papers allowing his underage daughter to marry Yoder, for which Aurelio Gomez just happened to get paid."

"Oh." Hazel was listening intently now, her forehead creased into faint lines under the soft awning of coppery bangs.

"Silvia didn't blame her father, she told me, because she was the oldest of eight and they were all hungry. Besides, she was tired of picking lettuce and thought it would be nice to live in a house with a bathroom for once in her life.''

Jess shifted his gaze to the make-believe family lined up on the small table in the corner. It was a nice setup, he thought. Inviting, but structured, with pictures of baby animals on the walls and pansies in an old teapot on the table. His gaze lingered for a moment on the stuffed figure of a man sprawled facedown, arms akimbo, as though in terrible pain.

''Thing was,'' he continued, choosing his words carefully, ''Silvia didn't know that Cleve liked his women submissive, and old Cleve didn't know that his virgin bride had a temper. The first time she stood up to him, he broke her nose. When she went crying to her father, Gomez just shrugged and told her that was the way a lot of Anglos treated their wives.''

Hazel drew a long breath. ''So she stayed with this Cleve because she had no place else to go?''

''Essentially, yes. After her third son was born, the doctor told her not to have any more children because it could kill her. When she told Cleve, he just laughed and said something about that being no big tragedy. One woman was just as good as another, and they all looked alike in the dark, anyway.''

''Men like that should be shot!'' Hazel exclaimed with heated vehemence, then started at his sudden chuckle.

''That's what Silvia thought, so she loaded his shotgun and waited for him in the barn.''

Her hand flew to her throat, drawing Jess's gaze for an instant before he shifted it upward a few inches. ''Did she kill him?''

''Damn near. If the man hadn't been strong as a bull, she would have. As it was, the bastard was in the hospital for a month.''

Although his expression was as carefully controlled as most things had to be in Jess's life, Hazel felt the waves of anger and frustration coming from him.

Jess was one of Sacramento's busiest criminal attorneys. Not because he was chasing a buck, but because he had trouble saying no.

"A soft touch in Big Bad Wolf's clothing" was how Ty McClane put it whenever he was set on riling his childhood buddy. Adversaries in the District Attorney's office called him a tough, bleeding heart, son of a bitch in public, while privately respecting him for his grit and integrity.

"And you're thinking of taking her case?" she asked.

"I already did—over two years ago."

"What happened?"

Jess picked up a ceramic paperweight bearing the hand print of a child, hefted it as though it were a weapon, then put it down.

"The jury didn't buy self-defense. Maybe if she'd grabbed the gun on impulse, but…" He shrugged. "The judge gave her four-to-eight in Santa Rita down in Pleasanton. Cleve got a divorce and sole custody of their sons."

"Too bad her aim was so bad."

A smile tugged his mouth briefly. "She claimed she closed her eyes right before she pulled the trigger. Didn't want to see the blood."

Hazel thought about the scarlet stains on the carpeting of the apartment she'd once shared with her husband. The landlord had had the rugs replaced after Ron's death, but Hazel still saw the blood whenever she walked into the bedroom. She'd finally moved. It hadn't helped.

"How long has she been in prison?" she found herself asking.

"Nearly two years. Long enough to get pregnant. She's due in a week or so."

Glancing up, she glimpsed a hard anger in his eyes. "Who's the father?"

"That's a good question. My money's on one of the guards, but so far, Silvia has refused to name names."

Frustration iced his already anger-cold eyes, but Hazel sensed both emotions were directed at himself.

"Maybe she loves the man and doesn't want him to suffer," she suggested in a deliberately mild tone.

His sudden cynical frown told her what he thought of love. "The message I got from the prison doctor said she's close to an emotional breakdown, which is why I'm here."

"But, Jess, I don't treat adults. Only children."

"Which means you know the child welfare system a lot better than I do."

"Well, yes, but—"

"Silvia's baby isn't even born yet, and already the by-the-book bureaucrats at Protective Services are making noises about the kid being a ward of the court. I need an expert in infant psychology to help me convince the suits to hold off, at least long enough to find out if Silvia can make parole."

He rested his palm on her desk and leaned forward. He had a big hand, with pads of thick muscle in the heel and prominent veins. Hazel sensed strength there, but little gentleness.

"I'd have to meet her first. Talk with her, get to know her, before I could even make a decision on whether or not I would feel comfortable as her advocate."

Jess nodded as though he'd foreseen that objection and was prepared to counter it. "Fourth of July holiday starts tomorrow, and court's recessed until Tuesday. I'm driving down to Pleasanton first thing in the morning to talk to Silvia. The best thing would be for you to come with me. I'll even spring for lunch. You choose the place."

"How long until her parole hearing?"

"Four months."

Hazel took a moment to consider. "In that case a postponement shouldn't hurt the baby too much," she said slowly, "although foster care is never the best choice for a newborn. The need to bond with the mother or mother figure is most critical in those first few months."

"So, how about it? Naturally I'll pay for the consultation, whatever you—"

"Lunch will be fine," she interrupted, glancing at the clock. Any minute now her next patient would be arriving. "If my schedule permits, that is."

She took her appointment book from the drawer and turned to the next day, Friday the first. "I'm sorry, Jess, but I have three appointments tomorrow," she murmured sucking absentmindedly on her pen. "Saturday, Sunday and Monday are free, however."

When she looked up again, Jess discovered there was a smudge of blue ink on her lower lip and found himself wondering if he would taste ink as well as woman if he kissed her.

"What time's your last appointment tomorrow?"

"Eleven, but—"

"I'll pick you up at noon sharp." He got to his feet, thought about kissing her again and decided against it, mostly because she looked far too adorable this afternoon. It was the tumbled hair, maybe, making her look as if she'd just left a man's bed. Or maybe it was the off-white dress he figured had to be silk, because it seemed to flow over her like colored water when she moved. Reminding himself that he'd made her off-limits a long time ago, he gave her a quick grin and turned to leave.

"Now wait a minute. I didn't say I'd go—" But Jess was already halfway to the waiting room.

"Jess, wait—"

The outer door opened, and Rhea Angelou and her mother walked in.

"Noon sharp," Jess repeated as he caught the door before it swung completely shut. He was gone by the time Hazel stopped sputtering.

Time to make his move.

Jess hugged the saddle tight and hard, urging the big gelding to the limit of his power. Beneath the leather of his chaps, he felt Stinger surge.

High desert brush whipped past in a blur, reminding him of the gauntlet of frenzied spectators who'd once cheered him on.

His fingers handled the reins with the sensitive touch of a lover, guiding the horse the way he'd once guided the sleekest of racing cars.

Iron-protected hooves pounded the hard earth in a throb of pure animal power, adding to the rush of adrenaline that flooded Jess's body.

Fifty yards ahead was the old stone post that served as the finish line. Next to him, Ty McClane shouted encouragement to his young Appaloosa stallion, his words whipped aside by the wind.

Jess noted the jut of Ty's chin and grinned. Ty was going to win this time or bust a gut trying.

Screw that! he thought, stretching lower over the bay's flying mane. Jess Dante never lost a race without a fight.

Ten yards from the finish the bay edged ahead, his powerful legs stretching for each inch. Jess sensed the animal's final spurt and felt a visceral surge inside himself like the rush a man got an instant before climax. Unable to stop himself, he let out a rebel yell loud enough to bounce off the Sierra foothills.

"Hot damn, Sting!" he shouted close to the horse's ear. "We did it!"

There was nothing like winning, he thought, patting the bay's lathered neck. It made a man feel strong again. Invincible.

Still high, Jess reined his horse to a walk, savoring the victory. Hat in hand, Tyler swerved the Appaloosa closer.

Jess grinned, enjoying the look of pure disgust on his old buddy's face. He'd seen that look before on other men he'd edged out in the stretch. Twice at Indy, once at LeMans.

But that had been a long time ago, when he still had both arms and a hunger for life in the fastest lane. Now the only races he won meant nothing to anyone but him. And even the thrill he got from that was beginning to wear thin.

"Thought I had you that time for sure," Tyler declared when the dust settled.

"Almost did. Would have, too, if Sting didn't hate the thought of losing to a kid half his age."

"Happens to us all, sooner or later."

"Like hell it does!"

Jess rode Stinger into the corral. The gelding strained at the reins in an effort to angle right toward the stone stable and dinner.

Some said Jess's maternal great-grandfather, an unreconstructed Rebel, had built the old barn shortly after the War Between the States. Others, Jess's father included, claimed that Spanish soldiers during the time of Father Serra were responsible.

No one knew for sure, and Jess didn't much care. He'd grown up loving every inch of that old barn and the land that held it.

As soon as he'd been old enough to sit in the saddle without sliding sideways, his daddy had taught him to ride in this same corral.

He'd learned to rope there, too, while his old man and the hands shouted advice. Every time he missed, the wrangler would be on his butt, egging him on.

Throw that loop, boy. Now! Before that little bitty bull has you singin' soprano the rest of your life.

Use your wrist, son, like I showed you.

Put your shoulders into it. Nothing better'n ropin' to make a man of you.

Jess smiled to himself. The first time he'd held a lariat, he'd been so scared his teeth had chattered and his knees had knocked together, but his pride hadn't let him quit until he'd made himself into the best roper in the county.

Jess reined Stinger toward the center of the corral, away from the old building. Tyler followed. Both horses would need a good cooling out before they were unsaddled and groomed.

Tyler waited until both men had dismounted before reaching into his shirt pocket for the twenty he'd put there earlier.

"Cait's gonna kill me when she finds out I lost again," he muttered as he stuffed the twenty into Jess's breast pocket.

"So don't tell her."

"You know Caitie. She has a way of finding out all my secrets sooner or later." Tyler shook his head. "I tell you, Jess. It's hell being married to a shrink."

"Yeah, I can see how miserable you are every time I stop by the house."

Thinking that Tyler was one lucky man, Jess rubbed Stinger's nose with the hand that still held the reins. On solid ground again, he was just a guy with a handicap he couldn't hide and a bunch of bittersweet memories.

Red's Place was little more than a dive, a patched-together shack where tired, thirsty ranch hands could wash down the dust with cheap beer and trade lies for hours at a time.

Jess bought. The remainder of Tyler's twenty was still on the bar. Both men had a boot firmly planted on the bar rail and a hand wrapped around a cold frosted schooner of Red's best—and only—lager.

"So how's Cait feeling these days?" Jess asked when he'd taken the edge off his thirst.

Ty's face softened the way it always did when he talked about his wife. "Great, now that the morning sickness has passed."

"How do you feel about having another kid?"

"Probably the same way you felt when you won at Indy the first time."

Returning Tyler's grin, Jess felt a familiar tightening in his gut. "That good, huh?" He kept his tone light, the way he always did when someone mentioned the past.

Tyler took a handful of peanuts from the old wooden bowl and tossed them down. "By the way, in case you haven't figured it out already, Cait and I would like you to act as godfather for the new baby. Okay with you?''

Jess ignored the sudden rasp in his throat. "Hell, yes, it's okay. As long as I get to spoil him like I spoiled Jesse.''

Tyler laughed. "Sorry, old son. *He's* a *she.*''

"No lie!''

"Not unless that sonogram operator turns out to be totally incompetent.''

"Heck's fire, Ty. You'll be an old man before Jesse and this new kid are out of high school.''

"Naw, Cait won't let me get old. Says we have too much time to make up.''

Jess had met Cait when Ty had been on trial the first time. Cait had been his sister-in-law then, instead of his wife, and instrumental in urging her sister to take her daughter's statement to the police. At the time no one had believed that a mother would coerce her own daughter into lying, but that was exactly what Crystal McClane had done. It was only after Crystal's death, when Kelsey had gone to live with Cait, that the truth had come out.

Jess had been hard-pressed to like the woman who'd helped send his best friend to prison. He'd changed his mind when she and Hazel had helped Jess win Tyler another trial.

After his acquittal, Ty had convinced Cait to take him on permanently, and a year later Jesse Fielding McClane had arrived with an enraged bellow and his father's stubborn disposition.

"Hazel's already agreed to act as godmother again,'' Ty added, as though it were an important afterthought.

Jess nodded before returning his attention to his beer.

He and Hazel had been in the waiting room when Jesse had been born. And at the christening, and at every one of Jesse's birthday parties. And every time he'd been with her, he'd wanted her.

That part had been easy to understand. O'Connor was what he and his adolescent buddies had called stacked. All her curves were generous and in just the right places to spike a man's blood with a restless, urgent heat.

But it was her smile that he liked best, that and the way she had of looking up at a guy with those golden eyes of hers, as though she considered him the most fascinating man she'd ever met.

His ex had had eyes like that, too. And she'd been just as sexy and intelligent and exciting. What she hadn't been was faithful or even particularly kind.

"Hey, is that clock right?" Ty asked the bartender just as Jess was about to suggest another round.

"Dead on," Red Arnold shouted back. A hair shy of seventy and still tough as a redwood burl, he'd lost most of his hearing working in the lumber mills and consequently never spoke in a normal tone.

"Then it's time for me to call it a day." Ty downed the last of his beer and got to his feet. "Hey, why don't you come along?" he said. "Kels and Jesse would love to see you."

Jess was tempted to pretend that he really was part of a normal, happy family for a few hours. Because he knew he wasn't and never could be, he forced himself to decline.

"Naw, I'll take a rain check, okay? I'm not like you world-famous surgeons who only work when you feel like it. I've got some work to catch up on tonight."

Ty grinned. "Same time next week? Same distance?"

"Why not? I need the money."

After Tyler left, Jess ordered another draft. Maybe he would stop for a pizza on the way home, he thought, watching Red draw off the beer. Or maybe he'd watch the guys in the back room shoot a few games of pool before he tackled the long drive down the hill.

Anything to keep from going home before he was tired enough to fall into a dead sleep the minute his head hit the pillow.

He rarely dreamed then, but when he did, he was never maimed in those dreams, never awkward or helpless or ugly.

And when he smiled at a woman in his dreams, she smiled back. And when he opened his arms, she melted into them.

Jess lifted the mug to his mouth and drank deeply. The cheap beer had a kick like a mule and a bitter aftertaste. But, like his law practice, his restored 1959 Mercedes, and a lot of memories he sometimes wished he could forget, it was better than nothing.

Chapter 2

Hazel closed her eyes and imagined herself on a beach on Maui, soaking up the radiant healing sunshine and sipping an icy Mai Tai.

Mentally, emotionally, she blocked out the clang of barred doors slamming shut deep within the prison's bowels and instead summoned the soothing swish of waves flowing across sand.

In her mind she changed the air from dank and sour to warm and benign, then perfumed it with plumeria and ginger instead of strong disinfectant.

Unlike the tepid coffee from the machine near the guard's station, the rum in her drink would be potent and laced with heat, like a man's eyes right before he makes love.

"O'Connor?"

"Hmm?"

Hazel allowed a lazy smile to curl the corners of her mouth. That same man would have a distinctive voice, deeper than most, with a gritty timbre and a hint of a western twang. She could grow to love a voice like that, she decided.

"Hey, wake up, O'Connor. No sleeping on the job."

A very large, very masculine hand hovered over her right shoulder, then gripped lightly, returning her instantly to the small bare room with dingy walls and a cold cement floor.

"Welcome back." Jess reclaimed the chair next to hers, abandoned earlier when he'd gone seeking information.

Hazel sat up straighter and rotated her neck, working out the kinks. "What time is it?"

Jess consulted his watch. "Just past five."

Santa Rita Women's Facility reminded Hazel of the Veteran's Hospital in San Diego, where she'd done her internship. Gray walls, dirty windows, even the clothing worn by the few inmates they'd passed in the halls was drab. It was enough to make even the most insensitive person hurt inside.

She and Jess had arrived at a few minutes past three, only to discover that the woman they'd come to see had gone into labor hours earlier. Since then, they'd been caged in the small anteroom off the infirmary wing.

His restlessness had been palpable from the moment they'd walked through the gates, his frustration at their inability to do more than wait even more evident.

While Jess had paced, she'd tried to meditate. After the first sixty minutes she had begun to feel the walls closing in. After the second she'd had to resort to mind games to keep from feeling smothered. Putting herself somewhere else was one of those.

"Looks like I dozed off for an instant," she murmured with a self-conscious shake of her head. "Sorry about that."

His smile came and went, no more than a brief lessening of tension in his dark, enigmatic face. "No problem. Happens that way sometimes after a long day."

"Any word on Silvia?"

"The infirmary clerk I collared said any minute now." His mouth flattened, and Hazel sensed the hard edge of the emotion he was holding inside.

"How's she doing?"

"Not well, from the look on the clerk's face."

"Too bad they couldn't lock up the guard who did this and throw away the key instead of slapping his wrist with a punitive transfer."

Upon arrival Jess had discovered that the man had been identified through an anonymous tip. He'd been demoted and sent to another prison, nothing more. Jess's fury had been carefully controlled, but Hazel sensed it nonetheless.

"Silvia refused to admit that it was rape."

"I take it you tried to change her mind."

"Yeah, I tried." He gave a snort of derision.

Hazel let her gaze linger on his face. He looked exhausted, like a man who'd pushed himself to the limit too often and wouldn't admit it.

Someone ought to convince him to ease up on himself now and then, she thought. Someone who saw him as a flesh-and-blood human being instead of a courtroom machine. Someone who cared about him, perhaps a bit more than he knew.

"Were you this tough on yourself when you were racing cars?" she asked very casually.

"Racing was my job. Tough had nothing to do with it."

"But you expected to be the best."

He shifted his gaze to a spot on the far wall, and his eyes narrowed until the blunt black lashes were nearly touching. Hazel wondered if he were looking back to a time before one decision had altered his life irreversibly, a time when his body was strong and whole and his spirit was intact.

"If you mean, did I expect to win every time I climbed into the car, the answer is no. Losing is part of learning how to win, and I could always tell myself that there was another race next week, and another after that. People like Silvia only get one shot at winning."

"But you can't possibly expect to win every case, either," she exclaimed softly. "Not even Clarence Darrow did that."

He turned slowly until his gaze was on hers. In the harsh light, his eyes seemed to splinter into shards of black ice.

"Are you telling me you don't expect to help every kid who comes through your office door?"

Hazel saw the cynical curve of his mouth and decided that Jess would be a devastatingly handsome man if those hard lips ever really relaxed into a genuine smile.

"I learned years ago not to demand the impossible of myself. But I'll admit I do believe in miracles, even with the toughest cases."

"No offense, O'Connor, but I learned a long time ago that relying on a miracle instead of yourself is a fool's game." His voice had turned flat. Like a smooth hard slab of granite. Like the wall he kept between himself and his emotions.

"Just like a lawyer," she countered, shooting him a teasing smile. "Already he's twisting my words."

"Who, me?" He didn't smile, but he looked as though he might—with the right encouragement.

"Yes, you, Clarence. Here I'm talking about believing in miracles, and you're telling me I'm really talking about relying on them." She shook her head and clucked her tongue. "Not the same thing at all."

"Does it matter?"

"Of course it does!"

He raised his eyebrows and contemplated her quizzically. "Why?"

"Well for one thing—"

"Mr. Dante?" The voice that interrupted them was lashed with weariness and had a French flavor. The woman wore surgical scrubs and a worried look.

"Yes?" Jess got to his feet immediately, his expression guarded.

"I'm Cecile Benoit, Silvia's doctor."

Jess offered his left hand, and Hazel caught the small stutter of surprise in the other woman's eyes before she gave him hers.

Because his chest was so wide, the absence of his arm gave him a slightly lopsided look. It hadn't taken her long to get used to it. Others sometimes had more difficulty.

"Silvia said that you were a man of your word, so she's let herself expect you," the doctor commented with a faint smile. "I wasn't as confident."

"Sounds like you're a cynic, Doctor."

"I've dealt with attorneys before."

"Not with me."

"Point taken, Mr. Dante."

Hazel thought she noticed a slight smile come into Dr. Benoit's eyes and mentally awarded the advantage to Jess as he glanced her way.

"Dr. Benoit, this is Dr. Hazel O'Connor. She's a child psychologist practicing in Sacramento, and I've asked her to come here to represent the baby's interests."

"I see."

As the doctor turned toward her to offer her hand, Hazel noticed shadows under the other woman's eyes and a cast of weariness to her full, pale lips. Too much responsibility and worry on too little sleep, she diagnosed, then felt an immediate affinity for the other woman.

"I assume the baby's been born?" she said softly.

Dr. Benoit nodded. "About thirty minutes ago. We've just taken Silvia back to the ward."

"How's she doing?" Jess asked.

"Poorly. She hemorrhaged badly before the birth. That and the lengthy delivery have sapped her strength, so much so her white count is dangerously low, even after multiple transfusions."

"And the baby?" Hazel put in.

"Normal, thank the good Lord. A girl. Six pounds, five ounces. Normal reflexes and response to stimuli."

Jess looked distinctly uncomfortable. "Sounds awfully tiny."

"Prison babies tend to be small," Dr. Benoit explained with a brief, humorless smile.

"Will the mother be able to breast-feed?" Hazel asked, thinking of the baby's need for nurturing and closeness.

"Unfortunately, no. Not only because it's against the rules, but because Silvia is far too weak to manage."

Dr. Benoit's eyes seethed with the very real frustration of a healer who'd done all she could and was still losing.

"Can we see her?" Jess asked.

"Ordinarily I'd say no, but I know how much she's been looking forward to your visit. Perhaps a talk with you would ease some of her concerns about the baby's future."

Jess looked uncomfortable but determined. "Anything we should know before we talk to her?"

"Just that she's very weak physically and even more fragile emotionally. Whatever you do, please don't upset her."

Turning abruptly, Dr. Benoit led the way.

The ward where Silvia was assigned was two doors up and across the hall. Hazel counted four beds in a room designed for two. All were filled. Two of the women were sleeping; the third was playing a desultory game of solitaire. The fourth bed was screened on two sides by curtains hanging from the ceiling.

On the far wall, the only window in the room let in a grid of bright yellow sunshine. Everything else was leached of color, including the thin blankets. Like the prison reception area, the room held no cheery cards, no flowers, not even a picture on the wall.

The doctor saw her looking around and paused. "We have a small OR here, but no ICU."

The doctor drew aside one of the curtains, revealing a young, hollow-eyed woman who looked more childlike than maternal. Hazel could see traces of the beauty she must have been in the long black hair, now stringy and limp, and in the provocative shape of her lips.

But the sunken brown eyes that might have danced with a girl's storybook fantasies were now haunted by shadows and rimmed with exhaustion. At that moment they were intently fixed on Jess's face.

He had to lean down to take her hand in his. "Hey, little mama," he said in a gruff tone that brought a sting to Hazel's eyes. "How're you doin'?"

Silvia's pale mouth trembled as she attempted a smile. "Not...so good."

"I've brought a friend to help. Her name is Dr. O'Connor, and she knows a lot about kids. You can trust her."

Silvia blinked, then slowly shifted her gaze until her tired brown eyes were fixed on Hazel's. "She has...a nice face," she murmured in a tone barely above a whisper. Hazel noticed then that Silvia's voice was sweet as a child's and flavored with the lilt of her Mexican heritage.

"She's a nice lady." Jess's quick glance beckoned Hazel closer.

"Hello, Silvia. We haven't seen your baby yet, but Dr. Benoit says she's adorable."

For an all-too-brief moment the woman's eyes brightened into rare beauty. "I...named her Francisca, after my mother."

"Oh, Silvia, that's such a beautiful name. I know she'll love it a lot when she grows up."

"I...hope so." Tears softened the haunting shadows in the sad brown eyes. "It's all I have to give her. It doesn't seem right...."

A sob racked her frail body, followed by another that ended in a coughing fit that left the young mother gasping.

Dr. Benoit poured water from a small plastic pitcher and helped Silvia drink. The water seemed to revive her, but Dr. Benoit kept a watchful eye on her patient as she took back the glass.

"Try not to make yourself so upset, Silvia, or Mr. Dante and Dr. O'Connor will have to leave."

"No...please," Silvia managed to get out between rasping breaths. "I have to make sure.... I don't want my little girl to grow up like me, no education, no talent but makin' babies with a man she hates."

Hazel bit her lip and glanced at Jess. His face was set in harsh lines, his jaw held at an angle just shy of pugnacious. "That's all over now, Silvia. You and Cleve are divorced. He can't hurt you anymore."

"His lawyer says I can't see my boys no more, even if I get parole."

"He's wrong. As soon as you're out of here, we'll haul him into court and make him let you see your boys."

Hazel heard a note of steel in Jess's deep voice and suddenly felt sorry for that other lawyer.

Silvia's gaze fell, and her free hand plucked weakly at the thin blanket. "Cleve says they hate me."

Hazel moved closer. "Silvia, listen to me. I work with kids every day. Big ones, little ones, sad ones, naughty ones—all kinds of kids. One thing that's the same in all of them is the love each one has for his mother. It's a special kind of love. A rare, beautiful, mystical love. And it's stronger than words or deeds or…even death sometimes. No matter what some idiot man says."

Tears slid from Silvia's eyes and ran down her thin, pale cheeks. "I loved my boys, Dr. O'Connor. You have to believe me." Her gaze swung to Jess's face. "Tell her, Mr. Dante, the way you told that jury. How I… I only wanted to scare Cleve into treatin' me right for their sakes. I'm not that awful person them welfare people say I am. I'm *not!*"

Her impassioned plea seemed to drain the last of her energy, and she sank back against the pillow, spent. Small beads of perspiration dotted her hairline, and her breathing took on a laborious heaviness, drawing a warning scowl from the doctor.

"It's okay, Silvia," Jess said with a burr of emotion roughening his tone. "Dr. O'Connor understands."

It was less than a glance he flicked her way, but Hazel noticed. "Of course I do," she said as soothingly as she could. "And I'll do everything I can to see that Francisca isn't taken away from you."

"She…the lady from the welfare who came to see me, she said there has to be a hearing, to see … who's best to raise Francisca."

"Don't worry, kid," Jess put in gruffly. "Nobody's gonna take Francisca away from you. You'll be back on your feet and out of here before I run out of appeals to file."

Hazel sensed the woman's struggle to draw strength and wished she could do something to help. But Silvia's hollow eyes were fixed on Jess's face, as though only he mattered.

"The man who made her doesn't want her," she whispered. "He said he loved me, but as soon as he got what he wanted, it was like I wasn't no good no more."

Jess leaned closer. "Don't worry, Silvia. I'm planning on attending that hearing. That lady you're talking about will find out she has a fight on her hands."

"The lady…she said there's lots of folks with good homes wantin' babies, and she said I could say who I wanted to adopt my baby. She called it private, uh—"

"Private placement," Jess finished quietly.

Silvia inhaled laboriously as she nodded. "She said if I loved my baby, I would do that for her."

Most of the time Hazel agreed with Protective Services. In this case, however, she found herself torn.

"Did she also tell you that you'd have to relinquish custody of Francisca?" she put in as gently as possible. "That you wouldn't have any rights where she was concerned, even after you're free again?"

There was no need for Silvia to answer. The tormented look in her eyes said it all.

"Is that what you want?" Jess questioned in his quiet, intense way. "To give your baby to someone else to raise?"

"I prayed and prayed to the Holy Mother to tell me the right person for Francisca."

Jess's jaw tightened, but his expression remained controlled. "And did she?"

Her nod was barely perceptible. "The welfare lady said I needed a lawyer to make things legal and all."

"It's not something I know a lot about," he said carefully, "but I know someone who does."

Silvia's hand had been lost in his. Now she tugged it free and struggled to sit up, but her weakened, emaciated frame failed her. Dr. Benoit helped by elevating the bed.

"No, I want you," Silvia said when enough strength returned to support speech. "Nobody but you. You're not like them other lawyers, the ones on Cleve's side. You know what it's like to be scared and alone. To feel all torn up inside.''

Hazel noticed that Jess was looking more and more uncomfortable. Somehow Silvia had seen through the armor to the wounded man inside.

"All them weeks ... the trial ... the bad things about me in the newspapers, I prayed and prayed for someone to help me, for someone to believe I wasn't a bad person—'' Gripped by a sudden coughing seizure, she broke off, gasping.

The doctor hastily counted Silvia's pulse, then met Jess's eyes. Nodding, he reached into the pocket of his corduroy jacket for a small notebook, which he flipped open, then laid on the bed before reaching into the same pocket for his pen.

"First I'll need the name of the person you've picked out to adopt your daughter," he told Silvia, more gentle than Hazel had ever seen him. "And an address if you have it.''

Silvia stared up at him with a strange look on her face. "I already said who,'' she whispered.

Jess frowned. "You did?''

"You, Mr. Dante. I want you to take Francisca.'' Fresh tears spilled from her eyes as she clutched his hand once more. "Promise me ... all I ask is that you don't let Francisca forget me.''

Hazel talked Jess into stopping by the makeshift nursery before they left. As soon as they stepped into the small room with a crib and a rocking chair, he knew he'd made a mistake.

The place might be fixed up like a nursery, but it still smelled like a hospital. He didn't believe in déjà vu. He did believe in some pretty rotten memories he would just as soon stayed buried.

"Is this where she was born?'' Hazel asked the doctor, glancing around them slowly, her expression grim.

Benoit nodded. "Through there," she said, indicating double doors to the left.

"It seems . . . obscene," Hazel murmured. "Prisons and babies, I mean."

Benoit sighed. "I tell myself I'll get used to it someday. Who knows, maybe I really will."

Jess dropped his gaze. Funny, he'd said the same thing a time or two to himself. He hadn't been talking about babies, however.

The nursing assistant on duty had a harried look about her, but she brightened considerably when Dr. Benoit relayed their request to see Baby Yoder.

The nurse's name was Arquette, and she spoke with an accent. Jess figured it was Australian.

"I'm always thrilled when I get to take care of a newborn," she said, bustling around with an efficient air about her that made Jess nervous.

"How is she doing?" Hazel asked, moving closer to the crib for a better look.

"Splendidly," the nurse murmured. "Would either of you like to hold her?"

Her gaze fell on Jess first, then skittered quickly to Hazel and remained there. Jess ground his teeth. He should be used to the stares by now.

"Me first," Hazel said softly, as though the nurse had given them a choice.

"Here, let me just fetch her up for you." The nurse lowered the crib's tall side and gently gathered the baby into her arms.

Hazel slung her purse over one shoulder, then took a deep breath. It was the first time Jess had seen her nervous, and he wondered if she'd ever wanted children of her own.

Had she been married? he wondered, and then realized that he didn't know because he'd never asked. Knowing too much about some women was dangerous. It made a man want to know more.

"Careful, the little lamb has just had an enormous bottle," the nurse murmured as she carefully nestled the baby into the crook of Hazel's arm. "There you go, love."

"Oh my, she's awake," Hazel whispered. "And so tiny."

Laughing softly, she brushed the black thatch of hair with her finger. "Look, Jess, she's smiling at you."

Feeling more and more awkward and out of place, Jess took a quick look at the small round face all but buried in the fuzzy pink blanket.

"Looks like she's mostly hair to me."

Hazel lifted her gaze from the baby's face to his, her smile still soft, her eyes filled with wonder. Jess had guarded his emotions so well and for so long that it took him a moment to realize how much he'd come to like Hazel O'Connor over the years, in spite of every intention not to.

"She's so precious," Hazel murmured, her voice wobbly and her eyes filling with tears. "This has to be breaking Silvia's heart."

Somewhere in the distance a woman cried out. Another shouted an obscenity. Jess couldn't remember a time when he'd been more desperate to escape a place.

"This isn't over yet," he vowed, his voice low and rough. "I'll talk to Silvia again tomorrow, when she's stronger. Convince her to fight."

Hazel nodded. "I want to help. Anything you need me to do…testify at the custody hearing, call in a few favors with Teri Grimes at Protective Services. Anything to help Silvia keep her baby."

"All of the above would help," he said.

It had been a long time since he'd allowed himself to trust a woman's motives without checking her out first. A man got burned when he let himself trust too deeply.

"If you'll excuse me," the doctor said quietly. "I'd better get back to my patient."

Jess caught the quick look she exchanged with the nurse and wondered about it. "Let me know if she needs anything," he told the doctor.

"Are you a praying man, Mr. Dante? Because if you are, that's what she could use most. Your prayers."

Without waiting for his answer, she nodded goodbye to Hazel, then beckoned for the nurse to accompany her into the corridor.

Hazel felt Jess's gaze come back to her. Since they'd walked into the sad little nursery, he'd been watching her with an intensity that she would have found intolerable in another man. She accepted it from Jess because intensity was as much a part of him as his imperious Roman nose and the subtle swagger in his walk.

"Would you like to hold her?" she asked softly. "She's no trouble."

Jess glanced down at the warm, pink baby waving her two miniature fists in the air. His experience with babies was thin at best. His niece Andrea had been born during the months when he'd been newly divorced, mad as hell at everyone who wasn't hurting as much as he'd been and generally behaving like a self-pitying jerk. While his brother Garrett had been learning to change diapers, he'd been trying his damnedest to drink himself to death.

When Jesse had been born, the kid had been a buster, practically walking and talking the moment he came into the world. Holding him had been a cinch, a lot like playing with a roly-poly puppy. But this little scrap of a thing was scarcely bigger than his hand. One mistake, one unexpected moment of clumsiness, and she could be badly hurt.

"No thanks. You're doing fine."

"Go ahead and take her. She won't break," Hazel urged, her voice soft and her eyes dark with an emotion he wasn't about to let himself share.

"Yeah, well, I'm not much for babies," he said gruffly. "Not much for hospitals, either, so if you don't mind, I'll wait for you outside."

Chapter 3

A rare California gully washer had hit the valley while they'd been inside the prison, making the interstate between Pleasanton and Sacramento an oil-slicked obstacle course.

It seemed foolish to spend two hours or more on the road, only to get in late and then have to leave early the next morning to visit with Silvia one more time. Staying over near Santa Rita had been the logical choice.

The nearest motel was part of a chain, unpretentious but comfortable. Jess had checked them in, insisting quietly but firmly on paying for both rooms. Hazel had protested, then argued, and finally conceded. Dante with his mind made up was as immovable as a brick wall.

It was nearly eight by the time they headed for the restaurant for something to eat. Like the motel, it was nothing to rave about, but neither of them seemed inclined to search for anything else.

Most of the tables and booths had been taken by the time they walked in, but the hostess managed to find them a booth near the rear.

Jess ordered two hamburgers and an extra order of fries, ate every bite and was already on his second cup of coffee by the time Hazel had worked her way through most of a tasteless chef salad.

"Do you always eat that much?" she asked when she couldn't eat another bite. Forty minutes of silence was her limit. Anything longer than that and she got squirrelly.

He glanced at the empty plate near his elbow and shrugged. "Not always. Sometimes I eat more."

Light from the overhead fixture picked up the silver salted into his hair and cast his eyes in shadow, making him look older and wearier. He had an animal-like magnetism, as well, something Hazel was determined to ignore.

"You realize you ate mostly grease. I hate to think what it's even now doing to your arteries."

Sipping coffee, he watched her with lazy, disinterested eyes. "I was raised on steak and frijoles. My arteries crave grease."

"Impossible," she hooted. "I can hear them choking from here."

Lifting an eyebrow, Jess glanced at the surrounding tables. "Me, all I hear is a bunch of grumpy travelers complaining about the rain," he said, returning his gaze to her face.

Even with the mingling smells of food and the acrid hint of cigarette smoke, he could detect her scent. It was something light and cheerful, and yet intense enough to give a man pause.

"Pooh on them," she said. "We need all the rain we can get. Besides, I like the way everything is always so much brighter and fresher after a good rain."

"Everything but the freeway in rush hour."

"Are you always this cynical?"

He shrugged. "Probably. I don't keep a log."

Hazel smiled. "Maybe you should."

He watched the busboy's eyes register masculine approval as he gave her a quick once-over while passing.

"Are you always so optimistic?" he asked. It had been a long time since he'd been so naive. Or perhaps so fortunate.

"Always. Does that bother you? I could try to work up a little cynicism, if that would make you feel more comfortable."

"Don't bother. I'm comfortable enough."

Hazel wasn't so sure. He gave off signals of a subtle shyness, waves of wariness. Unlike most of the men she'd encountered over the years, he seemed uninterested in impressing her with his memorable accomplishments, irresistible masculinity and monumental sex appeal. Undoubtedly that was the very reason she found him so compellingly attractive.

"At least eat some of my salad," she said, folding her arms primly in front of her.

"Why?"

It was Hazel's turn to shrug. "Because green stuff is good for you, that's why."

The arching of his bold, black eyebrows registered his disbelief. "What about all that dressing you slathered over everything?"

"Low cal," she crowed triumphantly. "Thirty-five teensy calories per tablespoon. It said so on the menu."

His gaze drifted over her assessingly, a wry half smile parting his hard lips. "Don't tell me you're one of those skin-and-bones nuts?"

Hazel glanced down and winced. "Do I look like it?"

He angled his back against one corner of the booth, stretched his long legs toward the other and reached out a long arm to drag her salad closer.

"You look very. . . healthy."

"Thanks a lot."

Jess studied her for a moment. Whenever he'd been with Hazel, she'd either been laughing at herself, or at some private joke she felt no neurotic need to share the way most people did.

He had trouble believing that life could be that placid for her or for anyone. Maybe that was why he always felt slightly off balance around her.

That and the fact that he had to keep a tight rein on his libido whenever she was within hailing distance.

"I meant that as a compliment," he said, spearing a chunk of lettuce. "Skinny women give me a pain."

Hazel felt a definite tug. He wasn't flirting with her. Jess Dante never flirted. But he wasn't being quite as abrupt as usual, either.

"Pardon me, but most men I've known wouldn't agree," she said with a dramatic sigh.

"Maybe that's because they were never married to a fashion model. I was."

He crunched the lettuce between his teeth. "No calories and no taste," he muttered before washing down the salad with coffee.

"Are you talking about the dressing or your ex-wife?"

Jess nearly choked and had to drop his fork in order to grab his water glass. When his gaze met hers again, Hazel expected to get blasted for daring to tease the caged lion without his permission.

"Both," he replied dryly. And then she saw it, a lopsided grin that softened the forbiddingly stern lines around his mouth and crinkled his eyes.

Dante at fourteen might have been memorable, but Dante at forty-plus was awesome. She took a slow breath and waited for her pulse to find a steady rhythm again.

"So how long have you been divorced from this fashion model?"

"Thirteen years." The warmth in his eyes faded. Hazel found that she missed it more than she should.

"And you don't want to talk about it."

"Not much, no."

An unusual woman, he thought. Exuding signals of sincerity and compassion when she'd been in the prison infirmary and now daring to do what even his friends hesitated to do—tease him when he'd made it plain he wasn't in the mood.

Instinct told him that she would be fun to know, and he found himself tempted to suggest a drink in the bar after dinner. And then he thought about the few times in the past he'd given in to a similar urge.

Sooner or later it always came down to a matter of sex— and whether or not the woman could handle his handicap. In this case he liked Hazel O'Connor too much to risk finding out that she couldn't.

"Can I get you guys anything else?" The waitress stood with coffeepot poised, her gaze darting from one to the other. "We've got some great strawberry pie on special."

Jess caught Hazel's disapproving look and fought a need to grin. "Sure, why not?" he told the woman. "We'll both have a piece."

"Comin' right up." She took Jess's empty plate with her when she went.

"Shame on you, Dante. Tempting me that way." Hazel shook her head and reached for the glass of wine she'd yet to taste.

"Not to mention your arteries."

"That too."

It was getting warm in the restaurant. Stuffy, too.

Hazel unbuttoned her cuffs and rolled the sleeves of her blouse above her wrists.

"I wonder how Silvia is doing," she said, glancing his way.

He looked up quickly, his fork poised over the last bite of salad, which he seemed to be enjoying in spite of himself. "Benoit seemed highly qualified."

"Yes, she did." She hesitated, then added slowly, "But I'd feel better if Silvia were in a regular hospital."

He put down his fork, pushed away the plate and picked up his coffee. As he sipped, he surveyed the room with cool, all-seeing eyes. An observer, she thought. But one who would catalog facts, while she absorbed emotions.

Finished with his coffee, he put the cup to one side and leaned his forearm on the table. He wore a watch but no other jewelry, not even his championship ring. "During the trial she struck me as a survivor."

"During the trial she still had hope."

"She has hope now."

"Does she, Jess? Really?" She shook her head. "Put yourself in her shoes for a minute. Her husband, who used her for a punching bag, now has sole custody of her sons and has already served notice that he intends to beat her up again—legally, this time—if she fights him."

"He can try." His tone was deceptively mild. The glint in his eyes was anything but.

"And then, when she's most vulnerable, another man she obviously trusted just…throws her away. So what does the state do? Tells her point-blank that she's not fit to raise her baby, that's what! It's barbaric."

"It's the law."

"It's a dumb law." Her emotions were in her eyes, he thought. Changing, flashing, stirring a man's imagination. The urge to know her better wasn't as easily suppressed this time.

"It's designed to protect kids. I thought you'd be all for it." He was deliberately prolonging the conversation past its logical conclusion just to watch the play of light on her hair and the life in her eyes.

"I am, but I can't help feeling sorry for Silvia all the same."

"Feeling sorry and ninety cents will get you a cup of coffee," he said, careful to keep his tone casual.

"And ignoring your feelings will give you an ulcer." Hazel took another sip of the wine and pretended to be unaffected by the sharp bitterness that had come into his eyes all of a sudden. It took some doing, she discovered.

"Maybe some of us have better control than that."

"Or maybe you just tell yourself you do."

The waitress arrived then, tray in hand, to serve the pie. "More coffee?" she asked, brandishing a full pot. Nodding, Jess moved his cup closer.

"How about you, ma'am?" she asked Hazel, coffee pot at the ready. "Coffee to go with the pie?"

"No, thanks. I still have my wine." She took a sip while the waitress cleared the rest of the dishes.

"I don't suppose there's any chance of getting Silvia a new trial?" she asked when the waitress had departed.

"None. And no chance of appeal. I've already gone that route."

Jess clawed his tie loose and slipped the top button of his plaid shirt. He'd already shucked his jacket, and the sleeve of his shirt pinned neatly to his shoulder had drawn its share of attention, especially from a group of giggling teenagers in the booth across from them.

"How about a compassionate pardon?" she suggested.

"It's been done."

"Not in this state."

"But maybe if *you* tried...."

For a long moment she thought he didn't intend to answer. When he finally spoke, his voice was stiff, as though he were admitting something shameful. "I did. No dice."

Hazel tasted the pie. It was sickeningly sweet. Nevertheless, for the sake of the cook's feelings, she ate a few more bites before shoving it away.

"I guess the next step would be to find out the name of the caseworker pushing for adoption," she murmured, as much to herself as to him.

"Lynn FitzGerald."

Hazel blinked. "How do you know that?"

Jess forked the last of his pie into his mouth, then reached for hers. "I asked Dr. Benoit while you were discussing 'bonding,' whatever the hell that is, with that Aussie nurse."

"I'm impressed." And she was. It hadn't occurred to her to ask, but it should have.

"Don't be. That's all I managed to find out."

Both plates were empty now, and Hazel wondered how he could eat like a stevedore and still manage to have a belly as hard as a slab.

"You might be interested to learn that I know Lynn. Not well, but I've worked with her before. She's...competent."

His gaze whipped to hers, dark and intense. "Suppose you translate 'competent' for us dumb lawyer types?"

"Lynn is professional, personable, knows the rules." She took the last sip of her wine before continuing. "But she doesn't have a lot of heart."

"Meaning what, exactly?"

She toyed with her empty glass, conscious that the teenagers at the next table were leaving, but not before giving her more than one curious look.

"Meaning she's probably never bent a rule in her life."

"Have you?" he asked.

"No, but I have wiggled one or two in a good cause."

His mouth relaxed for an instant. "I'm impressed," he drawled.

Hazel burst out laughing. "You should be," she murmured. "I don't admit that to everyone—only a select few, in fact."

"How select?"

"Well, counting Cait, there are two of you now."

His eyebrows tilted. "What made you include me in this select circle of yours?"

"I liked the way you were with Silvia. You went a long way toward restoring her faith in men."

"Don't kid yourself, O'Connor," he grated, frowning. "I'm not a very nice guy. Most lawyers aren't. We can't afford to be and do our job properly." He picked up the check and slid from the booth. "Ready?" he asked.

Hazel grabbed her purse and slipped her feet into her pumps. "Now I am," she answered, sliding across the slick seat and standing.

Jess stood back and let her precede him to the cashier's station. "On me, remember?" he said when she opened her purse. "I promised you dinner."

She smiled, showing just a hint of a dimple in one cheek. "Actually, you only promised me lunch, but thank you."

Lunch had turned out to be gourmet finger-food, packed by the chef at one of the best restaurants in Old Sacramento. They'd eaten in a shaded picnic spot off the interstate. Jess had even provided wine for her. Beer for him. Hazel had been instantly beguiled.

The cashier took the bill, and Jess handed over his credit card. "Thank you for coming," he said while the woman filled in the charge slip.

"I'm glad you insisted."

"So am I—for Silvia's sake."

The top of her head didn't quite reach his chin, even when she was tottering on high heels, and he noticed that her hair had hints of hidden gold in the bright, every-which-way curls.

"Everything all right?" the cashier asked as she handed over the slip for him to sign.

"Fine." His scrawl was nearly illegible, prompting the woman behind the counter to check it against the signature on the card.

"Sorry, but my boss insists," she said, obviously uncomfortable as she handed over the card and the receipt.

"Don't worry about it. I'm used to it."

He'd learned to do just about everything left-handed fairly well, everything but write—and make love.

It took a lot of booze to get Jess drunk. A man six-two, two-hundred fifteen pounds, had a hefty tolerance for the stuff.

Jess swirled his fourth—or was it his fifth?—Scotch in the bottom of the glass before letting it slide down his throat. He no longer noticed the taste nor cared about the brand. For all he cared, he could be drinking water.

For that matter, the bar side of the motel restaurant could have been one of a hundred in California's central valley. Dark, smoky, with decent booze and moderate prices—

perfect for a tired traveler who wanted to take the edge off his exhaustion.

From the look of the couples huddled in the dark booths in the back, it was also a place where the same tired traveler could get more than a few drinks for his money.

"Hit you again, friend?"

The bartender was the talkative sort, but Jess had made it plain after the first few minutes of the guy's practiced patter that he wanted to be left alone. Still, the man had a job to do. Jess couldn't fault him for that.

"Why not?" he said, pushing his glass forward.

After dinner Hazel had headed directly to her room for a hot shower, she'd told him, and to make a stab at the paperwork she professed to hate. He'd tried sacking out in his own room next door, only to find himself too restless to sleep.

"Double Scotch, neat." The bartender slapped a white napkin in front of him before serving the drink. "Just the way you like 'em."

Jess nodded his thanks. "What time you close up around here?" he asked without really caring.

"Two o'clock. You have plenty of time before last call. More'n enough time to put you under—if that's what you're aiming for."

"It's a thought." But not a good one for a man with a lot of thinking to do.

"If it's company you're interested in—"

"It's not."

The bartender raised both hands and took a step backward. "No offense, friend. It's just that you had the look of a man who needed loosenin' up, that's all."

The man walked away, and Jess went back to staring into his drink. A woman was the last thing he needed, he thought. Especially a pro.

He'd been with his share that first year after he'd gotten out of the rehab hospital. It had been easier to pay for sex than risk having his ego chopped into hamburger by a woman who couldn't quite keep the pity out of her eyes when he took off his shirt.

After the first few times he'd found himself lonelier than ever. Physically, the women were practiced and clever and outwardly willing, but the warmth he'd craved was missing. More often than not he'd ended up with empty pockets and an even emptier feeling inside.

These days he would rather live with loneliness and die celibate than put himself through that kind of hell again.

Here's to self-control, he thought, lifting his glass to his image in the mirror. Before he could drink, however, he found himself face-to-face with O'Connor.

Without makeup, she looked more like a hell-raising tomboy than a highly professional career woman. He decided that he liked her better this way, which didn't do a damn thing for his mood.

"I was heading for the restaurant and some hot chocolate when I saw you sitting in here," she murmured as she slipped onto the stool next to him and signaled the bartender.

"I'll have a glass of white wine, please," she said when he approached.

"Yes, ma'am."

The bartender gave Jess a look that said all the wrong things, but Jess let it pass. Instead he turned his attention to Hazel.

"How're you coming with the paperwork?"

"All done, thank goodness, and I feel very virtuous."

"So how come you're having trouble sleeping?" he asked when she seemed content to sit next to him without speaking.

"Every time I close my eyes, I see Silvia's face. I've been racking my brains, trying to figure out the best way I can help."

The bartender returned with her drink, left it in front of her and retreated to the other end of the bar—all without uttering a word.

"How about you?" she said after she'd tasted the wine.

He shrugged. She was sitting on his right side and that made him edgy. As casually as a man his size could manage, he turned on the stool until his body was angled toward hers. He felt more comfortable that way. More in charge.

"It's too early to turn in, and I'm not much for TV."

"Somehow I wouldn't have thought you were much for sitting alone in a bar, either," she commented before taking another sip.

"It's been a while."

"For me, too." She folded her hands on the bar and allowed a reminiscent smile to play over her lips. Jess felt desire tug at him and gave himself a moment to savor it before stamping it down.

"You want to tell me about it?" he asked, knowing full well that she did. Dark bars had a way of loosening tongues sometimes. Or forging temporary friendships.

He wasn't much for either these days, but the Scotch had made him lazy. Or maybe he was tired of drinking alone. He didn't care much which, just so long as he didn't have to think about Silvia Yoder.

Hazel gave him a curious look. "Promise you won't laugh?"

"Scout's honor."

Hazel adjusted the collar of her silk shirt, inadvertently drawing Jess's gaze to the slight shadow between the open lapels, and his blood pressure rose a notch.

"It was my thirty-seventh birthday, and my 'significant other' at the time had just called it quits because he'd fallen in love with his twenty-two-year-old graduate assistant. Remember him? I brought him to the McClanes's Christmas party that year. Tall blond guy, with a beard. He was head of the psych department at State. I thought he was very stable. He thought I was a prude."

Jess caught a flavor of defiance in her voice and wondered if she were more self-conscious about her age or being dumped.

"There's a lot of that going around, I hear," he reassured her without really knowing why. "Half the guys I know my age are working on second families."

"Tell me about it," she responded dryly.

Her tone was accented in three creased lines above a nose a bit too long to be called pert. Jess had an urge to pull her close and kiss away those lines, but he had a strong feeling he wouldn't be able to stop at one brief kiss.

"Anyway, I decided to get drunk and forget the bozo and his new little twit."

Jess tried to imagine Dr. Hazel O'Connor drunk, but the image didn't quite work. Now tipsy, that was something else. He had a feeling she would be more playful then, in the way that innately sensuous women often are. His mind veered into dangerous speculation before he could stop himself.

"Did it work?"

"Which part? Getting drunk or forgetting?"

"Forgetting. The drunk part is easy."

"Sure," she said with a grin that kindled intriguing little lights in her eyes. "Somewhere between my last drink and my first frantic trip to the bathroom to toss my cookies, I fell out of love."

About to take a drink, Jess sloshed Scotch on his thigh, then swore at his clumsiness. Slanting her a disbelieving look didn't help. She was still grinning like a kid who'd just pulled off a prank.

"What is this, O'Connor?" he drawled. "Shrink humor?"

Her lips pursed into a thoughtful pout, and her eyes went out of focus. "Nooo, more like an experiment."

She toyed with her napkin, making little pleats around the stem of the glass. She had small fingers, he noticed. Slender. And her nails were cut short and covered with clear polish instead of the blood red most of the other women he knew favored these days.

"What kind of experiment?"

"I wanted to see if I could keep you interested enough to break the world's record."

Her eyes gleamed like a small cat's in the dim light. Anticipating his next question, he figured. Ready to spring the punch line on him.

She wasn't flirting; he wasn't about to kid himself that the lady found him sexually attractive. But she wasn't the proper professional he usually encountered, either.

He shifted on the hard stool, more aware than he should be of the attraction he was feeling. "Okay, O'Connor. I'll bite. What world's record?"

"Hmm, just a minute, please."

She held her wrist to the dim light illuminating the bar and focused her gaze on the face of a small gold watch.

In the dim light her hair seemed a darker shade of red. Chestnut, maybe, like a cutting horse he'd had as a kid, but softer. Definitely softer.

He thumbed the condensation on his glass and wondered how hair that looked that soft would feel sliding through his fingers. Or brushing his neck.

And he wondered if her skin would be as warm and smooth to the touch as it looked in the dim bar light.

They'd bought a few necessities at the 7-Eleven after they'd checked in, things they'd needed for the unexpected overnight stay—toothbrushes and paste, a disposable razor for him, shampoo for her, odds and ends. One thing she hadn't bought, however, was a nightgown. Like him, she would be sleeping in the nude. Or damn near, anyway.

"Drumroll, please," she said, holding up one finger. Jess caught the amused look on the bartender's face and felt like a prize idiot.

"O'Connor—"

"You did it," she said with an exaggerated look of astonishment that had him scowling before he even knew why.

"Did what, damn it?"

"Remained in my presence for more than fifteen solid minutes before making an excuse to leave."

Jess muttered the first words that came to mind, which didn't faze the lady in the least. "We had dinner together, remember? And before that, we spent two hours driving down from Sacramento and another half a day sitting in the waiting room.

"Ah, but that was business."

"And this isn't?"

"Nope." She leaned her elbow on the bar and buried her chin in her palm. Noting his scowl, she wondered what it would feel like to have that hard, serious mouth capturing hers.

"So tell me, Dante, what was going on the last time you were sitting alone in a bar?"

She looked directly into his eyes, as though daring him to answer, and Jess wasn't sure he'd ever met a woman he'd wanted to kiss more. Her lips were silky, even without paint, and full enough to test a man's skill. The temptation to feel the texture and taste of that soft mouth was almost more than he could withstand.

When he spoke, his voice was cool, his gaze distant—for his sake, more than hers. "My not-quite-ex-wife had just had a baby with her new lover. His name was Stefano Giulliano. Ever hear of him?"

"Of course. He's a famous race-car driver, like you."

Not like me, Jess thought. The lucky bastard's still doing what he loves best instead of trying every day to convince himself that he doesn't miss the driving and the crowds and the winning.

"He's also the son of a bitch who was supposed to be my best friend."

"Ouch. That must have hurt."

"I got over it."

She made no attempt to hide the depth of feeling his words aroused in her. Jess had a feeling she would demand equal openness and emotional honesty from any man who wanted her.

"Where is she now? Your ex, I mean."

"Last I heard she was living in Paris and spending Stef's money as fast as he made it."

"And the child?"

"Probably in a boarding school someplace. Gayla wasn't what you'd call maternal."

Jess stared into his drink. He hadn't thought about Gayla and Stef in years, not consciously, anyway. Even then it had been triggered by something unexpected, like a glimpse of their faces in the grocery store tabloids.

Once, right after their fancy Monte Carlo wedding, the reporter had included pictures of Gayla as she'd been right after his accident, looking stricken and beautiful in the hospital chapel praying for his recovery.

And like the dutiful, loving wife she'd seemed in the photo, she'd been at his bedside when he'd come out of the anesthetic fog to discover the doctors had taken his arm at the shoulder.

The doctors had had to tie him down for a week before he'd calmed down. Even then they'd kept a watch on him for several more weeks. A suicide watch, they'd told him later.

Gayla had stuck it out until he was out of the hospital. He'd been trying to find something else to do with his time besides feel sorry for himself when she'd told him that she was divorcing him. No hard feelings, she'd said, but she'd married a world-class race-car driver, not a has-been who couldn't even make love properly.

A woman laughed somewhere behind them, low and throaty. Jess wondered if she and the man she was with would end the evening making love. Hazel started, as though she, too, had been lost in her own thoughts.

"So that brings us back to the current problem," she murmured as she brought her glass to her lips. "I phoned the prison, but they wouldn't put me through to the infirmary. Regulations, they said."

"Yes, I know." He'd gotten through to the office of the assistant warden, only to have some flunky gleefully inform him that the man was sick in bed with the flu. "I figured we'd get over there sometime around eight-thirty tomorrow.''

"I thought visiting hours didn't start until ten."

"They don't, but attorneys get special privileges." If they pushed hard enough and refused to take no for an answer.

"Have you decided what you're going to do first? Besides convincing Silvia to fight for the baby?"

Jess felt something hard thud in his belly. "Not for certain, no."

"What if Silvia still insists that she wants you to adopt Francisca? Then what?"

"I'll convince her to change her mind." He allowed himself one more sip before pushing aside the half-finished Scotch. He wasn't drunk, but he wasn't quite sober, either.

"I'm not sure that will be so easy."

Jess drew a long, deep breath that smelled of cigarettes and booze. Once it had been motor oil and grease filling his nostrils. He still missed the high they'd given him.

"The last thing I want to do is hurt the woman any more than she's been hurt. But what she's asking . . ." He shook his head. "Try to see it my way, O'Connor. Even if I petitioned for adoption, Protective Services would just haul out the rules and regs and a list of precedents showing that an over-forty bachelor with an obvious physical handicap isn't daddy material, and by the time the judge ruled against me, Francisca would have been stuck in a foster home someplace for months, maybe years."

"You might win."

"Don't kid yourself, Doctor. The system in this country has been stacked against minorities for more than three hundred years. And whether I like it or not, my disability makes me a minority."

Hazel wasn't one to admit defeat, but he was right. She'd fought the system too many times . . . and lost—to pretend otherwise.

"She'll be upset. You'd better prepare yourself."

Jess felt his face grow hot. "You think I don't know that?"

"I think you're a good man with a kind heart he works hard at hiding."

"Bull."

She challenged him with a look that invited him to share his innermost thoughts, but then, Jess told himself, that was her job, wasn't it? Drawing deeply buried secrets out into the light and then getting rid of the hurt.

Kids' secrets, he reminded himself. Kids' hurts. Not the kind that cut deep and went on cutting, no matter what kind of medicine a guy tried.

Jess reached for the drink he'd shoved aside and finished it in one gulp. "If I am, it's a private battle," he said as he signaled the bartender for another round.

"In other words, 'O'Connor, butt out.'"

"Exactly."

Her laughter was soft and directed more at herself than him. Or perhaps she'd just felt like laughing. Nothing was predictable with this woman. Nor out-of-bounds the way it was with most women he knew.

"There's so much that's good and strong and special in you," she murmured as though to herself. "And almost all of it hidden so deep I'm not even sure you know it's there."

He felt a stir, like the quick pause before a perfectly tuned engine unleashed its horses. And then she put a gentle hand on his mutilated shoulder, leaned forward and kissed him.

With the stain of shock still hot on his face, she took a twenty from her wallet and laid it on the bar before sliding gracefully from the stool.

"Don't be so hard on yourself, Dante. You don't deserve it."

Chapter 4

It was still early, but the restaurant was packed. Now that the weather had turned nice again, the tourists were eager to close the final gap between themselves and the bright lights of San Francisco.

Jess slitted his eyes against the sunshine streaming through the windows and wondered if his head was hard enough to handle the mother of all hangovers without busting wide open.

All those high-priced scientists who swore alcohol was an anesthetic were out of their collective minds. He figured there was at least a pint of Scotch still circulating in his veins, more, maybe, if the churning in his gut was even a halfway accurate gauge.

Just blinking hurt, he discovered as he popped the two aspirin he'd garnered from the waitress into his mouth and washed them down with bitter black coffee.

Tying one on had been a decision he'd made with his gut, not his head. And like most decisions made that way, it had been a mistake.

At least this mistake wouldn't cost him more than a splitting headache and a queasy belly, he told himself grimly. Others, like marrying the wrong woman and giving in to some idiotic idea of racetrack ethics, had been more costly.

Someplace close a baby cried suddenly, and he winced. A mom and dad and three kids were taking over the next booth. The hostess hovered, ready with a high chair.

Closing his eyes, he rubbed his aching temples and tried not to think of the next few hours. Or the sad, sick mother of another baby who'd had to turn to her attorney for help because no one else cared.

A spoon banged on the high-chair tray, and he all but groaned aloud at the painful spasm in his temple. At the same time he saw Hazel come in.

She had a quick smile for the harried hostess and a few words that made the overworked woman laugh.

Something moved inside him, like the first pangs of hunger after a long fast. Habit had him ignoring it as he watched her over his coffee cup.

Shorter than most women he knew, she had an exciting body, built more for endurance than a flash of speed. His ex-wife and her kind would sneer and call her plump, but Gayla and her friends had taken their standards from the shiny magazines, not a man's fantasy life. His never failed to kick start when Hazel was around.

She hesitated by the hostess station, scanning the nonsmoking section. Jess guessed that she was looking for him, a guess that proved correct when she spied him by the window and made a beeline in his direction.

People noticed, both men and women. If Hazel noticed them noticing, however, she didn't seem bothered one way or another.

As she approached, he tensed, waiting for her to throw him the same quick smile she'd given everyone else. When she didn't, he didn't know whether to be disappointed or pleased.

"Have you ordered yet?" she asked as she slipped into the seat across from him and dropped her purse onto the empty chair between them.

"Just coffee so far." He indicated the pot between the two place settings.

"A man after my own heart." She poured herself a cup and took a greedy sip, her eyes half-closed as though in ecstasy. "It's not officially morning until I've had my coffee," she murmured when she caught him looking at her.

"You look bright enough."

"You don't."

"Thanks, I needed that."

She raised both eyebrows, as though doing so helped her study of his face. His strength exerted the most pull on her, she decided. And the quiet resilience that showed in the occasional bursts of self-mocking humor directed toward his handicap. He was solid and dependable, a man who would be there for you if you fell—and then give you holy hell for being so clumsy.

She smiled, projecting both sympathy and scolding at the same time. "I thought you liked plain speaking?"

"A little tact now and then wouldn't hurt."

"I hate to tell you this, Jess, but I was *being* tactful."

After treating herself to another few sips, she cupped her coffee mug between her hands and rested it against her chin. Above the steam curling upward, her eyes took on a sleepy cast that made a man wonder if she woke up slow like a cat or quick like a nervous little doe.

Either way, he had a feeling she would be a pleasure to kiss first thing in the morning. Annoyed with himself and his thoughts, he concentrated on ignoring her. He wasn't used to talking to anyone but himself in the morning, and it was a hard habit to break.

"So, Counselor, what time did you get to bed last night?" she asked when the silence stretched.

Jess shrugged his good shoulder, then winced as pain burst in his head. "Burt and I closed the place."

"Burt?"

"The bartender."

"Ah, best friends are you, now?"

"Something like that, yeah."

The hint of perfume was gone, he noticed, replaced by the subtle tang of soap. Either suited her, he decided, although he preferred the natural scent as much as he'd preferred the absence of makeup.

"Good thing California has closing laws."

"Speak for yourself, Doctor."

"Uh-oh, we're in a lousy mood, are we?" She leaned back, taking her cup with her. He wondered if she were a tennis player. Or maybe a dancer. Something that combined grace and stamina.

"I'm in the mood for food."

"Looks like you tangled with that razor you bought yesterday—and lost."

It took Jess a second to realize that she was talking about the twin nicks along the edge of his jaw. He tested his recently shaven skin with his fingers and felt the fresh blood.

"I never did like disposable razors," he said as he wiped his bloody fingers on the paper napkin. At home he used an electric. Shaving with a blade one-handed cost him more time and frustration than it was worth. "Guess I'm lucky I didn't cut my throat."

"Nothing like camping out."

She saluted him with her cup before reaching for one of the menus lying on the table between them. As he scanned the other, Jess thought about the sleep he'd needed and hadn't gotten and wondered if she'd heard him pacing the floor through the wall between them.

If she had, she'd probably put down his restlessness to a guilty conscience. And she would be partly right, he decided, as he signaled the waitress.

As for the rest, some things a man kept to himself, things he couldn't do anything about—like pain in a limb that wasn't there and a need for a small, feisty, redheaded woman that was so strong it scared him.

Hazel had just put down her menu when the waitress reached them. The face was different from the woman's last night, but the weariness in the eyes was the same.

"Morning folks," she said, flipping her pad to a clean sheet. "Looks like the storm's past, don't it?"

Hazel darted him a glance before answering. "I'm not sure. Ask me again in ten minutes."

The waitress looked puzzled, then shrugged it off. She had little time for riddles during the breakfast rush. "What can I get you?"

Jess watched Hazel discuss the relative merits of waffles versus pancakes and noticed that she had a way of drawing her listener in, of making her an ally—or a coconspirator. Either way, it was a knack he'd worked hard to perfect in the courtroom. He had a feeling she came by it naturally.

"Number six, burn the bacon, eggs over easy and a large tomato juice," he said when the waitress turned to him. "And add a shot of vodka to that juice."

"Coming right up," the waitress said with a knowing grin before turning again to Hazel. "How about you, ma'am? Something else to drink besides the juice?"

"Just orange juice for me. I went to bed a lot earlier than my friend here."

Laughing, the waitress headed for the bar.

Jess stared into his cup, waiting for the throbbing in his head to ease. He would have given a month's worth of retainers to have this day over and done with.

"Jess, I've been thinking."

He glanced up to find her watching him again. Another of her annoying habits, like grinning when he wasn't in the mood to grin back, and prodding a man into talking about things he had no business sharing with anyone else.

"Sometimes that's not a good idea."

"I know," she said, sighing dramatically. "It's a bad habit I developed before I knew better, and now I can't seem to break it."

"Most habits are like that."

"True." She inhaled quickly; then, before she lost her courage, she blurted out, "I think you should give some thought to adopting Silvia's baby."

Shock rocked him hard, but training and habit kept it hidden behind the stare jurors had called intimidating.

"You're serious, aren't you?"

"Perfectly."

"I've been called a lot of things, but 'Daddy' isn't one of them, and for good reason. I'd be lousy at the job."

"How do you know, if you've never tried it?"

"I've never tried hanging, either, but I'm pretty sure I'd hate it."

Hazel watched the cynical curl of his mouth and decided that he hadn't been born that way. Life had done that to him. Or rather, he'd allowed it to happen. Jess might have been terribly injured at one time in his life, but he hadn't let himself become a victim. She didn't think it was in him to give up that much control to anything or anyone.

"You're almost a second father to Jesse and Kelsey," she reminded him with a smile.

"They're different."

"Simply older."

Jess tried to stare her down, but she hung in there, her gaze locked with his and her mouth set. Sipping coffee had blotted off most of her lipstick, leaving her lips pale and vulnerable.

The need to taste her came again, stronger this time. He tamped it down.

"That's just the point. Babies need feeding, changing, holding."

"Very true."

"And a little girl . . . hell, I couldn't even braid her hair."

"That would be a terrible tragedy, I agree."

His mouth relaxed for an instant, then slanted into a reluctant grin. "You're not helping, O'Connor."

"Funny, I thought I was doing the best I could."

Jess sat back suddenly, his gaze roaming her face intently. The smile she'd wrung from him was still lurking, mostly in the slight curve of his mouth and in the hint of a crease next to the harshly controlled corners. It suited him, she decided. That cautious, even reluctant, surrender to amusement that came from him at unexpected moments.

"It was a mistake bringing you along, I can see that now. You'd make a joke out of a hanging."

"Only if I'm the one being hanged. And don't try to change the subject. Or, what do you lawyer types call it? Misdirect the witness?"

She saw the waitress approaching, both hands full of dishes. "Now where were we? Oh yes, Francisca. She won't be a baby long, you know. Pretty soon she'll be walking and talking."

"Yeah, and then what?"

Hazel waited until the waitress had deftly placed food and condiments in the proper places and left again, promising to return shortly with the drinks.

"Then she'll grow up, just like the rest of us."

He slanted her an impatient look. "I don't know about you, O'Connor, but I grew up with a mother and a father and a couple of brothers. It wasn't a perfect family, but at least it worked at being normal."

"So?"

"So Francisca would grow up without a mother and—"

"It's been done before."

"—and a father who couldn't even hug her properly."

"I doubt that she'd mind as long as he *did* hug her."

"Damn it, O'Connor, stop being a bleeding heart for five minutes and face facts. A guy like me has no place trying to raise a kid alone—his own or anyone else's."

"So get married."

"Very funny."

The edge to his voice and the ice in his eyes warned her to back off. Jess rarely used the considerable power of his personality to intimidate, but when he did, the recipient took instant notice.

He'd heard it was usually that way with people who lived every day with an obvious handicap, especially men. Com-

pensation, the textbooks called it. The need to be tougher
and rougher and fiercely independent, so no one would dare
pity them.

"I'm serious, Jess," she continued with slightly more
force than necessary. "It's the 'in' thing to do now, didn't
you know? Part of the AIDS backlash. I just read an arti-
cle the other day that said marriage license bureaus all over
the country were being swamped."

His jaw edged forward. "I've been married. Once was
enough."

"Then hire a nanny. You can afford it."

"No thanks. I like my privacy."

"Aha!" she cried softly. "Now we get to the bottom line.
You don't want a child rearranging your nice tidy life."

His eyes narrowed and grew even icier. "That's not it at
all. If I really thought it was possible..." His voice trailed
off for an instant before he added with far more force, "But
it's not. No judge is going to give a baby to a guy like me,
period."

"You've taken on tough cases before and won."

"Not like this one. As far as I know, there's not one
precedent in the history of California law."

Hazel opened her mouth, then shut it again. It hurt her to
admit it, but what he was saying was very likely true. She
herself had been involved peripherally in such a case a year
or so ago, testifying for the petitioner, a man with cerebral
palsy who'd wanted to adopt a child with the same condi-
tion. His petition had been denied.

Jess saw the truth in her eyes. And the frustration. It
matched his own. "I rest my case."

Jess shoved aside his plate and leaned back against the
vinyl booth. When their eyes met again, Hazel sensed that
he was already regretting the unexpected glimpse he'd given
her into the man behind the intimidating scowl.

"What about Silvia?" she asked gently. "You heard what
she said."

Pain flashed in his eyes before he dropped his gaze. "All that stuff about praying... believe me, I'm nobody's answer to a prayer."

"No comment." She teased him with a smile and won a scowl in return.

"I'll explain everything to her. She'll understand."

The waitress returned with juice for Hazel and a Bloody Mary for him. Jess ignored the food and reached for his drink.

The vodka tasted foul on an already queasy stomach, like something dredged up from a storm drain. Flinching, he shoved it aside and washed away the taste with a slug of coffee.

"Serves you right," Hazel muttered as she picked up her fork and stabbed the pineapple garnish. Watching, Jess felt a new flare of pain in his head and fire in his gut. "Aw, hell," he muttered.

At the same time the baby in the next booth started crying again, causing the young mother to cast worried looks at nearby tables.

"I'd better take him out," she whispered loudly to her husband.

"No, you sit still," he ordered with a smile in his voice. "I'll do it."

"We'll be right there," his wife assured him as he hoisted the crying infant from the high chair and tucked him against his shoulder.

"How old is he?" Hazel asked when the other woman raised her eyebrows in silent apology.

"Almost six months." She sighed. "Wouldn't you know he'd wait until our vacation to cut his first tooth?"

Hazel laughed softly. "Of course. It's Murphy's Law."

"Isn't it, though?" the other woman said on a sigh before urging her other two children to drink their milk and wipe their mouths.

While their mother was counting out the tip, the two youngsters slipped from the booth, jostling each other in the process.

The boy—the oldest, by the looks of him—stumbled against Jess's edge of the booth and would have fallen if Jess hadn't grabbed him.

"Sorry," the boy mumbled, righting himself. "It's my sister's fault. She's always trying to act like a big shot."

"I hear sisters can be like that," Jess agreed gravely.

Interest sparked in the boy's blue eyes. "Do you have a sister?"

"Nope. Two big brothers, though. They were almost as bad."

"My little brother's already a pain."

"Maybe he doesn't mean to be."

The boy shrugged, then slid a glance toward his mother, who was greedily gulping the last of her coffee, as though fortifying herself for the next leg of the trip.

"What happened to your arm?" he asked, his gaze slicing to Jess's empty sleeve.

"I had an accident. The doctors had to amputate to save my life."

"What's amp... amp... that word?"

"Amputate means to cut off. The doctors cut off my arm because it was too badly smashed up to put together again."

"Yuck, that sounds gross!"

Jess managed a smile. "People tell me it was, but I was mostly asleep, so I don't remember."

"Don't you miss it? Your arm, I mean."

"Sometimes, but there's nothing I can do about it."

The boy frowned. "Yeah, but—"

"That's enough, Todd," the boy's mother declared in a low, embarrassed tone. "Daddy's waiting."

Taking both children firmly in hand, she met Jess's eyes reluctantly. "I'm sorry," she said, lifting her shoulders in a helpless shrug. "He doesn't mean anything."

"Forget it," Jess told her. "He's curious, that's all. Most people are, but not many have the guts to admit it."

Looking relieved, the mother murmured something about being late and shepherded the kids toward the cashier's counter.

"You handled that very well."

Jess glanced up to find Hazel watching him. "I've had practice."

"Some people might have blasted him."

"It was my own damn fault for not coming in for a tire change when I should have, not his."

"Do you miss racing?"

"What's the point of missing something you know you can't have?" Jess snatched his napkin from his lap and stood. "If you're ready, we might as well get this over with."

As soon as Dr. Benoit turned away from the window in her office, Hazel knew.

"Silvia didn't make it, did she?" she asked softly.

The doctor shook her head, and Hazel thought that she'd been crying.

"She died early this morning. The night aide called me around four to say that Silvia was unconscious, but by the time I got here, it was all over."

Hazel drew a shaky breath. Jess's mouth went white.

"Why didn't you call me?" he demanded of the doctor.

"Two reasons," she said calmly. "One, there wasn't time. And two, there wasn't anything you could have done for her."

Scowling, he walked to the window, braced his hand on the frame and stared at the concrete and steel beyond. "How did it happen?" he asked without turning.

"Technically, she had a stroke, but I think she really died because she didn't want to live any longer."

Jess didn't move, but somehow Hazel knew that he'd flinched.

"Dr. Benoit," she asked softly, "what about the baby? Have you notified Protective Services?"

"Yes, about an hour ago. Because adoption papers hadn't been drawn up, Francisca's caseworker is arranging for a foster placement. She said it would take a day or two to find the right situation. In the meantime—"

"In the meantime, we need to get that kid out of here." Jess turned suddenly, his shoulders squared and a dangerous glitter in his eyes.

The doctor shook her head. "I don't have that authority, Mr. Dante."

"Then give me the number of someone who does." Without asking permission, he picked up the phone and jammed it between his shoulder and jaw, his hand ready to punch out the number.

"It's on the pad, but I can't release the child to you or anyone without a written court order."

Jess slapped the phone onto the hook. "Where's the nearest fax machine?"

Benoit hesitated. "In the administration building."

Jess shot Hazel an impatient look. "You'd better do what you have to do to get the kid ready, because neither one of us is leaving without her."

Making love in the back seat of a car had never been a favorite of Hazel's. Changing a baby in such confined quarters, however, had zoomed right to the top of the list of things she never wanted to do again.

"What's wrong with her now?"

Hazel glanced up from the high-tech disposable diaper she was trying to unstick from her fingers and answered Jess's glare with one of her own.

"Don't ask me. I'm just as new at this as you are."

Lying half-bare on the blanket protecting the leather upholstery of Jess's beloved Mercedes, Francisca took a deep breath, hiccuped and started bellowing her outrage so loudly that the windows seemed to rattle. At the same time she bicycled her feet, making the task of changing her diaper an exercise in patience.

"It's okay, sweetheart. Just be patient with your Auntie Hazel okay?"

Bless her heart, little Francey had slept like a tiny pink-swaddled angel for the first hour, and then she'd started to squirm and fuss and generally exhibit signs of unhappiness.

At the first wail out of the baby's mouth, Jess had wanted to pull to the shoulder immediately. Hazel had convinced him, after a vigorous debate that had Francisca screaming even louder, to wait until the nearest rest stop. That had been ten minutes ago.

Jess scowled at her over the back of the seat. "Damn it, O'Connor," he ordered. "Do something. She's in pain."

"She's wet, that's all."

"Oh yeah? Then how come her face is all scrunched up like that?"

"Wouldn't yours be if your underdrawers were sopping wet?"

She nearly laughed out loud at the dumbfounded look on his face. "You have a point," he muttered as dusky color washed his olive complexion.

"Don't worry, she'll be fine—once I get this blasted thing on her properly."

"I still say you bought the wrong size."

"You heard me ask. The clerk recommended these."

"That clerk was seventy if she was a day. We should have gotten a second opinion."

Jess ran his hand through hair already furrowed by his long fingers. If she didn't know better, she would have sworn the man was on the verge of panic.

"Trust me, Jess. We got the right diapers."

"Then why is the kid still lying there buck-naked while you go through one after another, trying to make them fit?"

Hazel drew a quick breath. Beads of perspiration had broken out along her hairline, and her right leg had gone to sleep.

"Because I've only diapered two babies in my entire life, and I used cloth diapers and old-fashioned safety pins both times. These things were obviously invented by a committee of confirmed bachelors."

Hazel used her teeth to rip the sticky tab from her thumb. The plastic tore, and she muttered under her breath as she awkwardly extracted another folded diaper from the box.

Still scowling, Jess rearranged his long body in the old car's bucket seat one more time. "Are you sure Cait and Ty are expecting us?"

"I'm sure. Ty even promised to have Jesse's old port-a-crib cleaned up and waiting."

"What about clothes and things? All that junk you walked right by in the store."

"Everything's under control." Hazel used her chin to point toward the console. "However, this torpedo of yours is equipped with a phone. Call them yourself if you don't believe me."

His hand plowed the same furrows, wreaking more havoc. "I didn't say I didn't believe you," he muttered. "I just don't like loose ends."

"Ends you haven't tied up yourself, you mean."

Hazel concentrated on restraining the wildly kicking baby legs long enough to slip the diaper under the round baby fanny. Francey's skin was like velvet, her bones small as a bunny's, but the adorable little girl had the lungs of an opera diva.

"Now, if I can just get this thing...now the other... there!"

"She's still crying," Jess accused harshly.

"In case you haven't noticed, I do have ears," Hazel murmured as she wrapped the baby in the snuggly blanket.

"It's okay, darling girl," she crooned. "Auntie Hazel's got you." Cooing softly, she lifted the warm bundle to her shoulder and patted the screaming little girl's back.

Francey gave one more yell, hiccuped, and then to Hazel's amazement shut her small mouth and closed her eyes. Scarcely daring to breathe, Hazel looked up and grinned.

She'd surprised Jess with his guard down and his emotions exposed. Hazel knew that she'd never seen such abject longing in anyone before. Not in the patients she'd treated, adult or child. And not in herself, even during her blackest moments.

She drew a quick breath, her grin fading. Like a fast freeze in a movie, they were locked in a glance. And then, quick as the blinking of his heavy eyelashes, he changed from a man who had suffered terribly, who was still suffering, to the remote, self-proclaimed cynic who worked hard at keeping her and everyone else at a distance.

"Guess you were right," he said a shade too gruffly. "About her crying, I mean."

He'd been right about their not leaving without the baby. It had taken most of the morning, but Jess had gotten his court order—signed, witnessed and faxed to the warden's office by Judge Henry W. Pollard.

Both Dr. Benoit and the Protective Services caseworker had been stunned that he'd managed so quickly—and the doctor was also pleased.

Hazel wondered how many other authority figures had bent the rules when Jess Dante had asked. Must have something to do with his size, she told herself. Or possibly that hard, flat, commanding tone that overrode the sexy timbre of his voice when he wanted something.

"Jess, tell me the truth," she said softly as she patted the baby's back and waited for the tiny body to relax again. "How did you get Judge Pollard to grant you temporary custody?"

"I told him that I was arranging a private adoption pursuant to the mother's deathbed wishes."

Hazel's mouth went dry, and she hugged Francey closer. "You did?"

"What the hell. Like you said, it's worth a shot."

Chapter 5

Jess sprawled on the big leather sofa in the McClanes's den and watched Ty splashing brandy into a glass. Over their heads in the guest room Hazel and Cait were getting the baby settled in the small folding crib.

"Make it a double," he said when Ty lifted his eyebrows in his direction.

"That bad, huh?"

"If you call having my life turned upside down in a little less than thirty-six hours bad, yeah."

Ty made it a triple. "I'd join you, but I'm on call," he told him, recapping the decanter.

"The downside of being a world-class surgeon," Jess said as he accepted the balloon glass. While Jess sipped, Ty settled his still-lean frame into "his" chair, the one Cait tried to give away at least once a year without success, and hoisted a long leg over the arm.

"How long did you say it took you to drive up from Pleasanton?"

"Four hours." For a trip that had rarely taken Jess more than two in the past. "My car still smells like sour milk."

Ty grinned. "What can I say, buddy? Babies spit up."

"And mess their pants—"

"Diapers."

Jess poured a big slug of brandy down his throat and waited for the knots in his gut to ease. "Pants, diapers, whatever you call 'em. Hazel must have gone through half the box we bought before we left Pleasanton."

"Sounds familiar."

"Every time I got up to speed, she was having me pull over. Hell if I know how folks with kids ever get anywhere on time."

"Careful planning—and a lot of luck."

Ty made it sound easy, Jess thought, but then, Ty was crazy in love. He would do anything for Caitie and those kids of theirs.

"Have you found me a baby nurse yet?"

Ty rested his head against one of the padded wings. He and Jess were the same age, but Ty's hair was nearly all gray now, while Jess's still had more black than gray.

"Not yet, but I just put out the feelers a few hours ago."

"You know a lot of nurses. There must be one or two who you trust to take care of a newborn."

Ty shot him a wry look. "Seems to me you said you learned patience after they hacked off your arm."

"I did."

"How about showing me some, then?"

Jess studied the brandy in his glass. "Odds say we're just wasting our time, anyway."

"You're really serious about trying to adopt this baby, then?"

"I gave my word to Henry Pollard that I am, so I'd better be."

"Why? Because you feel an obligation to the baby's mother?"

Leaning forward, Jess set his glass on the coffee table in front of him. He'd had enough to drink.

"Partly. And partly because, corny as it sounds, I can't stand the idea of a total stranger taking Silvia's child. Not when they took just about everything else from her."

He shook his head and leaned back against the soft cushions again. "But now that I've had some time to consider it, I think I have to be out of my mind."

Tyler propped both arms behind his head and regarded Jess thoughtfully. "Sounds to me like you're scared."

"Damn straight I am! What do I know about raising a little girl?"

"About as much as I did, I imagine. Which is about as much as most fathers."

Too restless to sit any longer, Jess got to his feet and walked to the window overlooking the big backyard. Toy trucks littered the sandbox he'd helped Ty build, and twelve-year-old Kelsey's bathing suit was hanging over the mesh fence ringing the pool. Two cats, one gray and one a startling white, were curled in separate chairs, sleeping.

"Hell, Ty, my life is arranged around the things I can do, not the things I can't. But with a child . . ." he shrugged " . . . that's not always going to be possible."

"You've done all right so far."

Jess turned his back to the window and angled a hip against the wide sill. He respected Ty as much as he'd ever respected anyone in his life, and he still shuddered when he remembered the times he'd visited Ty in state prison.

Somehow, though, Ty had survived hell and come back a better man. But then, Ty had always had a need to put others first. Until that fateful afternoon at the track, Jess Dante had always been number one to Jess Dante.

He drew a deep breath. "I'm not sure I can hack it if all of a sudden she decides she's ashamed of her old man because he's a cripple. Dumb, huh?"

"No, not dumb. Understandable." Ty glanced around the comfortable, well-appointed room before returning his gaze to Jess. "I'm still an ex-con, even if my name has been cleared. There's always a chance my kids will someday be ashamed of me for that."

"It's not the same thing. You were innocent."

"And you're still as much of a man as you were before you lost your arm."

Jess stared down at the ornate pattern woven with such care and skill into a valuable oriental rug. There had been a time when he'd considered himself a man because he had the ribbons and trophies and the notches on his bedpost to prove it. These days he didn't quite know what he was. Sometimes he thought he was afraid to find out.

"Maybe, but I'm also a realist." He glanced up to find Tyler watching him.

"Yeah, right, Dante. That's why you're going to fight the odds and the system and your own doubts in order to adopt a child who you're not even sure will appreciate it if you win."

"Look, Ty, I've already been through this with O'Connor and—"

Ty's pager trilled, interrupting the conversation. Flipping it off, he got to his feet and reached for the phone. "This is Dr. McClane," he said when the call went through.

While Tyler listened to the voice on the other end, Jess walked to the big stone fireplace and looked at the framed snapshots crowding the mantel.

His favorite was the one of Hazel and him taken at Jesse's christening. She was holding Jesse in her arms and smiling for the camera, but the lens had caught a strange, wistful look in her eyes. Sometimes he wondered if a man could fall in love with a photograph, and then reminded himself that a man had to believe in love first.

"Okay, give me ten minutes."

Tyler's crisp command whipped Jess from the past to the present. Turning, he asked, "Problems?"

Tyler nodded, his expression grave. "An accident on the freeway, two dead, two critical. One is a four-year-old with a crushed chest. She's on her way to the hospital now via Life Flight."

Jess thought about a child's tiny bones and the damage sharp steel and broken glass could do in the wink of an eye. "Poor kid. I hope she makes it."

"Yeah, me too." Tyler grabbed his car keys from the drawer. "Gotta go. I'll see you when I get back."

"Good luck."

"Thanks."

Ty opened the door just as Hazel was raising her hand to knock. "Oops, sorry," she said with a tired grin as she and Tyler nearly collided.

"My fault." He bent down to kiss her cheek, then jerked his head in Jess's direction. "Sorry I have to run out on you all. Daddy there will explain."

Without waiting for an answer, Tyler loped down the hall, yelling his wife's name. Jess thought about the quiet rooms in his own house, filled only with the sound of his own voice or the TV he snapped on as soon as he walked in.

"Cait said that he was on call," Hazel said as she came into the den. "Looks like he got one."

Jess nodded. She'd shed her linen and silk as soon as they'd arrived at the McClanes's. Dressed now in a shirt and jeans borrowed from Cait, she seemed very different from the efficient professional who had gotten the baby packed up and ready to travel with very little fuss.

"Apparently there's been a bad accident on one of the freeways," he explained. "Ty's been called in to operate on a little girl with a crushed chest."

Hazel grimaced. "At least she's in good hands."

"If she makes it to the hospital."

Even then the poor little thing would go through hell and back before the splintered bones finally mended and the intractable pain stopped clawing at bruised nerves and torn flesh. Hang in there, kid, he thought. You can make it.

Hating the memories, he slipped his hand into his pocket and manufactured a smile. "How's the baby? All settled?"

"Sleeping like the adorable little angel she is."

"When her underdrawers aren't wet, you mean?"

Hazel grinned. "A minor glitch in her heavenly persona."

"Spoken like a doting aunt."

She grinned, but Jess saw the same wistful look in her eyes that he'd just noticed in the photograph behind him.

"Actually, I came down to tell you and Ty that Cait and I are going shopping."

"Shopping?"

She nodded. "For baby things. Cait made a list of the things you'll need before you take her home."

"Uh, right. I hadn't thought...you'll need my credit card."

"I think it would be easier if I used mine, and we can settle up later."

Jess nodded. "How long will you be gone?"

"No more than a couple of hours."

Jess frowned. "What about the baby?"

"I'll leave a bottle in the fridge. To warm it, just stick it in the microwave at half power for about a minute. Without the nipple, of course."

Jess had visions of scalding the kid's tiny little throat. "What if it's too hot?"

Hazel was busy rolling down the sleeves of the shirt she'd borrowed from Cait. It was some kind of almost white shiny material that looked terrific on her. Glancing up, she gave him a quick smile that had him thinking of his teen years, when he would get embarrassingly hard just looking at a pretty girl.

"Just shake a few drops on your wrist to test it before you give it to her."

Jess stiffened. "Oh yeah?" he drawled, deliberately loading his words with hard-edged sarcasm. "How am I supposed to do that—with my teeth?"

He waited for the fumbled apology, the flustered look, the carefully disguised pity that he hated about as much as he hated to look at himself in a full-length mirror.

Instead, impatience crossed her face as she glanced at his empty sleeve. "If that's what it takes, yes."

She consulted her watch before adding coolly, "We should be back by six, but if we're not, there are plenty of diapers on the bureau next to the crib."

Without waiting for an answer, she turned and walked out.

Hazel held up a doll-size shirt with tiny shell-pink ruffles around the sleeves and neck.

"How about this?"

Cait looked up from the terry sleepers she was sorting. They'd hit every department store in the mall, filling three shopping bags before Cait had remembered this baby boutique.

"It's adorable," she said with a tender smile, "but she'd only be in it a week or so before it would be too small."

Reluctantly, Hazel refolded the soft little shirt and replaced it on top of the stack before sorting through another pile for a larger size.

"Why do I feel like I've suddenly dropped about a hundred IQ points?"

Cait laughed. "When I was carrying Jesse, I read all the books, attended every class the Ob/Gyn clinic offered, even made out the ideal schedule for a newborn. Let me tell you, I was ready."

"I was there, remember?" Hazel said dryly. "By the time you delivered, I was seriously considering selling my practice and moving to Maui."

"It wasn't that bad," Cait grumbled.

"Worse. Remember the night you called me at three in the morning because you couldn't decide whether to use disposable or cloth diapers?" Hazel shook her head. "Let me tell you, Cait—at three o'clock, I couldn't have cared less."

Hazel watched Cait's cheeks turn pink. "Well, there was all that talk about landfills and the ecology versus the absolute horrors of diaper rash and water waste."

Hazel held up her hand. "Please! Save all that for Jess. I'm just Francey's honorary aunt, remember?"

Cait selected six sleepers in various colors and sizes and added them to the items already piled on the corner of one of the display tables.

"I assume Jess plans to hire a nanny."

"He's going to have to. At least until Francey's considerably older." Hazel fingered a fluffy rainbow quilt and thought about his awkwardly endearing attempt at gentleness when he'd held Silvia's hand.

"He claims he doesn't like children."

Cait's startled look probably mirrored her own earlier look. "Are you kidding? He's crazy about Kels and Jesse. He'd spoil them rotten if we'd let him."

"I mentioned that. He said that they're different." She added the quilt to the pile.

Cait shook her head. "Still, the thought of Jess actually becoming a father is a bit mind-boggling."

Hazel glanced at her friend questioningly. "Because of his disability?"

"Oh Lord, no! Mostly because he's such a man's man. All hard edges and tough surfaces. It's hard to picture him playing dolls and choosing school clothes and discussing the facts of life with a daughter."

Hazel worried her lower lip, debating how much to reveal. "It all happened so fast, the baby's birth, Silvia's death. And to tell you the truth, I all but shamed Jess into petitioning for adoption."

"Hazel, there are a lot of things I'm unsure about but one thing I'm not—no one forces Jess Dante to do something he doesn't want to do."

Hazel took scant comfort in Cait's words. Jess had a deep vein of decency that could push him into doing something he might regret.

"He didn't say much, but he took Silvia's death hard."

"Deep down, Jess is a very emotional man. Trouble is, he doesn't know it."

"Or maybe he deals with his emotions differently than we do."

"Most men do."

Cait nodded. "He's not like other men, though, is he? And I'm not just talking about his disability."

"He does tend to keep a person off balance, that's for sure."

Off balance and up half the night trying to erase the memory of a brief kiss that had been meant to soothe and ended up lighting fires.

"Did you ever see pictures of him when he was racing?"

Hazel glanced up in time to see Cait roll her eyes. "Talk about a stud! Thick black hair to his shoulders, the devil's own smile. Lord, I can't imagine anyone resisting Jess Dante when he was in his prime."

Or ever, Hazel added silently, thinking about the funny feeling in the vicinity of her diaphragm whenever he was around.

"He talked a little about his wife last night. Apparently she was pregnant when she left him—with his best friend's child no less."

Cait's eyebrows flew up. "He told you that?"

Hazel nodded. "Among other things. Why?"

Cait turned her back to the counter and sagged against it. "Hazel, Jess has been as close as a brother to Ty and me for five years and never . . . not even once—has he ever talked about his ex."

"Maybe you didn't ask."

"Are you kidding? You know me and my insatiable curiosity. Of course I asked. He was very sweet about it, but let me know in very clear terms that his past was not, I repeat, *not* a subject he cared to discuss.

"With Ty, then—"

"Nope. I know, because I asked. Ty said the same thing. When it comes to the ex-Mrs. Dante, Jess is a clam."

Hazel stared down at the miniature shirt in her hands. Instead of Francey, however, she was seeing Jess and the loneliness she'd sensed in him before he'd looked into the mirror behind the bar and seen her watching him.

"He'd had some Scotch. Maybe that's why."

"Or maybe there's something about you that gets to him, Hazel. Something he trusts in you and no one else."

Hazel felt her lips curve. "Whatever the reason, I'm not about to fool myself into believing I'm anything more to Jess than a sometime friend—and a darn good shrink he can count on in a pinch."

Cait made a small sound of protest. "C'mon, Hazel, where's your spirit of adventure? Of romance?" She manufactured a leer. "Of lust?"

Hazel laughed. "Tucked away where it'll be safe from idiots like you." And safe from a haunted, deeply caring man who had locked away far more than that.

"May I ring these things up for you?"

Neither Hazel nor Cait had noticed the clerk approaching, and her cheery question gave them both a start.

"Yes, please," Hazel said, digging in her bag for her checkbook, while Cait and the clerk carried everything to the cash register.

"What's the next step?" Cait asked, while the clerk folded each garment before ringing everything up.

Hazel watched a young mother pushing a stroller between the counters. Her baby was bigger than Francey, but she had the same look of wonder in her dark eyes.

"The next step is to draw up the papers giving Jess temporary custody while his application for adoption is being processed."

"I thought that had already been done."

Hazel shook her head. "Francey is still a ward of the court. Jess is simply acting as a foster parent at the moment."

"Sounds complicated."

"It is. Apparently the lines of legal responsibility get fuzzy when the mother is an inmate and the birth father has relinquished all rights."

"What about the mother's deathbed request for Jess to take the baby?"

"*Verbal* wishes. It could have helped if she'd written it down and had it witnessed. Still, Dr. Benoit and I have already agreed to sign depositions to that fact."

Cait grimaced. "Jess didn't exactly endear himself to Teri Grimes and some of the others at Protective Services when he was trying to get Ty access to Kelsey."

"I know. That's why I promised to go to bat for him."

"I don't have to tell you how tough Teri can be, especially now, when there are more strongly qualified, hopeful couples than there are babies."

"It's not fair, Cait. Just because Jess is missing an arm, he has to fight just to do the right thing."

"Let me know if I can help, okay?"

"You *are* helping by giving Jess a place to bring Francey until he can make permanent arrangements."

Hazel watched while the clerk rang up one purchase after another. These things were to be her present to Silvia's baby. In a way they would be her goodbye, as well. Jess just didn't know that yet.

"When is your baby due?" the clerk asked as Hazel handed over her check.

"Actually, she's two days old."

The clerk's jaw dropped, and at the same time her gaze darted to Hazel's waist, where Cait's braided belt cinched the borrowed jeans.

"Must have been an easy delivery," the woman said, trying an uneasy smile.

While Cait tried to keep a straight face, Hazel took pity on the earnest young woman. "I'm buying these for a friend. He's adopting the cutest little girl in the world."

"I'm sure she is." The clerk handed over two bulging shopping bags. "And please accept my best wishes—for your friend."

"Thanks," Hazel said grimly. "I have a feeling he's going to need all the help he can get."

The question was, would a man as proud as Jess allow himself to accept it?

Chapter 6

Jess woke up in the McClanes' guest room feeling drugged. While Hazel and Cait were out shopping he'd fallen asleep and had no idea how long he'd been out.

The house was quiet—no pack of little boys playing in the backyard, no music blaring from Kelsey's CD player.

His right arm had fallen asleep again, just above the wrist.

Instinct had him reaching to rub it with his left hand before his mind sharpened and he remembered. He had no wrist because he had no arm.

Scowling against the pain that nothing but the caprice of phantom nerves could ease, he turned to his side and closed his eyes again. At that same moment he heard a sharp cry, followed by a crescendo of lusty, angry wails.

Francisca was wide-awake and screaming.

His mind went blank, and adrenaline drove his blood pressure sky-high, which didn't do much to control the panic.

"Uh, don't cry, kid, okay?" he pleaded, getting himself off the bed fast and over to the crib. "Just give me a minute to figure out what I'm supposed to do first."

Instead of lessening, the cries only increased, accompanied now by the jerky flailing of tiny arms and legs. Taking a deep breath and screwing up his courage, he tugged the blanket free. As he did, he was engulfed in a pungent odor that reminded him of the foaling barn at his brother's ranch.

It took him just about his entire repertoire of youthful cuss words to extricate Francisca from the wet long johns covering her from neck to toe, and another burst of creative profanity picked up from various pit crews before he had her wiped clean and powdered and ready for the diaper.

By this time the baby was alternating between frantic screaming and furious sucking on her fist. Jess was drenched in sweat and had all but gnawed one corner of his mouth raw.

"Now, listen, kid...Francey," he said somewhat desperately, "this is my first time at this, so help me out, okay?"

The diaper reminded him of a fat pressure bandage like the ones that had covered half his body for weeks, only this one was encased in plastic.

He'd forgotten that the thing had tabs, and by the time he managed to free them from the plastic, he had already murdered Hazel three times in his mind for leaving him alone.

"Okay now, don't kick, so I can slide this sucker under," he muttered. He leaned closer, only to catch a foot in the nose.

"Hey, watch that, okay? It's already been broken three times."

The baby stopped crying suddenly and stared up at him, her eyes big and round and deep, deep blue—like barn kittens right after their mother had cleaned them up.

Francisca's were going to be dark, though, he decided. Like Silvia's. And like his.

Hazel's eyes were light, somewhere between green and gold. It occurred to him that they might be called hazel and wondered if that was her given name, or a name she'd picked up as a kid. Not that it mattered much one way or another, he told himself as he gritted his teeth for another try at this diapering business.

"It's not that I don't want to be your daddy, honey," he assured her gruffly, fumbling with the tab while trying to avoid another kick in the face. "But the people who watch out for kids like you might not let me, not without a whale of a fight and even then, the odds are outta sight against a beat-up guy like me."

One tab was secured, so he turned his attention to the other. Francisca was no longer screaming bloody murder. Instead, her big solemn eyes were fastened on his face with the kind of rapt attention he worked hard to win from every juror he faced.

Keeping the lower part of the diaper in place long enough to maneuver the top into the right position was taxing his patience and straining the tendons of his hand. Worse, the baby kept kicking, especially when his fingers brushed her tummy.

"Ticklish? Yeah, me too, only don't tell anyone, okay?"

When she puckered her mouth for another try at shattering the windows, Jess rushed into speech, figuring that the sound of his voice might make her feel more secure than silence.

"Don't get me wrong, honey. I'm going to fight for you. But the thing is, I'm not all that sure I'm the best person to take care of you. So what happens to you and me if I do win, and then find out I can't manage?"

He would have to give her up, that was what. Something that would be difficult to do even now—and damn near heartbreaking once he'd gotten to know her better.

A guy with any self-protective instinct at all would know that and pull back now, while he still had some control over his feelings.

And then what, Dante? Spend the rest of your life thinking about the trust in Silvia's eyes?

One final awkward tug of his fingers and the tab was safely stuck to the plastic. Allowing himself a grin, he took a moment to savor his success.

It wasn't the greatest job in the world, but hot damn, he'd done it! He hadn't felt so cocky since he'd learned to button his shirt one-handed.

"Feels better, too, right, kid?" he said with a grin. The baby kicked and cooed, as sweet now as she smelled.

"Okay, now what?"

Jess eyed the sodden sleeper, decided that it wouldn't do and looked around for something to replace it.

Hazel had left a few items of clothing on the bed, which he'd carefully moved to the dresser before he'd sacked out. With one eye on the baby, he quickly sorted through them. Everything was made in miniature, even the tiny undershirts, and the soft material snagged against his callused fingers.

"How about this sack thing?" he asked, holding it up for the baby to see. Impatient now, Francey pulled her crescent eyebrows into a frown.

"Don't much care for it, huh? Kinda plain for a stylish little lady like you, but it'll have to do for now."

He had to take a minute to figure out whether the thing was supposed to snap in the front or the back, and then a few more minutes to work out the best way to handle both a wiggling, slippery baby and a nightie that wasn't much bigger than his hand.

Five minutes later Francisca was wearing the soft little nightie and Jess was exhausted. He was also beginning to wonder where in the hell he was going to find the courage to give Francey up if the courts denied his petition.

Cait parked the car while Hazel hurried inside, shopping bags banging crazily against her legs. All the way home she'd been convinced that the baby was screaming her head off or working on a bad case of diaper rash, or both.

Letting the screen door slam behind her, she bolted through the kitchen to the hall. She'd just started up the stairs when she heard a definite baby gurgle coming from the den.

Heart in her throat, she changed direction and headed for the French doors at the far end of the foyer. As she neared, she heard the rumble of a deep male voice, followed by soft babbling.

Francey was apparently wide-awake. Poor Jess, she thought with a sharp pang of guilt.

"Poor Jess" was sitting on the floor with his back against the sofa and his knees raised. The dress shirt and trousers he'd worn since yesterday had been replaced by a T-shirt she would have consigned to the rag bag long ago and jeans that looked uncomfortably snug.

The baby, dressed in one of Jesse's much washed gowns and a sadly wrinkled, crooked diaper, was cradled on Jess's thighs, vigorously kicking him in the belly. One tiny hand was clasped around Jess's forefinger, which Francey was gumming with complete absorption.

Jess looked up as she entered, greeting her with one of his rare grins. Someday she would have to stop fantasizing about the sexy man lurking behind that flashing white grin, she told herself.

"Lose your watch, did you?" he asked in a desert-dry voice.

Feeling guilty was one thing. Admitting it when you didn't have to was another. "You wouldn't believe the traffic," she said airily, dropping the bags by the door before crossing the room.

Raising both eyebrows, he leaned forward until he was almost nose to nose with the baby—one nose very masculine and slightly hooked, the other cute as a bunny's. "Sounds like a pretty flimsy excuse to me, sugar babe. What do you think?"

The baby's response couldn't really be called a smile, Hazel knew, because all the books said newborns couldn't smile. But it looked so much like a smile that it brought a lump to her throat.

"Hi, punkin," she cooed as she plunked her bottom on the plump cushion and smiled down at the baby. "How's darling Francey?"

"Darling Francey is fine and dandy," Jess said in a grumpy voice. "Darling Jess is damn near worn to a nub."

In spite of the frown on his face, Hazel thought that he sounded smugly pleased with himself, and her heart gave a few unnecessary beats. He looked more rested, too, as though he'd just gotten up from a nap.

She'd made a bad mistake last night, giving in to the impulse to comfort him with a kiss. Unfortunately, however, she'd done just that, and, like the genie in the bottle, all those feelings for Jess that she'd successfully avoided for so long refused every effort to stuff them back in. Her only option now was to ignore them.

"So," she said, sitting up straighter, "did she have her bottle?"

"About an hour ago, every drop of the stuff." His eyebrows drew together over an impressive Roman nose. "Her appetite's the biggest thing about her."

Hazel returned her gaze to the baby propped so securely against his hard thighs, and she felt herself softening. "At the moment it looks like she's trying to make a meal out of your finger."

"Yeah, well, I tried that rubber thing the nurse gave you, but she kept spitting it out." He shot a disgusted look at the pacifier on the coffee table. "Not that I blame her much," he added irritably. "Seems like a poor substitute for the real thing."

He returned his gaze to hers and kept it there. Sensitivity to nuance was second nature to a psychotherapist, but Hazel detected nothing remotely suggestive about the look on his face.

So why, she wondered, did she feel as though he'd just managed a very thorough, very erotic study of her breasts?

"A lot of neonatal experts would certainly agree," she said evenly.

"Would they?" There wasn't even a hint of a smile on his lips, and his eyes were completely innocent. Wickedly innocent.

"Absolutely," she murmured.

As though agreeing, the baby gave a sharp gurgle and at the same time waved one minuscule fist in the air.

Hazel laughed softly as she reached over to smooth the mop of baby-fine hair. Letting her fingers linger for a moment, she felt an instant surge of tenderness welling inside her.

How I wish you were mine, sweet Franccy, she thought. Already I love you so much it hurts.

"Looks like you didn't do too badly while I was gone, little miss," she murmured, her voice soft. "Even if Daddy did get your gown on backward."

"The hell he did," Jess drawled in an equally low tone. "I was stuck in enough of these things in the hospital to know what goes where."

Hazel pictured a gown designed for a man of ordinary size draped on Jess's extraordinary body and figured the hem would hit him just about mid thigh. As for the opening . . . Hazel found her pulse quickening and her skin heating.

"This is a nightie, not a hospital gown," she said with a blandness that impressed the heck out of her, given the nature of her thoughts. "Which means the opening goes in the front, not the back."

Jess glanced at the baby cooing away happily. "What do you think, sugar? Front or back?"

Francey crinkled her face into a gigantic yawn, and Hazel burst out laughing. "Looks like she has other things on her mind."

"Just like a woman. A guy thinks he's making headway and all of sudden, wham, the door slams in his face."

He was kidding, and yet, Hazel realized, he wasn't. "Don't worry about it," she advised in a tone no heavier than she figured he could handle. "Bonding takes a while. The trick is to keep at it."

"Bonding? Who, Francey and me?"

Hazel couldn't decide if the idea pleased him or not. Jess was an expert at keeping his deepest feelings hidden.

"Sure. If she were a baby duck, she'd have pretty much decided that you were the dominant drake, and that, therefore, she was a very lucky little duckling."

Hazel wasn't sure how a man as big and virile as Jess could manage to look so boyishly pleased, but he did. His mouth was already relaxing into a smile when, suddenly, he stopped himself.

"Yeah, well, she's not a duck, and I'm not a daddy yet. Sort of makes us even, doesn't it?"

"It was an analogy."

"I know what it was, O'Connor. Maybe I didn't get terrific grades in school, but I managed to snag a couple of degrees here and there."

And passed the bar on the first try, she recalled, a feat that struck her as pretty terrific for a guy who'd relied on muscle and endurance and lightning reflexes instead of brain power for more than half his lifetime.

"C'mon, Jess," she teased, "stop being so touchy and—"

"I'm not touchy, and I don't need analysis from you or anyone else, okay?"

Hazel heard the silky warning and promptly ignored it. "Is that why you're always getting your back up around me? Because you think I'm going to poke and prod and uncover all your deep, dark secrets?"

"A guy like me doesn't have secrets!"

The sudden force in Jess's retort startled the baby into a sudden yelp. Hazel leapt up as the baby's wispy eyebrows drew together and her face puckered.

"Whoa there, I didn't mean to scare you," Jess said to her in a voice so gentle it made Hazel wish he would find a reason to use it with her.

In response, Francey let go of his finger and began screaming with a force that turned her satin skin a blotchy red.

"Now see what you've done!" Hazel exclaimed as she plucked the baby from his cradling thighs and tucked her against her shoulder. The baby smelled of talcum and milk, and seemed to weigh nothing in her arms.

"Don't cry, precious," she crooned next to the baby's ear. "Daddy didn't mean to upset you."

Jess pushed himself to his feet so quickly that Hazel found herself staring at a distinctly masculine throat above the ragged neckline of the faded blue shirt.

Hastily, she fine tuned her sights and found him watching her, his eyes already smoked over with his customary wariness.

"We need to talk."

"We do?"

"About putting her gown on backward, feeding her the right things, I'm going to need some help—until I can get things arranged."

"You could hire a practical nurse."

"And I'm trying to do just that, but there's this bonding thing. Wouldn't that just confuse her? Too many new people in her life all at once, I mean?"

"It could, yes. But at this point there aren't that many options open."

"You could move in with me."

"*What!*"

"Hi, guys," Cait said, sailing in tummy first with a cheery smile that suddenly faltered as she glanced from one to the other.

"Oops, sorry. Is this a private conversation?"

"No." Jess looked relieved.

Hazel couldn't say a word.

Cait looked from one to the other, her eyes bright with speculation. "Well, as I was, um, saying, I just came in to make sure you're both staying for dinner."

"I shouldn't...." Hazel murmured, avoiding Jess's gaze.

"Sure you should," Cait said with a wide grin. "You too, right, Jess? I'm making lasagna."

Jess looked anything but thrilled, which made his words all the more surprising. "Yeah, sure. Only now that you two are back, I have to go downtown for a while."

"No problem. We won't eat until seven anyway—unless Ty gets held up at the hospital. Then we play it by ear."

"Anything you need while I'm downtown?"

"Nope. Just your smiling presence, you handsome devil you."

One side of his mouth slanted. "You got it, toots."

Francey began to fret again, flailing her small fists like tiny warning flags. Very gently Jess caught one fist in his big hand and gave it a gentle shake.

"Impatient little squirt, isn't she?" he said, his gaze meeting Hazel's.

"Seems to be," she agreed.

Jess held her gaze a beat longer, then leaned down to brush a kiss across the baby's head. "Be good while I'm gone, okay, kid?"

The baby hiccuped, then snuggled her face into the warmth of Hazel's neck.

As his eyes met hers again, Hazel felt a definite stirring. She wanted a kiss, too. But not the kind meant to soothe.

As though reading her mind, his gaze dropped to her lips and his eyes darkened to charcoal, like smoke over flame.

He aimed for her cheek as always, but ended up brushing her mouth with his, lingering ever so slightly before breaking the moist contact of hard lips on soft.

"We'll continue this discussion later." The rasp in his voice could have been a threat or a promise. Perhaps both.

"If that's what you want." Her voice was more than a whisper, but far less than a normal tone.

"What I want and what's possible are usually two different things."

Smoothing his tousled hair with his hand, he headed out. Seconds later the front door opened and then closed again. Hazel and Cait exchanged looks.

"Whoa," Cait exclaimed softly. "Did I or did I not feel a definite buzz of sexual tension between you two just now?"

Drawing a sharp breath, Hazel nestled Francey closer. "I'm beginning to think you did."

"I knew there was something lurking under all that brooding moodiness he hides behind. All it took was a little concentrated exposure to your considerable charms to coax it to the surface."

Hazel forced a smile. "Cait, I hate to tell you this, but those pregnant hormones of yours have softened your brain."

Cait smoothed the baby's hair, her expression thoughtful. "In some cultures, a pregnant woman is considered psychic."

"Not in ours."

"Hmm, don't be so sure. When I was carrying Jesse, I told Ty that I was certain you had a crush on Jess. Looks like I was right."

"Don't be silly, Cait. I like Jess just fine as a friend, but that's as far as it goes."

"Yeah, right. That's why your face is as pink as Francey's bottom."

Hazel's free hand went to her cheek, causing Cait to grin knowingly. "What'd I tell you? Psychic."

"Weird is more like it."

"Let's split the difference and call it fey."

Hazel shook her head. "Call it whatever you want to, I'm going to take this little darling upstairs and work on my diaper changing skills."

"Good idea. And I'd better get to work on Jess's lasagna. It's not his favorite, but we both pretend it is."

"You do? Why?"

"Because it's just about impossible for him to eat anything he has to cut with a knife."

"Oh. I see. I never thought of that."

"Most people don't. But Jess has to."

In silence, they walked from the den.

An hour later, Jess shook the sweat from his eyes and fought for one more pull-up, even as strain burned deep into his muscles and turned his tendons to ropes from his wrist to his shoulder.

Teeth gritted against the pain, he inched his chin over the bar and, even though no one was holding a stopwatch on him, held himself motionless for a count of three before he allowed himself to let go.

"Working out a tough case, Dante?"

Jess glanced up in time to catch the towel tossed his way from the direction of the bench press, where Mitch Scanlon had just hoisted two-hundred and eighty pounds, a walk in the park for a man of his considerable strength.

"Might say that, yeah." Jess used the towel to mop his wet face before draping it round his neck.

"Another lost cause."

"Probably, although I haven't made up my mind yet." Jess angled a hip against the rack used to hold the weights and watched Scanlon move from the bench to his wheel-chair. A mega-famous NFL quarterback in a former life, Mitch had lost the use of his legs when he'd surprised a gang of kids attempting to steal his Porsche and been slammed in the back full force with a crowbar.

These days he mainly concentrated on regaining as much mobility and strength as possible while at the same time avoiding media questions and cameras.

Friends from the days when they'd taken turns being on the cover of sports magazines, he and Jess were co-owners of the gym which had been specially designed for use by the disabled.

"Buy you a beer?" Mitch offered with a grin.

"Thanks, but I'm expected someplace in an hour."

"Yeah? Business or pleasure?"

Jess hesitated. "Business."

Mitch clucked his tongue. "Here I was hoping you finally got yourself a hot date."

Straightening, Jess snatched the towel from his neck and tossed it at Scanlon's head. "Haven't you heard? Cripples don't have sex," he said over his shoulder as he headed for the showers.

"Hey man, speak for yourself," he heard Scanlon throw at his back. Jess kept on going. The last thing he wanted to talk about was sex.

Trading stories about women had never been a favorite of his in the past, when he'd had stories to tell. Now that he didn't, he liked it even less.

The shower room was deserted. The dinner hour was the slow time at the gym, which was one of the reasons Jess had come then. He needed to think, and he did that best when he was alone.

Reaching into the shower stall, he turned on the hot water full force, then methodically stripped out of his sweats and stepped into the steam.

Like a warm lush woman, the hot moisture embraced him wholly, eagerly. Closing his eyes, he braced his palm against the slick, sweating tile and leaned into the heat, allowing the pounding water to work its magic on the knots in his shoulders and back.

Willing himself to relax, he surrendered to the hot stinging needles. The water felt good against his skin, but good as it was, he craved more. He wanted a woman. Not just for sex, but to hold, to touch, to smell.

He wanted the gentleness a woman offered, the soft warmth, the acceptance.

Who was he kidding? He wanted O'Connor.

He prided himself on having his life under control, on keeping his physical needs under tight rein, but there were times when he dreaded being alone one more minute of one more day.

Lifting his head, Jess let the water pound his face, hoping the heat would scald away the remembered pleasure of her mouth whispering across his cheek. Or the even sharper pleasure of his mouth on hers.

He prided himself on his logic. Others called him ruthless. So why couldn't he get a handle on what it was, precisely, that he wanted from her?

It had to be more than her ability to make him see himself in gentler, more accepting ways. More than the knack she had of making him want to smile when she smiled and laugh when she laughed. Damn it, it had to be more complicated than that, he told himself as he dropped his head so that the water could pound the sudden spasm in his neck. Nothing could be that simple.

Nothing else in his life was. Things he used to take for granted now took ingenuity and persistence and patience. Like eating and driving a car and handling his briefcase together with a door that had to be opened manually.

Problems like that were a nuisance, but they were also easily defined. A man could handle what he could define.

But feelings, needs—things he couldn't touch or see or analyze piece by piece, like the need he had to be close to O'Connor, to listen to her voice and watch the dance of emotions in her eyes—all of his life he'd avoided things like that.

Clenching his jaw, he reached for the soap. His body was familiar territory to him now—one side the same as it had been for a lifetime, the other irreversibly changed.

Like Jekyll and Hyde, he thought as his finger worked suds into the scarred, cratered flesh of his shoulder and side. Ugly, mutilated, pathetic.

He'd heard all the words, felt the stares. He'd accepted his ugliness because he'd had no choice.

A woman as bright and pretty and sexy as O'Connor had a world of choices. Why on God's green earth did he have the gall to think she might want him?

Chapter 7

"There's one more piece of pie left," Cait called from the doorway between the kitchen and the dining room. "How about you two guys splitting it?"

"Give the whole piece to Dante," Tyler said, aiming a grin Jess's way. "He's been looking a little scrawny lately."

Surgery on the small accident victim had gone well, which was why Tyler had made it home in time for dinner.

"You wish."

Jess slanted his friend a rude look before shifting his gaze to Cait. "He's just ticked because he's gone through three horses to my one and he still can't outride me. Problem is, he and I are the same size, but he's carrying twenty pounds extra in the gut."

"Like hell," Tyler grumbled, patting his belly. "I can still get into the same jeans I wore as an intern."

"That's true, sweetheart," Cait put in with a saucy grin for her husband of almost five years. "You just can't sit down in them."

Tyler looked abashed. "Hey, no fair spilling family secrets."

"Jess *is* family," Cait threw back. "Besides, I notice that he had as much trouble fitting into the jeans he borrowed from you as you did, which is why, I suspect, he went home to change into a pair of his own."

"Whoa, I resent that," Jess proclaimed staunchly. "I went home because I needed to check my mail and return some calls."

Ty snorted his disbelief, and Cait grinned. Hazel remained silent, her gaze fixed in her wineglass. She'd been in the kitchen helping Cait when he'd come looking for her earlier, his hair still damp and his jaw freshly shaved. It was an odd experience, being sought out by the man who usually shunned her, one she wasn't sure she understood. Or even particularly trusted.

"I still can't believe there's a baby in the house," Kelsey said as she breezed in with a glass of milk in one hand and a dish of ice cream in the other.

Finished with his dinner and fidgeting under all the adult conversation, Jesse had been excused to take his dessert into the family room, where the faint strains of a children's video could be heard whenever conversation lagged.

"Talk about a surprise! I mean, coming home from cheerleading practice and finding Auntie Hazel with a baby in her arms. Wow!"

Kelsey flopped into her seat, put down her glass and picked up her spoon, all during the space of one breath. "And *then* come to find out the baby is going to be Uncle Jess's adopted daughter. Double wow!" She stopped to dig in.

Jess marveled at the effervescence in Kelsey's tone. She was just two months shy of her thirteenth birthday and trying hard to be "adult." Sometimes, though, she forgot herself.

"So when are you taking Francey home with you, Uncle Jess?" Kelsey asked with her mouth full of dessert.

Jess met Hazel's eyes and saw the same question written there before she looked away. "I'm not sure," he hedged.

"I'm in the middle of a trial that resumes Tuesday, and I'm not sure how I'm going to deal with child care yet."

"You can always leave Francisca here," Cait said as she returned to the table with a dish of apple pie in one hand and a full pot of coffee in the other. "I would be thrilled to have another little one around."

"Yeah, Uncle Jess!" Kelsey exclaimed. "I'd love to baby-sit."

"That's great," her mother interjected as she refilled cups all around. "But what happens when you go to cheerleading practice or your tennis lesson or out with friends?"

"No problem. I'll take Francey with me."

Putting the pot on the straw mat, Cait resumed her seat. "Sorry, sweetie, it's not that easy."

"Why not?"

"Well, for one thing you have to take her diapers and wipes and bottles and a change of clothes whenever you take her, remember?"

Kelsey grimaced. "Yuck. That sounds too much like work."

Cait burst out laughing, and Hazel bit her lip. Kelsey looked utterly offended. "I was just making a point," she said huffily.

Extreme swings in mood must be a stage, Jess decided. A teenage thing. And then he wondered how he would handle Francey without a mother's help when she was that age.

"And you're absolutely right," Cait told her solemnly. "Which is why I suggested to Uncle Jess that the only sensible thing to do right now is to leave Francey with me, since I'm only working two days a week until your sister is born."

Mollified, Kelsey scraped her spoon against her bowl, scooping up the last bite before turning her attention to Hazel again.

"I bet it's going to be hard for you to let go of that little darling, but maybe Uncle Jess will let you baby-sit now and then."

"Actually I'm trying to get her to do more than that," Jess put in before Hazel could answer.

Eyes bright with curiosity, Kelsey looked first at Hazel and then at Jess. "Oh yeah? Like what?"

"Like move in with me and help me take care of Francey until the court decides if I'm really going to be her father or not."

Jess was taking a chance, and he knew it. Still, he figured he had a fifty-fifty shot at making a good case, which was better odds than he usually took into trial with him.

"*All right!*" Kelsey cried. "Like this movie I saw once, only the baby was a little boy and he was the son of this woman's sister and her husband who was the brother of this guy."

Kelsey glanced around the table expectantly. When no one spoke, she went on. "Anyway, these two, the parents I mean, are killed in a plane crash, leaving the baby an orphan, like Francey. See what I mean?"

Jess realized that he was expected to comment. "I believe I do," he said dryly.

"And then . . . where was I?"

"Plane crash," her father put in.

"Oh yeah. So these two, the baby's aunt and uncle see, start fighting over who should adopt the baby—"

"Wouldn't happen, not if the parents left a will," Jess interjected. Kelsey looked annoyed. "Yeah, but see, that was part of the problem. They hadn't expected to die so young, and so they hadn't got around to making a will or serious junk like that. Anyway there was this big custody fight, see, and these two were acting like enemies, only they were really falling in love and didn't know it. And then the baby gets kidnapped and—"

Jess groaned. "Enough, Kels. This story of yours is giving me heartburn."

Undaunted, Kelsey grinned. "Well, it was a *killer* movie."

"I'm sure it was," Hazel said before Kelsey could get started again. "But Uncle Jess isn't really serious about my moving in with him."

She seemed perfectly relaxed, and her smile was casual, but he was perceptive enough to sense the world of emotions under the calm. A week ago, he wouldn't have noticed. A week ago, he wouldn't have cared.

"Sure I am. Cait has her own kids to take care of. You and I are both self-employed and our schedules are at least somewhat flexible."

"Yours maybe. Not mine."

Pushing back his chair, he stood up, walked around the table and positioned himself between her chair and the door. He wanted to touch her but reminded himself that this was about Francey's needs, not his.

"C'mon, let's you and me take a walk to settle the lasagna."

She looked at him as though he'd suggested something ridiculous. "Jess, I have to get home. I have mail to read and calls to return, too, you know."

"Fine, I'll drive you."

From the corner of his eye, he saw Ty and Cait exchange looks and wondered what they would do if he suddenly grabbed Hazel by the hair and hauled her out of there.

"No... oh, all right, but just remember, I'm not some wide-eyed juror to be swayed by glib words and one of those patented Jess Dante glares."

Kelsey giggled, but her eyes were round with surprise, and her hand was clutching her throat.

"Look at it this way, O'Connor. I make my living talking, and you make yours listening. That's all we're going to do. For now, anyway."

Hazel's house was an architect's nightmare of turrets and gingerbread and windows that didn't match, all painted a soothing gray with sparkling white trim.

Jess hadn't gotten much past the front door before he realized the place was as contradictory as its owner. Unlike the exterior, the entry was a sensory barrage of primary colors.

The paintings and artifacts decorating the walls were both traditional and irreverent and showed absolutely no sense of organization at all. It was as though she'd hung some new treasure wherever she'd found room to fit.

"Interesting," he said when he caught her looking at him.

"I'm glad you like it."

"I didn't say that."

She laughed, a light breezy sound that he absorbed almost hungrily. "Make yourself at home."

She dropped her purse and briefcase on the nearest solid object, an odd-looking chair with a dragon carved into the back.

"The parlor has the most ambiance. I'll just check my machine, and then I'll put on a pot of coffee."

Jess glanced to the right and saw French doors leading to what he took to be the dining room. At least it had a table and chairs in it, along with a huge painting of peacock feathers and an antique Victrola, the kind with a crank. By the process of elimination, the "parlor" had to be to the left.

Definitely unusual, he thought, turning slowly in a circle. The furniture was dignified, even stuffy. Victorian, he decided. But the silk-screened print covering the cushions was clearly twentieth century, and there were pillows everywhere. Soft cushy ones, plump ones with tassels, others with ruffles.

There was even a red silk job on the pink and gold love seat that looked as though it had come from the nineteenth-century bordello that now housed his office.

"Fantastic, isn't it?" she exclaimed when she caught him running his fingertips over the slick material. "I got it for a song at this little antique store in Diamond Springs."

"I bet you did at that."

She came toward him, a grin on her face and a mug of steaming coffee in each hand. He noticed that she'd kicked off her shoes and done something to her hair. Made it fluffier, he decided. More touchable.

"Black, no sugar, right?" she said as she set both mugs on the old chicken-crate coffee table and curled into one corner of the settee.

"Right."

He chose a platform rocking chair that looked sturdy enough and sat down. The old chair creaked as it took Jess's weight, and the sound startled both of them.

"You should have seen that chair before I fixed it," she said, intensely aware of the long legs stretching within touching distance. "A real disaster."

"You like fixing things, I take it."

She reached her cup and cradled it on her thigh. "Is that an insult or a compliment?"

"Let's see if the thing holds me up before we decide, shall we?" he said, his tone almost droll.

"You have a point."

Was there a sense of fun trapped beneath the reserve? she wondered, intrigued and beguiled at the thought of releasing it.

"It's the oddest thing, but I feel as though I've been away from home for weeks instead of hours."

She took a sip, then cradled the mug between both her hands and leaned her head against the back of the settee. Her throat was smooth and creamy and just the right angle for a man's mouth to explore slowly.

Jess reached for his own mug and downed half the contents in two long swallows. It was hot enough to burn all the way to his stomach. The distraction was welcome.

"How about you?" She let her eyes drift open. "Do you have the same feeling?"

"No. I'm used to settling in wherever I am. Comes from my years on the racing circuit."

Something had changed about him, Hazel thought, but she couldn't quite pin it down to specifics. He was still solemn, still very reserved when he looked at her, his eyes seeing everything and revealing so very little. But there was something . . .

Hazel smiled at him, testing the waters. "I'm listening," she said softly.

"Pardon?"

"You talk, I listen, remember?"

Jess relished the give-and-take of a criminal trial because he'd always rigorously done his homework well before the gavel came down for the first time. The more difficult the defense, the more he tore into it.

But O'Connor wasn't a defendant, nor was she a hostile witness. Instead she was a woman he respected, a woman who had rearranged her crowded schedule to give comfort to a woman she'd never met, simply because he'd asked it of her.

Jess lowered his mug carefully to the table and edged forward until he was sitting straight. It was always better to face an unknown curve with too much confidence rather than too little.

"Look, we both care about Francey, that's a given."

That won him a small smile, giving him the courage to plunge ahead. "And I feel at least a certain responsibility to carry out Silvia's last request."

"In a strange way, so do I."

"I keep thinking about what she said. That she wanted her daughter to have a better life, and if the court does give me custody, I want you to know I intend to do the best I know how to be a good father."

"I know that."

"But a little girl . . . I had brothers. I don't even know the first thing about girls. And the idea of a nanny, well, it seems so impersonal."

Impatience had her cocking her chin and staring up at him. "Then tell me, Jess, what is it exactly that you do want?"

"Damn it, Hazel, I thought women were supposed to have a sixth sense about these things."

"*What* things?"

Jess took a deep breath. His palm was sweating, and his throat was dry. "I told you. I want you to move in with me."

"To be Francey's nanny?"

"Well, not exactly. More like her . . . mother."

"I . . . you—"

"Exactly. You and me. You yourself said that marriage was 'in' these days."

Jess was beginning to feel foolish. This was supposed to be a straightforward merger, but Hazel O'Connor had a way of looking into his eyes that had him thinking of a houseful of children with red hair and green eyes and a smile just like hers. Boys, maybe, to spoil their big sister.

"I realize there are things you need to know." He cleared his throat, more nervous suddenly than he'd ever been even for a summation in a capital case.

"I'm just shy of forty-six, in decent shape financially and in excellent health. I'm easy to please and don't have too many bad habits, not any that are against the law, anyway."

"That *is* reassuring."

Jess saw the smile in her eyes and allowed himself to smile back. So far so good.

"I'll pay the household expenses, but now that I've seen your place, it might be better if I moved in here instead of the reverse. Your house is twice as big as mine and has a yard." And a homey warmth that not even the expensive decorator he'd hired had been able to give his.

"And a tree for a swing."

"Yeah, right. A swing."

"And maybe a sandbox."

"Whatever you want."

"You mean whatever is best for the baby?" There was a hint of a smile in her voice.

"That's assumed."

"Of course."

"If you prefer, I'll have all of this stipulated in a contract."

His eyes were very dark, very intense. Meeting them, she felt herself being pulled by the shadows faintly visible even in the inky depths. A dangerous man to love, she thought. Heartache in any relationship with him would be a given, but something told her that the pleasure he could give her with that hard body would outweigh the risk.

"A prenuptial agreement, you mean?"

"You could call it that, yes."

"Notarized?"

His eyes narrowed. Clearly she'd pushed him as far as he intended to allow. "Most people I know accept my word."

"Ah, but will you accept mine?"

"Yes."

His eyes flashed a subtle but clear warning. This was not a man to lose control with, she told herself. He wouldn't be gentle, and he wouldn't be kind—not unless one or the other served his purposes. But he would be fair and in many ways exciting.

As a lover, perhaps, a small voice of sanity reminded her. Not as a husband.

"That's it?" She allowed a smile to play over her mouth. "One proposal wrapped up in legal ribbons and ready for my signature?"

"That's it. Say the word, and I'll have the papers drawn up."

She pressed both hands against the settee's cushion and swung her legs out in front of her. She had small, tidy feet, and her toenails were painted a wild pink, not the kind of image he would expect a kiddy shrink to project.

Jess shifted his gaze from ankles that were far too slender for his peace of mind to her face. Her mouth was pursed into a pensive frown, and her lowered lashes hid her eyes.

"Well, it's not the most . . . romantic proposal I've ever had," she said, studying those same bright toes while he studied her.

"I'm not much for the candlelight and wine bit, O'Connor. You might as well know that up-front."

She lowered her legs and lifted her gaze. "So what I see is, um, what I would get? Is that it?"

"Exactly."

Hazel heard the smile in his voice and searched for it on his lips. Instead she found his mouth bracketed by deep grooves that hadn't been there earlier.

"Why marriage?" she questioned in a neutral tone. "Why not draw up a custody agreement between us? Wouldn't that serve the same purpose?"

"I thought of that, but it wouldn't work." Tension banded his shoulders and sharpened his tone.

"It wouldn't?"

"No. For example, what if you met someone and decided to get married? Who would be Francey's daddy then?"

"Yes, I see your point."

She studied the veins on the backs of her hands. She'd worn a wedding ring for almost five years and spent another two in mourning for the man who'd given it to her.

After that, she'd thought about remarrying a time or two. She'd even set the date once, with a man who'd promised to fill her old house with children. At the last minute she'd realized that she wasn't in love with him and called it off.

"And, of course, you might meet someone and fall in love," she added when he remained silent. "Someone you would naturally want to be Francey's mother."

"Unlikely at best."

Her chin lifted slowly until her eyes were in line with his. "Just so I have this straight," she said in a tone that seemed far too calm. "This is to be a marriage of convenience between two consenting adults, with the welfare of the baby uppermost."

Jess wondered why her words sounded so cold when she was simply paraphrasing his own. "Exactly."

"And what about marital relations? Sex?"

Jess rubbed his hand over his thigh, realized what he was doing and closed his fingers into a loose fist. A trickle of sweat was slowly making its way down his backbone, and his skin felt hot and tight, the way it had when he'd gotten himself stuck in the back of the pack with no way out. Taking a calculated risk had been his only choice then, and he'd been paying for it ever since.

"That's up to you," he said in a tone that implied his own indifference. "I'm not so desperate for sex that I'd force you to do something you would hate."

"That's very generous of you," she replied, standing suddenly. "I'll give it some thought, along with the rest of the items you put on the table."

Jess got to his feet quickly. Even though she radiated an unnatural calm, her face had paled to the color of newly skimmed cream. His own felt as hot as a fresh burn.

"I don't expect an answer now," he said, when the prolonged silence had him ready to squirm.

"Good," she murmured, her voice dry. "Because I'm still in shock."

"Take all the time you need—as long as you give me an answer by Thursday night."

"Why Thursday night?"

"Because Friday I have my first appointment with Lynn FitzGerald. It would help my cause considerably to be able to tell her that you and I are engaged."

Hazel ran an unsteady hand through her hair. "Of course," she murmured, her composure wobbling. "That makes perfect sense."

Jess watched the sunlight come through the etched window glass to splinter into a dozen shades of red and gold in her hair. He liked the casual way she kept it, and the way the soft curls seemed to draw attention to the graceful slant of her cheekbones.

She smoothed her borrowed slacks over her thighs, then stuck out her hand. He saw the tension then, in the stiff way she held her shoulders and the hint of strain in her smile. "Nice listening to you," she said, her tone wry.

Her hand slid into his, and her grip was firm, the way he'd remembered. Her fingers gently pressed his before she let go.

"Jess? Is something wrong?"

"Ah, hell," he muttered, and then his mouth brushed hers, so desperately gentle, so heartbreakingly tentative, as though it had been a long, long time since he'd kissed a woman.

Hazel's eyes grew damp, but whatever pity she might be tempted to feel was instantly smothered by the heat generated by the growing pressure of his hard lips over hers.

No matter how vulnerable he might or might not be, at this moment he was kissing her with an impatient man's passion and a strong man's restraint. Kisses tasting of coffee and hunger.

Jess had meant the kiss to be brief, without feeling, or so he'd told himself in the split second it had taken him to make up his mind. But her mouth was warm silk, and he had been lonely for a very long time.

Her hands balled against his shoulders, pushing hard, but her mouth was busily softening under his. He felt need stir, the kind that he'd denied for so long—sharp and yet sweet, like the first biting swallow of Scotch.

His hand moved lower until his palm found the curve of her spine. Tugging slowly, he arched her upward, taking most of her weight on his arm, until she was molded to him, her body pliant and warm and tempting.

He kept the kiss soft, too afraid of the need he would unleash in himself if he didn't. His tongue tasted instead of plunging deep. His body ached to push hard against the yielding softness of her belly, but he remained motionless, letting his mouth do what his body dared not, drawing every ounce of pleasure he could from her until they were both breathless and shaken.

Reluctantly, too close to the edge to risk going over, he drew back and waited for her to open her eyes, supporting her until she found her footing.

"Was that about the baby, too?" she asked, her eyes full of confusion and lingering intimacy.

"No," he said with a bite in his voice. "That was because I was damn tired of talking myself out of it."

Looking like a man who was already regretting his actions, he turned abruptly and walked out.

Chapter 8

"A marriage of convenience, huh?" Cait filched a walnut from the pile she'd just finished chopping for the brownies Hazel was making. "You know, I've always wanted you two to get together, but somehow I didn't picture it quite the way you described it."

"The way Jess described it, you mean."

Hazel licked the brownie batter from her fingers and dropped the spoon into the sink. It was Sunday afternoon. Francey was with Jess and Tyler. According to Cait, Ty was teaching Jess how to give the baby a bath without drowning her, himself and the bathroom in the process.

"I feel as though pride has me by one hand and Jess by the other, pulling like holy Ned." Hazel carried the bowl to the table and added the walnuts. "If I let go of my pride, I'll get my chance to be a mother, but I'll also be the wife of a man who doesn't love me. If I hang on to my pride, I'll lose Francey."

"What do you want to do?"

Hazel poured the batter into the pan. She'd never been able to deny herself chocolate, no matter how bad it might turn out to be for her well-being.

"Honestly, Cait, I don't know," she said as she scraped the last speck of chocolate from the bowl's slick sides. "That's why I sent out an SOS for you."

Cait gave her a sympathetic look. "And you knew that I would go anywhere, anytime, for brownies," she joked, watching Hazel slip the pan into a hot oven.

"But of course," Hazel replied with a chuckle, though her heart wasn't in it.

"Do you love him?" Cait asked softly, catching her off balance.

"No, but I could far too easily," she admitted, flopping into the nearest kitchen chair. "If he'd give me a chance, that is, which he won't."

"How do you know he won't?"

"Because, when I asked him if sex was included in this 'partnership' he was proposing, he said that it didn't matter much one way or the other. Whatever I wanted was the way he put it."

Cait stared. "Jess said that? The same Jess Dante who's second only to my husband in the sexiest-man-of-all-time department?"

"The very same, except that I'd rate him number one—no offense intended." Hazel managed a wisp of a smile for Cait's benefit.

Cait smiled back. "None taken." Leaning back, she let her smile fade and replaced it with a thoughtful pursing of her lips.

"If I'm reading you right, you're saying that a man who doesn't care whether or not he sleeps with his wife can't possibly be in love with her. Nor can he care whether or not she's in love with him."

"Exactly." As usual, Cait was right on target, and the truth hurt.

"In which case a woman with any self-respect at all would be a fool to fall in love with that man."

Hazel nodded. "Exactly," she said again.

They sat in silence for a few seconds before Hazel got to her feet and set about boiling water for herbal tea. She had a new kind that was supposed to calm frazzled nerves. She was hoping it would also do something for the low hum of desire that ran through her whenever she thought of becoming Dante's wife.

"I've often tried to imagine what life must be like for him, but in all honesty, I can't." She glanced over her shoulder to find Cait watching her.

"I know. When Ty broke his wrist and was in a cast, he nearly went crazy—and that was only for four weeks. Jess has had fourteen years of restrictions and obstacles and just about every other kind of frustration known to man, I imagine."

Hazel carried the mugs of hot water and two tea bags to the table and sat down again. "Not to mention the stares and questions and misplaced pity," she said, dunking one bag.

Cait plunked her own bag into the hot water, then wrinkled her nose at the pungent scent. "He handles it well. At least, he has whenever I've been around him in a public place. In private..." Cait shrugged. "Who knows?"

Hazel ran her tongue along the inside of her lower lip. Jess kissed like a man who'd had more than his share of practice. And his need hadn't been feigned. She'd felt it in the faint trembling of his hand when it pressed her spine and in the hard tension of his thighs.

At that moment, at least, he had wanted her. But there were still some things that required both hands, no matter how skillfully a person compensated or how strong he made himself. She wondered if making love was one of those things.

Hazel tried the tea, then made a face. The stuff tasted awful; therefore it had to be good for her.

Sipping determinedly, she glanced toward the window facing the backyard. Outside, a brilliant blue jay was doing a courting dance in the oleander bushes while the smaller, drabber female perched nearby, playing hard to get.

Did birds mate for life? she wondered. Did they feel love and anguish and desire, or were they simply driven by primal juices to mate in order to continue the species? And did it really matter why the babies were born, as long as the adults were around to protect them?

"Cait, were you in love with Ty when you went to see him in that saloon in Sutter Creek?" she asked, still watching the courtship rite beyond the pane.

"No, but like you said earlier, I knew I could be."

Hazel brought her gaze to Cait's face. "And if he hadn't fallen in love with you, would you still have married him in order to reunite Kelsey with her father?"

Cait looked thoughtful. "I admit I've wondered that myself, mostly in the middle of the night when I'm snuggled in his arms. The truth is, I truly don't know for sure. Oh, I tell myself, no, that I would have had too much self-respect, but I'm also extremely glad I didn't have to make that choice."

Hazel thought about the control Jess had imposed on the two of them. And the explosive kindling of desire that had made that control necessary. Other marriages had started with less and succeeded very well.

The problem was, Hazel needed a man to cherish her and laugh with her and share his hopes and dreams and fears with her more than she needed a skillful lover.

"Stubborn man, he'll never let anyone get past that wall he put up when his wife walked out."

She wasn't aware that she'd spoken her thoughts aloud until Cait shot her a startled look. "A classic response, but perhaps understandable in a man as sensitive and proud as Jess must have been. Still is, for that matter."

"More like bullheaded and dictatorial."

"Dreadful traits in a man, I agree." Cait grinned. "Reminds me of Ty, actually, when he was on parole and ready to snarl at anyone who looked at him crosswise."

"He had a reason to be so prickly."

"A lot of people would say that Jess does, too."

Hazel gave a most unladylike snort. "Well, I'm not one of them. He's got a few problems, but so does everyone else. His are just more visible than most."

"Something the press loved, Ty told me once."

Hazel got up to check on the brownies. As soon as she opened the oven door, the tantalizing smell of chocolate filled the kitchen. Ten more minutes, she thought, inhaling as she reluctantly closed the door again.

"What do you mean, the press?" she asked, taking her seat again.

"Seems they even sneaked into his hospital room and snapped pictures of him when he was sleeping."

"That's sick!"

"Ty said that one of the tabloids bribed a nurse into describing Jess's reaction when he found out he'd lost his arm. The headlines said something like 'famous race-car driver Jess Dante goes berserk when he realizes he's become a freak.'"

Horrified beyond words, Hazel found herself thinking about Jess lying helpless in a hospital bed, unable even to come to grips with his changed body in privacy.

"No wonder he keeps so much to himself," she said slowly.

Cait nodded. "Wouldn't you, if you had his memories?"

Hazel expelled a ragged breath. "After Ron's funeral, I spent months alone in our apartment eating junk food and feeling sorry for myself."

"You're not doing that now. Well, the feeling sorry part, anyway."

"Don't be so sure about that." Hazel propped her head on her elbow. "Tell me the truth, Cait. What would you do?"

Cait pushed aside her cup in order to prop her hands under her chin. "I would marry the man on his terms and then seduce the bejabbers out of him."

Hazel leaned back, her hand resting on the table. "And if he refused to be seduced? Then what? A platonic marriage until Francey goes off to college?'' She shook her head.

''I want to be a mother—Francey's mother—but I'm not sure I could handle that kind of pain.''

She pushed back her chair and went to fetch the brownies. Done or not, they were history.

A call to Santa Rita told Hazel that Silvia was to be buried in the small central valley community of Hargrove. The service was held late Tuesday afternoon. It took some juggling, but she cleared her schedule so she could pay her respects.

Located halfway between Sacramento and Pleasanton, Hargrove was unincorporated and appeared on few maps, a fact she hadn't discovered until she was already late.

Asking directions along Highway 99 got her to the town, where a paperboy on a bicycle pointed her toward the church. Simple in design and in desperate need of a fresh coat of paint, it sat alone on a windswept rise near a grove of drought-withered eucalyptus.

What little grass that had survived the wind and drought had been killed by neglect. Someone had planted annuals in ragged rows by the cracked sidewalk, only to see them wither and die, too, because water was too scarce in the valley to waste on mere beauty.

Except for the hearse parked near the entrance and a few dented, dusty pickup trucks, the lot in front of the sad little building was empty.

As she pulled in, however, she spied another car parked to the rear, in the sparse shade of one of the few remaining trees.

It, too, was far from new, but unlike the trucks in the front, Jess's Mercedes had been lovingly restored and carefully maintained.

She hadn't expected to see him there, even though she knew that he was paying Silvia's funeral expenses, something she'd discovered when she'd called the prison to inquire about doing the same thing.

Her heart thudded beneath her black dress, driven by a rush of adrenaline. She hadn't seen him since he'd left her house on Saturday night.

She parked where the Mercedes could block the worst of the wind, checked the rearview mirror to make sure she didn't have lipstick on her teeth and stepped from the air-conditioned comfort of her BMW into what she felt like a blast from an oven.

Central California in summer was hell, pure and simple. By the time she reached the door to the church, her face was damp and her hair was windblown and crackling with static electricity.

The church was too small to have a foyer. Inside, the air was only a few degrees cooler and smelled of candle wax and old wood.

The altar was simple pine, but the white lacy cloth covering it was spotless, and the statues of Mary and Jesus on either side of the hand-carved wooden crucifix showed signs of loving attention.

Because she was afraid no one else would, Hazel had sent flowers. Now she realized her fears had been groundless.

There were flowers everywhere. Marigolds and black-eyed Susans from someone's backyard, carnations, roses and others she didn't recognize in formal urns, and a heartbreakingly simple spray of pearly roses on the casket itself.

The few people in attendance were sitting in the first few rows, listening to the priest, who was standing near the simple but clearly expensive casket.

He was speaking in Spanish, and it took her ear a moment to adjust to the softer vowels and quicker cadence. Without pausing he glanced her way and nodded as she slipped silently into a back pew.

Jess was sitting in the front on the right, along with about a dozen others, who Hazel took to be Silvia's family. There were mostly women and children, she noticed, and several of the women were quietly weeping.

The service was brief, the words simple and strangely comforting, even though Hazel's Spanish wasn't as polished as she would have liked it to be.

Because the church had no organ or even a piano, the final hymn was sung without music, the voices of the adults and children blending in a ragged, heartfelt chorus, making the song all the more touching.

Hazel's eyes were blurry with tears by the time the last notes faded. She was frantically searching in her purse for a tissue when the funeral director wheeled the casket up the aisle, followed by the solemn-faced priest and the rest of the silent mourners.

Jess was the last in line, and to her surprise, she saw that he was accompanied by three dark-haired, dark-eyed little boys, one of whom, the smallest, was clinging tightly to Jess's hand.

Silvia's sons? she wondered, and then knew that was exactly who they were.

When Jess and the boys reached her pew, he stopped. If he was surprised to see her there, he gave no sign as he quietly introduced her to the children.

The eldest, a skinny sullen boy of about eight named Cleve Junior, had yellow eyes and a faceful of half-faded but still painful-looking bruises. The middle boy, Randall, was shy and seemed to resemble Silvia the most in appearance and temperament, while Johnny, the youngest, stuttered incoherently when he tried to reply to her greeting.

"I'm sorry about your mother, boys," she said solemnly, "but I know she loved you very much. Her last thoughts were of you and your new baby sister."

"Mommy's not ever coming back," Randall piped up in a reedy voice.

"No," she agreed gently, knowing that acceptance was painful, but necessary to the healing process.

"Mr. Dante said that Mommy's in heaven now and she's going to be our guardian angel." His nervous little fingers worrying a button on his jacket, Randall glanced up at Jess's face and asked, "Do you really think she's watching us right now, Mr. Dante?"

"Yes, Randall, I do."

"So do I," Hazel told him. "And she'll always be there for you in your thoughts."

"My old lady was a convict, and everybody knows it," Cleve Junior muttered to no one—and everyone.

"Your mother was a good woman, son. She did what she had to do to survive. Someday I intend to make sure you understand that." Jess didn't raise his voice, but Cleve Junior's sullen face took on a sudden red tinge, and his mouth shut with an audible snap.

Jess was at his impressive best in a dark suit and white shirt, but even without the somber clothing, he would have projected the kind of unmistakable integrity and authority children instinctively understood.

Without another word, Cleve broke into a run, racing down the aisle and into the blinding sunlight beyond the door. Left behind, Randall stood silently, biting his lip. Johnny began to cry.

"I know you're sad, and that's okay," Hazel murmured, dropping to her knees. She tried to take the shaking little boy into her arms, but he stiffened and shied away.

"Daddy says that only sissies cry," Randall declared with little boy bravado.

The effect was marred, however, when he cast a furtive look toward the back of the church as though he expected his father to rise up in judgment.

"I think everyone cries when they're sad," she said, choosing her words with great care. "Sometimes people do it where others can see them, sometimes they don't, but either way, crying isn't a bad thing."

"Is too," Randall muttered, looking more like Cleve Junior now than his mother. "Daddy said Johnny's a crybaby just like—" The boy stopped short, his gaze fixed on a spot behind Hazel's shoulder.

"Go on, boy," an annoyingly nasal voice boomed. "Tell the little lady what I done told you."

Hazel rose quickly, turning toward the intruder at the same time. The man striding toward them was above average height and barrel-chested, with a head shaped like a bullet and soulless eyes the color of wet straw.

So this was Cleve Yoder, she thought, with a small private shudder of sympathy for Silvia. Looking smug, Cleve Junior matched his father step for step. The closer his father got, the more Randall seemed to shrink. His brother Johnny had already taken refuge behind Jess's long legs.

"Well, boy, cat got your tongue? I told you to tell the lady what I told you about crybabies."

Randall flushed and dropped his gaze. "Like our mom was," he mumbled, cowering under his father's glare.

Yoder's fishhook mouth quirked. "That's right, like that no-good, candy-ass mother of yours. Always whining about something that didn't matter a diddly damn, and don't you forget it."

For a terrible instant Hazel was certain he meant to hit the boy, but before she could take action, Jess stepped between Yoder and the children. His face was hard, his eyes harder still.

"You're out of line, Yoder." His words were deliberate, balanced on a knife-edge.

Cleve's nostrils flared, the reaction of even the most savage of animals in the presence of clear danger.

"That's rich, coming from a blackmailer like you, Dante."

"I meant what I said. Silvia asked me to watch over her children, and I intend to do just that."

"You and how many others to help you?"

Hazel saw the shimmer of chilled steel appear suddenly in the jet depths of Jess's eyes. "Rash words from a big, brave wife beater like you, Yoder."

Yoder sucked in his breath, his eyes bulging and his skin blooming with unhealthy color. "So help me, if you weren't a cripple—"

"Hey, don't let that stop you."

Yoder's eyes slitted, and his chunky face stilled, reminding Hazel of a rattlesnake sizing up his prey.

"You'd like that, wouldn't you, Dante? Get yourself beat up fair and square and then sue me for assault. All you lawyers are alike, bloodsuckers all of you. But I ain't gonna fall for no shyster's game, not me."

Jess's expression didn't change. "Suit yourself. Just don't forget what I told you. Silvia's sons are under my protection now. One way or another, I'm not going to let them forget their mother."

Yoder mouthed an ugly obscenity, then ordered Cleve Junior to grab his baby brother's hand. He himself took hold of his middle son so violently the boy cried out.

"I ain't hurting you, you wimp," Yoder snarled before aiming a look of pure hatred Jess's way. "This isn't the last there'll be between us, Dante. I give you my word on it."

Hazel watched Yoder stalk up the aisle, his three boys in his wake. The door creaked on unoiled hinges, then slammed against the jamb as Yoder charged out. Hazel exhaled slowly, her gaze returning to Jess's face.

"Too bad Silvia had lousy aim," she murmured with heartfelt vehemence.

Jess looked startled; then the ice in his eyes cracked, and the corners crinkled. "Yeah, that would have solved a lot of problems."

"Meaning the bruises on Cleve Junior and Johnny?"

"You noticed those, did you?" Jess met Hazel's eyes steadily.

She nodded, suddenly chilled even though the sun had shifted slightly, drenching the chapel's interior with light. "Do you think he's started in on them now that he doesn't have Silvia to knock around?"

His expression turned grim. "I'd bet big money on it."

Hazel watched dust motes jerk crazily in the light flooding the plain windows. "We have to do something—"

"Already done. Someone from the county children's services will be waiting for Cleve at his place with a writ. The boys will be safely in foster care by nightfall."

Hazel blinked. "You called them?"

He nodded. "From my car before the service started. While Silvia's sisters were busy getting reacquainted with the boys Cleve never let them see."

"They never should have been allowed to remain with him in the first place."

Jess frowned. "After Silvia admitted under oath that she was the only one he'd brutalized, the court had no reason to remove them."

Hazel glanced toward the altar. Suddenly the flowers didn't seem so comforting, nor the words of the service so healing.

"Why did Yoder accuse you of blackmail?"

"Because I threatened him with legal action if he didn't allow the boys to say goodbye to their mother."

"Could you have done that?"

"Not in time, no, but he didn't know that."

Hazel wondered if Jess had ever played poker. "What happens next?" she asked, shifting her gaze to Jess's face again. The daylight brought out the wash of silver at his temples and deepened the grooves framing his mouth.

"Next I file a petition to transfer temporary custody to Silvia's sister, Yolanda, while the authorities look into the charges of child abuse I intend to file."

His jaw was suddenly tight and his expression bleak. Hazel had a feeling he'd been berating himself for not doing enough for Silvia while she was alive, perhaps even blaming himself for her death.

She started walking up the aisle. Jess fell in step, fitting his longer stride to hers, and she noticed that once again he'd maneuvered so that she was on his left.

As soon as they stepped outside, Jess worried the knot of his tie loose and hooked a finger under the collar button to free it from the buttonhole.

Hazel hid a smile. Jess was only barely civilized when it came to the clothes he wore. As for his ties, they were the most god-awful things she'd ever seen hanging around a man's neck.

"I've always meant to ask you—how do you tie a tie one-handed?"

Hazel saw the sudden stillness in his eyes. Some questions he handled well, others not. Which was this? she wondered, knowing that she wouldn't stop asking no matter what his response.

"I don't," he said finally, his tone impassive. "The clerk in the men's store ties it for me and I never untie it."

"Ah, very clever."

Neither spoke until they'd reached the driver's side of her car. The hearse was gone, the parking lot deserted.

"I didn't expect to see you here," he said, looking around as though suddenly seeing the place for the first time. Already the brutal heat had sheened his skin with moisture, and his hair was beginning to curl where it lay against his neck.

She'd expected him to take off his suit coat as soon as the funeral had ended. When he hadn't, she'd wondered if he made it a habit to wait until he was alone to do things that took more than normal effort.

"I very nearly didn't make it in time," she confided, pushing back her damp bangs. "I'm usually good about getting directions ahead of time, but lately everything seems topsy-turvy."

"Must be going around."

Tensing, Hazel wondered what she'd said to put the rasp of irritation in his voice. "How's Francey?"

"Doing well." He hesitated. "She's still with Cait."

"Yes, I know, and I've been thinking about that." She wet her suddenly dry lips, then plunged in. "My next-door neighbor, Mrs. Weller, is a licensed care giver. She's not working at the moment, because her grandchildren have been visiting, but they're leaving tomorrow."

"Are you recommending her as a nanny?"

"At least temporarily." She took a deep breath. "I thought I could keep Francey at night, and then Mrs. Weller could come in when I leave for the office. I have room, and, well, Cait was looking pretty tired last time I saw her."

Instead of responding, he drew a pair of aviator sunglasses from his breast pocket, shook them open and fitted them over the bridge of his nose. To avoid eye contact? she wondered, looking up at him and seeing a reflection of herself in the opaque lenses.

"Does that mean you're accepting my proposal?"

She sensed a leashed tension in him now. Like a wild predator masquerading as a docile pet.

"You promised to give me until Thursday to give you my answer."

"But I didn't promise not to plead my case one more time," he said, his mouth descending.

His mouth sought hers slowly, as though he were giving her time to draw back, an opportunity to escape. To reject him as he'd been rejected before.

Incapable of moving, unable to breathe, Hazel let her eyelids drift closed, accepting him, sealing the image of his lived-in face into her mind.

This time his kisses were more demanding—moist, draining kisses that had her thoughts and senses swirling and her arms slipping around his neck. His shoulders were iron stiff, his skin on fire beneath her palms, his hair thick and cool and very springy where her knuckles burrowed.

At the first sign of response, he shuddered hard, as though flinching from sudden pain, and then his fingers were tightening, holding her and yet caressing her at the same time.

When she moaned, he drew her closer, then abruptly drew his mouth from hers, leaving her lips bruised and damp.

"Have dinner with me tomorrow night. We'll talk about this Mrs. Weller of yours." His voice was ragged, his breathing far less controlled than it should have been for a man so intensely fit and strong.

"All right." She dropped her arms and took an unsteady step backward.

He withdrew his hand slowly, letting his fingers trail gently over the fragile bones of her throat. "I'll pick you up at six."

"At the office."

Jess opened the door for her and waited until she got in before bending lower to kiss her one last, lingering time.

"At the office," he repeated before shutting her door. "And O'Connor?" he asked through the open window.

"Hmm?"

"Time *is* running out."

Chapter 9

Neil Kenyon had been Hazel's patient for almost three months. A strapping, good-looking seventeen-year-old with startling blue eyes and a marked resemblance to a young Clint Eastwood, he had been diagnosed as severely depressed and potentially suicidal after he'd broken his neck in a diving competition.

Instead of helping ease the boy into his new life, his seven months in a rehabilitation center had left him embittered and suspicious of everyone who tried to get close to him—including Hazel.

According to his mother, he'd been a big man on campus, star quarterback on his team, popular with his teachers and fellow students alike—and, Hazel suspected, pretty much able to date any girl he fancied.

Since the accident, however, he had isolated himself at home and cut off communication with old friends. Hazel's first goal had been to bring him out of his self-imposed exile and into the world again.

"So what are you going to do for your birthday on Saturday?" Hazel asked toward the end of their session.

Neil glanced down at the wheelchair that would be a part of him for the rest of his life. "Well, it's like this, Doc," he said, his mouth stiff with self-pity. "I'm trying to decide between horseback riding or Roller-blading."

Hazel raised her eyebrows. "I'd go for the riding if I were you."

"Yeah, right."

She leaned back and looked at him with lazy eyes, as though nothing he could say would shock her. "True story. I have other paraplegic patients who ride just about every week and love it."

He shot her a skeptical look, which was far better than the blank apathy that had been his stock response during most of his earlier sessions.

Rocking her chair back and forth on its heavy spring, she held her gaze steady on his. "I understand it's great exercise."

"Yeah, well, pushing this damn chair everywhere is all the exercise I can handle right now."

"What about working out with the team the way you'd planned?"

His gaze shied from hers, and he slumped lower in the chair. "Changed my mind."

"You seemed very excited about it last week. 'Ready, willing, and able to tear up trees' was the way you put it."

He looked away again, but his hands were slowly clenching around the arms of his chair. Hazel waited, giving him the time and emotional space he needed to decide whether or not to trust her with his deepest feelings.

"It was the guys!" he burst out finally, his tone trembling with hurt. "They tried not to, but most of 'em kept looking at me like I was some kind of freak."

Hazel kept her expression calm. "Do you think you're a freak?"

His face turned crimson, and his eyes flashed a heartbreaking hurt. "No, just a cripple who can't even get it up."

Hazel leaned back and used her toes to swivel her chair slowly right and left. "You mean you can't get an erection?"

He looked away again, this time without answering, misery radiating from every line of his body.

"Have you tried to masturbate yourself to arousal?" she asked matter-of-factly.

He flicked her a glance she took as an affirmative. "And don't ask me if I've tried screwing my girlfriend," he exclaimed in a tight, furious voice, "because I haven't. And I won't."

"Why not?"

He shrugged. "You're so smart, you figure it out."

"I could, I suppose," she said with perfect seriousness. "But that would be wasting my time and yours, so why don't you just tell me now and save a lot of hassle?"

Neil leaned on the arm of his chair, his deep blue eyes seething with despair. "I don't want her to see my legs," he mumbled, his eyes downcast. "It's like... like they're a couple of limp noodles attached to my body."

"You're more than your body, you know."

"Yeah, right," he sneered. "Tell that to the guys who don't want to know me anymore and the girls who act like I got some kind of disease worse than AIDS."

Hazel glanced at the notes she'd made earlier. "What about your girl, Lisa? Does she look at you like you have a disease?"

Neil clenched his teeth and shook his head. At the same time, his hands clenched on thighs that had once been muscular and strong, something they would never be again.

"I hate being crippled," he grated, his voice hoarse. "You hear me, Doc? I hate it!"

A strangled cry like a sob broke from his lips, followed by others. Harsh explosions of sound. Painful as it was to hear, however, she knew that the outburst was cathartic and necessary to the healing process.

"I know it hurts," she said gently. "On some level it might always hurt."

Neil dragged the back of his hand over his eyes. "Why me? What did I ever do to make God mad at me?" He choked on a sob and took a moment to compose himself again.

"Every morning... it's like I wake up not remembering. Like I can just get up and get dressed and run to school like always. Only... all of a sudden I can't feel my legs."

He glanced up, tears clumping his lashes and his mouth trembling. "And then I remember. I can't run to school 'cause I can't walk. Not ever again!"

"No wonder you hate being a paraplegic," Hazel said as she pushed the box of tissues within easy reach. "I can't think of anyone who wouldn't hate it."

As she'd hoped, her calm acceptance encouraged him to continue. "Lisa swears it doesn't matter to her if I can walk or dance or play football anymore, but when... when she touches me, I can see this funny look in her eyes. Like she's cringing inside and trying not to show it."

He tore a handful of tissues from the box and angrily swiped his eyes. "And whenever I try to talk about what it's like to be in this chair, she changes the subject real quick, like she can't stand to hear stuff like that."

"Maybe she's afraid talking about your feelings will make them worse."

"What makes it worse is her always talking about a miracle cure, like all of a sudden some scientist someplace is going to come up with a pill that'll make my spine grow back together again. Only that's not gonna happen, just like she's never gonna accept me like I am now."

"Perhaps not. And that may mean your relationship will have to end. But there are other girls who won't feel the same way."

Neil's expression hardened, then grew sharply cynical, reminding her of Jess's expression that night in the motel bar when he'd been talking about his ex-wife.

"Yeah, right. And there's this guy in a red suit and a big white beard who comes down my chimney every Christmas with a bag of toys."

"Is that why you think you might like to kill yourself?" she asked gently. "Because of Lisa and the way she looks at you?"

Surprise stuttered into his eyes, then turned slowly to uncertainty. "I thought it was, yeah, but..." He trailed off, staring at her as though he'd suddenly had an astonishing thought.

"But what?" she prodded with a calm she was far from feeling.

"But now I'm not sure she's worth dying over. Or any other girl, either."

"I certainly agree with that," Hazel said with a vehemence that won her a small, crooked grin.

"I kinda thought you would."

Hazel chuckled. "I see being paralyzed hasn't taken the edge off that wise guy attitude of yours."

That seemed to please him, and he sat up just a bit straighter. "Maybe we ought to talk about my sex life again," he challenged, then blushed.

Hazel laughed. "Next time, okay?"

Neil wiggled his eyebrows and leered. "Is that a promise?"

"Yes, Groucho, that's a promise." Still grinning, she got up to circle the desk. "Now give me a hug and get out of here. I've got people with real problems waiting to see me."

In fact, Neil was the last appointment of the day, but he didn't know that.

"You don't have to tell me twice," he said, accepting her hug with a lot more spirit than the previous week.

Still bantering, she walked him to the door but let him open it himself. Seated alone in the small anteroom, Neil's mother looked up from the magazine she'd been reading and watched him wheel himself across the carpet.

"All set?" she asked, getting quickly to her feet.

"Yeah, let's blow this joint!" Neil exclaimed, but he was grinning.

Mrs. Kenyon's gaze whipped to Hazel, who smiled. It's going to be a long, rocky road, she wanted to tell the anxious woman, but today he took a very big step. Instead, she caught Neil's eye and said meaningfully, "Same time next week, okay, wise guy?"

"You got it, Doc."

Mrs. Kenyon looked startled for an instant before a spontaneous grin replaced the worn look around her mouth.

"We'll be here."

Neil reached up to open the outer door, only to have it swing away from his fingertips. "Hey, watch it, dude!" he said. "You could jerk a guy out of his chair that way."

"Sorry, dude," Jess apologized, stepping back. The tailored trousers and impeccably shined loafers told her he'd been in court, but somewhere along the way from the courthouse to her office he had discarded his suit coat and tie. Today he was wearing suspenders, the wide kind that made him look more rugged than trendy.

Neil did a double take before turning in his chair to give Hazel a curious look. "Whoa, doc, is Dante here one of those problems you were talking about?"

Hazel blinked. "Uh, not exactly."

Jess rumpled Neil's hair as he sidestepped the wheelchair and entered. "How are you, Mrs. Kenyon?"

"Much better since the last time I saw you, Mr. Dante. As you can see, so is Neil."

Jess cocked one eyebrow and gave the teenager a critical stare. "You still mad at the world, kid?"

Neil looked abashed. "Only parts of it this week."

"Works for me."

Hazel watched the subtle affection pass between the man and boy and felt strangely left out, as though they were part of a very exclusive club she could never join.

"I didn't know you two knew each other," she said, glancing from Neil to Jess and holding his gaze.

"I thought you knew, O'Connor. Us crippled types 'bond' well." Hazel heard the dry humor in Jess's tone and shook her head.

"Okay, okay, I get the point."

"Mr. Dante came to the hospital to see Neil when he was still in traction," the boy's mother explained.

"Yelled at me real good, didn't you, Dante?" Neil grumbled before shifting his gaze to Hazel. "Even threatened to whip my butt good if I didn't agree to dump all my troubles on you. Claimed you were the best in the city and he—how did he put it?—strongly recommended I get my tail over here pronto, or he would drag me to your office himself." His grin flashed suddenly, giving Hazel a perfect view of an adult male charmer in the making. "Not that he could, you understand, but you have to humor these old guys, you know?"

"So I've heard," she replied, meeting Jess's gaze. Even though he looked as though one of his deepest secrets had suddenly been exposed, there was a light in his eyes that made her want to cuddle close and tell him just how wonderful she thought he was—when he thought no one was looking, that is.

"Smart kid," he said with a crooked smile.

"With a wiseacre attitude," Hazel teased. "We had a discussion about that earlier."

Neil shrugged, then seemed struck by a sudden thought. "Hey, Doc, if Dante here isn't one of your patients, what is he? Your old man or something?"

"Neil!" his mother exclaimed, embarrassed and yet pleased to see some of her son's spirit returning.

"Or something," Hazel replied, laughing. "We have mutual friends."

"Don't let her con you, kid," Jess drawled. "She's so crazy for my body I'm about to let her marry me, just to get me some peace and quiet."

Hazel's mouth dropped open. "Jess Dante! You know that's not true."

"Which part?" His tone was flavored with masculine irony, as though he wanted his words to be true, but knew they couldn't possibly be.

"I . . . we'll talk about this later."

Madeline Kenyon cleared her throat. "We'd better get going if we're going to beat the traffic." She held out her hand. "Good luck, Mr. Dante," she said as he gave her his. "If anyone deserves to be happy, it's you."

Neil rolled his eyes and grabbed the wheels of his chair. "Let me outta here before it gets too deep for the chair to move."

His mother swatted him on the head before grabbing the handles of the chair. "Mush, you," she said lightly, but Hazel thought she detected a small catch of emotion beneath the teasing words.

"Be good, Doc," Neil threw over his shoulder as his mother wheeled him out. "You too, Dante! But not too good, if you get my meaning."

The look on Jess's face and the tension tightening his shoulders told her that he'd taken Neil's meaning very well. So had Hazel, which was already threatening her vow to remain rationally composed in Jess's presence.

"Ready?" he asked when they were alone.

"Don't give me that innocent look, Dante. I want to know what just went on here."

"Not much," he said with the shrug she'd come to expect from him and a heart-stopping grin that she hadn't. "But I have high hopes."

Before she could catch her breath, he leaned forward to give her a quick, hungry kiss that was over far too quickly, leaving her disoriented.

"Don't think I'm rushing you, but we're late."

"You said six. It's not quite five to."

"Yeah, but we have a long drive before we can eat, and I missed lunch."

So had she. "I thought we could run over to this little Italian place I know. Unless you have a better choice."

He picked up the magazine Neil's mother had left on her chair and tossed it onto the square table in the center of the small room. "O'Connor, you might as well know now— you're looking at one distant son of Italy who hates tomato sauce."

She threw him a disbelieving look. "I saw you eat three helpings of Cait's lasagna."

He shrugged. "It's her way of pampering the starving bachelor. I wouldn't want to hurt her feelings by telling her I'd rather have beans and rice."

"Very considerate."

"Considerate, hell. Caitie might look like a cream puff, but she's got a mouth on her that could strip the hide off a bull buffalo."

Hazel laughed softly. "You have a point," she murmured, taking ridiculous delight in watching his eyes crinkle and his mouth quirk.

His mood seemed different, too. Lighter, in a way, and yet he had the same fierce, focused intensity of purpose he'd carried into Tyler's retrial. As though not even the demons of hell could keep him from getting what he wanted.

"So where is it that we *are* going?" she asked lightly.

"All the way to Placerville."

"What's in Placerville?" she asked, heading for the inner office, her purse and a chance to gather the wits he was busy scattering.

"The best ribs in the state, for one thing."

"And for another?" she asked, slinging her purse over her shoulder before turning off her desk lamp.

"My brother's ranch." Jess flipped out the lights and closed the door behind her as she exited.

To her surprise, he took her arm possessively as they passed the other offices, as though he wanted anyone watching to think that the two of them were going on a proper date.

He had a powerful grip and a way of making a woman feel protected just because he was at her side. With or without both his arms, Jess Dante was a very sexy man.

"Your brother the rodeo champion?" she asked as they approached the door to the parking lot. He released her—reluctantly, it seemed—to open the door for her.

"My brother the rich, successful vet turned stock breeder," he said as he claimed her arm again. "I figured it might help my cause if you met at least one Dante with company manners.''

Even one-handed, Jess drove with the same superb skill she would have expected from an ex-race driver. But it was more than just skill, she decided, watching him covertly. It was as though he and the powerful, low-slung car were one entity.

Only when he had to insert the key into the ignition on the right and shove the gear lever into drive did he seem the least bit awkward.

He also kept the old Mercedes close to the speed limit, something she'd first noticed when he'd driven them down to Pleasanton and again on the way back. Then, as now, his was far from the fastest vehicle on the road.

''Something wrong?'' he asked, catching her looking at the speedometer.

''I'm just surprised that you're such a conservative driver.'' Hazel watched a balding yuppie in a Corvette whip past them in the left lane.

''Most race drivers are.''

''Except on the track,'' she surmised.

''Especially on the track. Too many things can go wrong if you're not.''

She let her gaze linger for a moment on his profile. He was driving with the window down, and the wind had teased a few stray curls into his normally straight hair. It gave his severe face a softened look she had trouble resisting.

''I never thought of it that way,'' she said, clearing her throat of a sudden tickle.

He glanced her way, catching her watching him. ''That's because you haven't spent much time around a track.''

''None, actually,'' she admitted, shifting her gaze to the front and keeping it there. ''And I've never even seen the 500 on TV, mostly because I'm afraid there might be an accident, and I'd just as soon not be an eyewitness.''

"Chances are you wouldn't be. Not recently, anyway. Not the way the cars are designed to protect the driver these days."

"Are you kidding? I've seen pictures of those cars. I had a kiddy car when I was five that looked stronger."

He chuckled, and the creases framing his mouth deepened like long shallow dimples. "If you'd ever seen a race, you would know that the engineers have figured out a way for the car to fly apart on impact, diffusing the kinetic force from the cockpit, which pretty much stays intact."

"What about fire?"

"Formula One engines burn pure alcohol. It's not as volatile as high octane gasoline, and it's easier to extinguish."

Hazel took a deep breath. "Was there a fire when you had your accident?"

"Some."

"Were you burned?"

"No, the rescue crew got me out before the tank exploded." His tone conveyed very little emotion, as though he were talking about a routine point of law.

Telling herself to follow his lead, she took a deep breath, drawing in the aroma of leather and his musky after-shave along with the fresh air coming through the windows.

"How much of it do you remember?" she asked in a matter-of-fact tone.

"All of it."

He used his index finger to flip on the signal for the first Placerville exit. "When you're racing, time slows down, which is one of the reasons you can handle a car at two-hundred plus. It's the same with a smashup."

Hazel waited until he'd navigated the serpentine curves of the exit before asking, "Do you have nightmares about the crash?"

This time there was a nearly imperceptible pause before he answered. "No. Not now."

"But you did?"

"More like flashbacks. The shrink in the hospital told me to expect them, but I thought she was talking through her hat." He glanced her way, his mouth wryly mocking. "She wasn't."

"How long did you have them?"

"A few years. Until my second or third year of law school."

He stopped at an intersection, then took the road to the left that looked as though it led off into nowhere. Hazel had been to Placerville before but had never ventured this far into the boonies.

She'd heard it said somewhere that the northern section of the California Sierra Nevada was more west Texas than west Texas, and she was beginning to see why.

"I can almost see John Wayne riding hell-bent over that rise over there," she said, craning her neck.

"Me, I was always the Lone Ranger when my brothers and I got a chance to play cowboys and Indians."

She laughed, then tried to picture a younger version of the man she knew galloping over these hills, a gangly kid in dungarees and a checkered shirt. She had limited success, however, mostly because images of a man's broad chest and hard lean thighs in tight jeans kept intruding.

"Looks like good cattle rustlin' country, Kemo Sabe," she murmured when her thoughts became too unsettling.

"More like good grazing land," he said, sparing her an amused look that should have made her laugh and instead had her thinking about the leashed hunger of his mouth when he'd kissed her.

"Is that what your brother raises? Cattle?"

"No, Appaloosas and quarter horses. Before him, though, the Dantes were cattlemen, man and boy. Three generations back."

"So how come you ended up driving race cars? It doesn't quite compute."

"Sure it does. I've always liked horses. I just wanted to drive more than one at a time."

Hazel shook her head. "That makes sense—I think."

They drove in silence for a time, heading up a winding road and through a stand of gnarled live oaks, then along a sturdy, well-maintained rail fence and up a long unpaved lane.

"How's the kid doing?" Jess asked after having her shift into low for him. Occupied with the gear lever, it took Hazel a moment to realize that he meant Neil.

"He's doing better, finally."

A muscle low on his jaw flattened, then eased. "Does he still want to blow his brains out?" His tone was completely dispassionate, as though they were discussing the latest baseball scores.

A week ago she would have been disgusted by his utter lack of emotion. Now she knew better. Jess was simply more adept at hiding his feelings than most people.

"You know I can't discuss specifics," she said, chiding him with a smile that he seemed inclined to return.

"At least he's still hanging in there. That's something."

Hazel drew a cautious breath, then said lightly, "I was surprised to hear that you were the one who recommended me to the Kenyons."

He flicked her a look that could have meant anything from irritation to surprise. "Why? You're good, aren't you?"

"Very. I didn't realize you knew that, however."

"Why wouldn't I? I was around when you were treating Kels, remember?"

Hazel folded her hands around her purse and held a quick private debate with herself. Should she or shouldn't she?

She should, she decided. After all, Jess had asked her to be his wife. She had every right to display curiosity about his life, past and present.

"How did you come to know Neil and his family well enough to recommend anyone, let alone me?"

Tensing, he seemed to be considering his answer, perhaps weighing how much of his privacy he was willing to give up.

"I read about his accident in the paper," he said finally. "One day when I was at the rehab center I dropped in to see him."

"The rehab center? Do you still take therapy?"

"No." He hesitated, then frowned. "I volunteer now and then. Sometimes it helps new patients to talk to someone who's been through the drill."

"Did someone talk to you?"

"No."

Slowing to a crawl, he turned right into a track passing under a rustic wooden sign bearing a rocking D brand and the name Dante Brothers.

"I didn't know you owned part of the ranch," she said, straining against the lap belt for a better look at the land where Jess grew up.

"I don't. Garrett used to be partners with our brother Rafe before he was killed. Somehow he never got around to taking down the sign."

Before Hazel could ask him what had happened to his brother, they had crested a small rise and were heading toward a setting right out of the same John Wayne movie she'd thought of earlier.

The house was a two-story adobe with deep shaded balconies, built in the midst of a gorgeous stand of eucalyptus trees that had to be a good hundred years old or more.

A lush lawn of Bermuda grass surrounded the house, and there appeared to be a pool on the other side of a grape stake fence to the rear.

The outbuildings were adobe, as well, with the exception of a large barn made of stone. Jess pulled up next to the corral gate and killed the engine.

"Home, sweet home," he declared, half turning toward her in order to remove the keys and set the brake. "Garrett said to meet him in the barn. He's mending tack."

"Oh, Jess, it's wonderful," she said, trying to see everything at once.

"Yeah, well, don't fall in love with it," he warned, opening his door. "Garrett lives here. I live in a bungalow in Fair Oaks."

She had just freed herself from the old-fashioned lap belt when Jess opened the door and extended his hand, obviously intending to help her out of the lower than normal bucket seat.

Expecting him to let her go once she was on her feet, she found herself suddenly pulled against him instead. Before she could make a sound, his hand had slipped deftly into the hollow of her back and his mouth had come down on hers for a hard, demanding kiss.

Her heart was pounding and her legs were remarkably unsteady when he lifted his mouth from hers.

"That's just to remind you which Dante wants to marry you," he said before releasing her.

"Don't worry, I'm not about to forget," she assured him, straightening her skirt. Just as she wasn't about to let herself forget the reason—a dark-haired, adorable orphan named Francisca who needed a mother.

Chapter 10

Once inside the barn, Hazel felt as though she had stepped into a different century. Life seemed simpler here, more in tune with the rhythms of nature than the clock.

The interior was cool, the space impressive. The sweetly seductive scent of alfalfa wafted from the loft to mingle with the more pungent odors of manure and horse flesh below.

Glancing up, she saw massive hand-hewn oak beams and age-darkened timber. Stark, solid reminders of a rugged demanding life-style and the men and women who had survived it.

"This is one great barn," she murmured, turning slowly in a circle.

Standing near the door, Jess found himself watching her every reaction, measuring her response to the place he loved like a kid bringing his best date home to meet his folks.

Somehow he'd pictured her feeling as ill at ease here a he'd been in her house, her world. Certainly she was dressed more for that parlor of hers than a working spread. Tailored slacks, simple blouse without frills or ruffles, gold a her ears and throat. Nothing overtly sexy or even subtly hinting at a female come-on. No reason at all why he should be standing there feeling as randy as a stallion confronted with a skittish mare needing more gentleness than he possessed.

"I have to tell you, Jess, this is *nothing* like the puny little stable where I boarded Pizzazz."

"Pizzazz?"

How long had it been since he'd made love to a woman? he wondered, forcing himself to concentrate on her words instead of her lips. How many years of living like a monk and telling himself celibacy was good for him?

"Pizzazz was my Arab. Father bought her for me as an investment. 'Your college fund' he called her, and let it be known that I was to win enough prize money on her to increase her value substantially."

"Did you?"

"Enough to pay for four years of grad school by the time he made me sell her." She inhaled deeply. "Being here reminds me of her."

She came closer, testing the promise he'd made to himself to press his case slowly and logically. The whisper of her perfume and the proximity of her soft mouth gave him a few bad seconds before he had his control shored up again.

"Being here reminds *me* of damn hard work."

He was at home here, she thought. At one with this old place as he was one with the Mercedes he cherished—and constantly threatened to sell when it gave him trouble.

Was that the way Jess handled his deepest feelings? she wondered. By denying them with the same fervency?

"Did you really hate it?" she asked, giving in to the need to know as easily as she gave in to impulse. "Or are you just telling yourself that because you can't do it any longer?"

Jess froze. "I can still do it," he told her, his voice clipped. "It just takes me longer."

"And you're angry at me for bringing it up, right?"

His face was stone, like the barn, all the emotion she'd been feeling from him withdrawn behind that impenetrable wall.

"Did you ever think that you'd be angry with me if I ignored the fact that you face limitations I don't?" She rested both hands on his shoulders and made him look at her. "Jess? Tell me how you want me to handle the fact that you're, um, 'differently abled,' I think the term is these days?"

Jess recognized the attempt to put him at ease with an openness about his handicap that he'd learned never to expect from a woman. Or anyone else, for that matter. Although he himself wasn't a particularly kind person, he recognised kindness in others. Hazel had more than her share.

But lying helpless as a baby in a hospital bed had taught him that kindness generally came with a kicker, the kind that stripped a man of his dignity and left him raw inside. He realized that he liked it better when she was yelling at him.

"I don't want you to 'handle' it at all." he said.

"Too bad, because we both know it's not going to go away. As someone told me once, it's not as though some scientist someplace was suddenly going to figure out a way to grow you a new arm. And if we can't be honest with each other about our feelings concerning this one small problem, how can we possibly handle a marriage?"

Turning away before he could answer, she moved eagerly toward the stalls. Like a room of kindergarten kids, the mares lined up to greet the visitors with soft nickers and inquisitive stares.

"Oh, what a beauty!" she exclaimed softly, stopping in front of an Appaloosa yearling.

Jess told himself to hold on to his anger. It was safer that way. But Hazel had a way of making a man want to take risks with her that he would never consider taking with anyone else.

"That's Madonna, my niece Andi's pride and joy."

The mare pricked her ears and whinnied. "Hiya, lady," Jess murmured, rubbing the eager nose with his knuckles.

"She likes you," Hazel remarked, glancing up at him speculatively.

"I helped Garrett deliver her. We—"

"If you say 'bonded,' I swear I'll sock you a good one," she exclaimed softly, her eyes sparkling. In the barn's dim light, they appeared more golden than green. Like a mama cat's when she was feeling frisky early in the morning. Or late at night.

Because he wanted very badly to draw her down in a bed of clean hay and make very slow, very careful love to her, he made it impossible by calling out his brother's name.

As he expected, Garrett stuck his head out of the tack room and waved. "Yo, J.D.! Thought I heard that bomb of... yours." Garrett's welcoming grin froze as he caught sight of Hazel. "You didn't tell me you were bringing a guest for dinner."

Jess sensed immediately that Hazel liked his brother on sight. But then, most people did, especially women. Garrett had been the stud of the county before he'd married his high school sweetheart. Now that he was a widower, he was in more demand than ever.

"Hazel O'Connor," he said, slipping his hand under her arm and leading her forward. "Meet the rock of the Dante family, my big brother, Garrett."

Hazel found herself looking up at an older, leaner version of Jess, with the same dark eyes and strongly shaped mouth. Meeting his frank, open gaze, she sensed some of Jess's sharp intelligence beneath the weathered facade, as well.

"Hello, Garrett. I'm very glad to meet you."

Hazel stuck out her hand. Garrett ignored it and instead gave her one of his patented bear hugs. Watching, Jess realized just how tiny she seemed when she was wrapped up like a cuddly package in Garrett's big arms. He also realized at that precise moment just how much he wanted to slug his brother in the gut.

"I'm running a little behind mending Andi's show saddle," Garrett said when he released Hazel. Damn reluctantly, too, it seemed to Jess. "How 'bout you two having a cup of coffee while I finish up? There's still plenty left in the thermos. Made it myself.''

Jess groaned. "Sure you haven't got a jug someplace instead? Hazel is partial to white wine, but I'll drink anything that isn't right out of a still someplace.''

Garrett threw a long leg over the stool pulled close to the most beautiful silver-encrusted saddle Hazel had ever seen and reached for the half-mended stirrup.

"Sorry, no jug. Just coffee.''

"Sounds lovely,'' Hazel murmured, smiling up at Garrett with a free and easy warmth Jess envied. He wasn't a jealous man, but the sharp catch in his gut was hard to ignore.

"Don't say I didn't warn you,'' he grumbled, handing her one of the cups Garrett kept in a drawer for visitors.

"I like strong coffee,'' she insisted, unscrewing the cap on the thermos.

"Strong doesn't begin to cover cowboy coffee.''

Jess hooked a cup for himself and held it out toward her. She poured for both of them, then topped up Garrett's cup.

Jess tested the coffee and found it worse than usual. After his sister-in-law's death a few years back, his brother had learned to cook and keep a passable house, but he hadn't learned squat about brewing a decent pot of coffee.

"Strong, isn't it?'' he said, eyeing her closely.

Hazel took a tentative sip, then nodded. "Very.''

He seemed more at ease here than anywhere she'd been with him. More the rugged cowhand than the sophisticated attorney. And far more difficult to resist, she was discovering, especially when he was looking at her with eyes dark and enigmatic one moment, lashed with heat the next.

Excitement ran through her, chased by a mental shiver of warning. Once released, passion as deep and potent as his, passion that had been dammed up so strongly and for so long, could easily destroy anyone not strong enough to withstand the torrent.

"Very strong,'' she repeated, forcing another tiny taste. "A real challenge to the system.''

His mouth slanted. "Most women prefer something easier to handle."

"And some don't."

"Hard to tell sometimes, though, isn't it?"

Wanting her with a hunger that strained even his will to endure, Jess leaned against the drug cabinet and watched Garrett's fingers manipulate leather and awl. It was a job that he had once hated. Now he would give anything just to be able to do it again.

"Where's Andi?" he asked Garrett when the silence started to make him edgy.

"4-H meeting." Garrett wet the end of a leather thong with his tongue. "County Fair's next month," he added for Hazel's benefit. "My daughter's entered Madonna this year."

"Do you think she'll win?" Hazel asked.

"Damn, I hope so. Otherwise she won't be fit to live with for months." Garrett pierced the leather wrap on the stirrup with the needle-sharp awl before glancing up. "Takes after her Uncle J.D., hates like fire to lose."

"Really?" Hazel murmured, her voice reeking of a playful innocence Jess was more and more inclined to kiss out of her. "You could have fooled me."

While Jess scowled, Garrett glanced at the long line of dusty blue ribbons tacked to one of the rough-hewn rafters.

"See those awards there? My old man hung the first one the year I took the bronc-busting prize at the junior rodeo. J.D. was six that year, and he musta liked all the attention I got, 'cause the next thing we know, he's out in the far pasture, trying to ride anything that would stand still long enough for him to climb on."

Garrett threw Jess a grin that wasn't returned. "Broke his leg once, dislocated his shoulder another time. Even managed to get himself a coupla concussions before he learned how to hang on properly."

"Don't listen to him," Jess told her with a dark look for his brother. She'd already sensed the subtle thread of love between the two males, even though she doubted if either would openly admit it to the other.

"How many of those up there are yours?" she asked Jess with a smile.

"Hell if I know. Ask Garrett. He likes telling stories so much."

Garrett chuckled. "Five are mine, six are his. There would have been more, but he discovered cars could go faster and farther, and that was that. Got himself an old hot rod and took to racing deer out on Old Placer Road."

"So that's how you got started," Hazel said, watching him intently with those soft golden eyes as though she'd never quite seen anyone like him before.

Being watched made him nervous, no matter who was doing the watching or why. In the courtroom, he had learned to start out slow and easy with a new jury, giving them time to get used to the homely guy with one arm before he showed them the attorney.

There were still times, however, when he wondered if he too often won concessions from the jury or other attorneys out of sheer pity, something he hated but couldn't prevent.

Downing his coffee in two quick gulps, he stood up and gave his brother an impatient look.

"Finish that later, okay? I promised the lady ribs, and I'd like her to taste them before she's too damned starved to appreciate Marvella's sauce."

Garrett drew the thong taut, then looped a knot close to the stirrup before slicing it cleanly with his knife. "How about it, Hazel?" he asked, putting down his tools before standing and reaching for his hat. "Ready for a once in a lifetime treat?"

"Lead the way," she said, setting aside her cup and getting to her feet in one graceful movement.

As they walked back through the cavernous barn, Jess had to stifle a strong urge to loop his arm around her shoulder and stake the kind of claim even his thickheaded flirt of a brother would understand. Instead, he settled for putting himself between them all the way to the car.

The shadows had grown longer while they'd been inside and the air slightly cooler. Hazel inhaled deeply, then wrinkled her nose at the faint odor of skunk.

"Country perfume," Jess said with a wry look that made her warm all over.

"Where's your cowboy hat?" she teased in return.

"Must've lost it somewhere."

"Truth is, he can't find one to fit that swelled head he got when he won the Grand Prix," Garrett tossed over his shoulder.

When they reached the Mercedes, Hazel took one look at Garrett's long legs and volunteered to sit in the back.

"No need," Garrett said, crooking his elbow and jerking his chin toward a row of vehicles lined up in a low shed to the right. "You're gonna ride with me."

"I am?"

"Sure. We always take two cars when we go to Marvella's. That way J.D. doesn't have to double back here to bring me home before he heads back to Sacramento."

Hazel glanced at Jess, who simply shrugged. "The man drives like a half-soused trail cook, but go ahead and humor him if you'd like. Just don't say I didn't warn you."

"Don't listen to him, sugar," Garrett said, taking her arm, since she hadn't taken his. "These days *he* drives like a little old lady out for a Sunday ramble."

Hazel let Jess's brother lead her to a white pickup parked in a sturdy shed to the right, along with a dark blue mini-van and a wicked-looking black Jaguar convertible.

Behind her, she heard a car door slam, more violently than seemed necessary. Garrett slanted her a look, then winked.

"Do him good not to call the shots all the time," he said as he helped her into the passenger side of the pickup.

Hazel didn't question why they were taking that instead of one of the other vehicles. Like Jess, Garrett had his own way of doing things and didn't seem all that amenable to questions or second-guessing.

The inside of the pickup was almost as comfortable as her car, with just about the same luxuries. Before shifting into first, Garrett shoved a tape into the cassette player, and the sounds of Beethoven filled the spacious cab.

Hazel smiled to herself. In his own way, Garrett was as much of an enigma as Jess.

"I can taste those ribs now," he drawled, backing quickly and skillfully in a tight circle before leading the way down the lane. Jess followed.

"You must be very important to my brother," he said, glancing in the rearview mirror.

"Why do you say that?" Hazel asked, as dubious as she was puzzled.

"For one thing, he hasn't brought a woman out to the ranch since he came back to the area to stay." Garrett shot her a quick grin. "For another, he's behind us."

Hazel glanced in the side mirror. The old sportscar looked low and wide from the front. And, she admitted, very sexy.

"I guess I'm not getting your point," she told Garrett.

"Usually he leads the way when we go to Marvella's 'cause he claims it slows me down. Tonight he seems in a big hurry for some reason."

"Maybe he's hungry."

"Or maybe he doesn't want to give me much time to warn you off." His voice was suddenly dead serious, and Hazel realized that Garrett was like his brother in another way as well. He never did anything without a good reason.

"I'm ... very fond of Jess," she said softly, but with a seriousness to match his. "I'd never deliberately hurt him, if that's what you're worried about."

She sensed a shift in the atmosphere and realized she'd guessed right. "Not worried, but wondering."

"I can understand that. After all, Jess is your brother."

"Yeah, which is why I'm more worried about you and wondering if you know what you're doing when you take on an *hombre* like him."

He moved so that his broad back crowded the door, making it easier for him to study her. "I don't know if you know it or not, but Gayla, his ex, really did a job on him. Butchered him worse than the surgeons, in fact."

Hazel waited, knowing now that Garrett had a purpose in shanghaiing her. "I'm not saying he hates women, you understand, but..." He paused.

"But he doesn't trust us all that much, either."

Hazel took his grunt for an affirmative. "It's a funny thing," he went on after a moment's thoughtful silence. "But in her own way, Gayla truly loved Jess. I think she wanted to stay with him, but he made it impossible."

Hazel picked at the stitching on the strap of her purse. "She was pregnant with another man's child when she left."

"I'm not saying she was perfect, but neither is my brother."

"Are you saying he cheated on her first?"

Garrett shook his head. "Jess takes promises very seriously which is why he rarely makes them. No, with Gayla, after the accident, he just shut her out like she was a part of his life that no longer existed. Maybe that made it easier for him to handle not being able to race again, but it still hurt her badly."

Hazel heard censure shading his voice and frowned. "He was going through a stressful time. Losing a limb is like suffering a death in a way."

"I'm not saying he wasn't hurting. He was. And I'm not saying Gayla didn't make things worse by some of the things she did and said. But a man who truly loves a woman..." His eyebrows bunched. "He'll forgive her for being human. Jess didn't."

"Maybe he tried."

"You're right. Maybe he did. There's a lot about my brother he keeps strictly private." Garrett shot her a quick glance. "Like the fact that he's thinking about getting married again."

"How do you know he is?"

"He dropped a few hints when he called to let me know he was coming over for ribs tonight. I figured he was angling for his big brother's words of wisdom."

He grinned at her, as though the idea of Jess asking him for anything was blatantly outrageous.

Grinning back, Hazel managed to hide her surprise. She'd give a lot to know exactly what Jess had told his brother about her.

"How do you know I'm the bride-to-be?"

"Have to be. J.D. is not what you call a jealous man, but he was sure showing signs of it tonight."

Jealous? Jess? Hazel considered Garrett's words carefully. Was it possible?

Rounding a curve, they met another pickup approaching, driven by a man in a Stetson about as broken-in as Garrett's. Both men tooted.

"You know what I think?" Garrett said when the pickup had passed. "If anyone is strong enough to take on my brother without getting too bruised in the process, it's you."

Hazel laughed. "Lucky me, huh?"

It was Garrett's turn to laugh. "Ask me on your first anniversary."

Hazel hesitated, trying to decide how much she could tell Jess's brother without violating Jess's privacy. "I haven't said yes yet."

"You will. J.D. has a way of getting what he wants. Sometimes it just takes him a little longer." Garrett slanted her a measuring look. "'Course he doesn't always want what he thinks he does."

Remembering the heated look in Jess's eyes had her frowning in the dimly lit interior. "You'd know that better than I would."

"He thought he wanted Gayla. Swore he was in love with her. Maybe he was, although she was never the most important part of his life, even in the good times. That was reserved for racing. Winning, that's what got him high. I'm not sure that's changed—even if he has."

"You sound skeptical."

"It's hard to know what to think about him sometimes." Garrett shrugged. "Jess was wild when he was younger. More full of himself. Insensitive, my wife called him. Me, I just figured he was long on what the papers called animal magnetism and short on character.''

Hazel studied his face and saw blunt honesty. "Why do I think you didn't like him very much then?"

"Because I didn't." His tone was a whisper shy of anger. "Not many folks around here did, except Ty McClane, that is. Those two were more like brothers than Jess and me."

"And now?" she asked softly.

He chuckled, but there was little humor in the throaty sound. "He's learned a few things—or maybe we both have. Anyway, we're both older."

Hazel stared at the lighted instrument panel until the colors blurred. "He's different out here," she mused. "Tougher, but in an odd sort of way, gentler, too."

Garrett glanced at her, disbelief clearly etched on his shadowed face. "Hazel, take my word for it. There's nothing gentle about my brother. If he hadn't had such a need to be the best at everything he tried, if he hadn't been born with this obsession to win, he might have been a nicer person. More tolerant, maybe. But gentle?" He shook his head, sorrowfully, it seemed to her. "Not in this lifetime. Not unless he's changed more than I know."

"You're wrong, Garrett," she said fervently. "I saw that side of him in the hospital, when he was with Francey's mother. He cared deeply about that woman. So deeply it shook me."

They were passing through a sad-looking hamlet whose boarded-up gas stations and abandoned diners had served countless customers before Highway 50 had become a limited access freeway between the coast and the mountains.

The town still boasted a stop sign, however. Garrett paused, then turned right. The road was rougher, and the truck bounced hard on the shocks, jarring Hazel's spine and rattling her teeth.

"Maybe he's changed more than I know. But when a man..." He grinned ruefully. "...or a woman, makes winning into some kind of god to worship, everything else gets shoved aside. That's part of the process. In Jess's case, he took chances that no one else would take, drove cars that weren't safe, even lied a time or two to get the ride he wanted. All because he couldn't stand coming in second."

Hazel frowned. "But he almost died because he was thinking of the other drivers."

"Who told you that?"

"I . . . a friend."

"Your friend was wrong. He smashed up his car and himself because he was trying to pass when it wasn't safe, on tires that were too worn to hold the track. Maybe he had a chance to choose between hitting the wall or the car next to him, but I doubt it."

His mouth tightened. "Jess is crippled today because he made a mistake. He made that mistake because he was willing to risk everything to take that checkered flag. Don't quote me, but I have a hunch that's the real reason he's so bitter about Gayla's problem accepting his handicap. It's easier to blame her for the pain he's carrying with him than to blame himself."

He braked for a dark-colored cat streaking across the road ahead, his gaze darting to the mirror. "There's a lot of anger left in Jess, Hazel, and even more resentment. He's been down a rough road, rougher than most of us ever have to travel, and it's left him with some deep scars. I don't mean just physical ones, either."

"Yes, I know."

This time the look he gave her was almost tentative. "Then you've seen him without his shirt?"

Hazel wasn't a prude, but Garrett's question gave her an odd jolt. "No, and if you're asking if we've been to bed together—"

"I'm not," he hastened to reassure her. "That's your business."

Hazel smiled. "Yes, it is. But I don't mind telling you that we haven't been intimate. In fact, this is our first real date."

Garrett looked disquieted, but determined. "I was afraid of that."

It was Hazel's turn to feel disquieted. Her session with Neil was still fresh in her mind, including his words about his sexual dysfunction. "Is there something I should know?" she asked softly.

Garrett was silent for an uncomfortably long time before he sighed and said, "It's been fourteen years since I saw my brother without his shirt. He's worked horses for me, shoveled manure, helped mend fences on days when the temperature hit one-seventeen in the shade, and never once shucked his shirt.

Hazel remained silent, sensing that Garrett was taking his time to make his point for a reason. "I might be all wrong, Hazel. Lord knows it's happened a time or two." He grinned. Sensing his need to ease the strain he had to be feeling, she did, too.

"Big of you to admit that," she murmured.

As he took his eyes from the road to study her, his grin slowly faded until his face was grim again. "He's embarrassed by his body, Hazel. Maybe even ashamed of it." He frowned, as though suddenly in pain. "I guess what I'm fumblin' around, trying to say is just this. If you do take him on, be patient with him. Don't expect too much right away. He might not be as confident in the sack as he once was."

Hazel expelled a shaky breath. Sensing that herself was one thing; but having Jess's closest relative confirm it gave her mixed feelings.

"Thank you for telling me that," she said, touching his arm. "I know it wasn't easy for you."

His expression told her that she'd guessed right. "I'm not much for giving unsolicited advice, I want you to know that."

She smiled. "Consider it solicited, then."

He slowed, then turned left again. The neighborhood was seedy, mostly boarded-up businesses that had gone belly-up long ago.

The blinker clicked loudly as Garrett steered the truck into the crowded parking lot surrounding a ramshackle stucco hacienda.

Finding a spot between a pickup and a battered sedan, he pulled in and shut off the engine. Jess had to circle to find a place for the Mercedes.

While they waited, delicious smells wafted through the partially opened window, and the sound of western music throbbed into the growing dusk.

"Are you saying I shouldn't marry him?" she said when Garrett would have opened his door and gotten out.

He took a moment to reflect, then shook his head. "Marry the man if that's what you want, be the mother of his children and appreciate him for the good qualities he has. Just don't fall in love with him the way Gayla did."

Hazel drew a long, unsteady breath. "It's too late, Garrett. I already have."

Chapter 11

Hazel poured hot water into the teapot and replaced the lid. Jess was in the den, phoning Cait to check on Francey.

She'd had a good time at Marvella's. As promised, the ribs had been the best she'd ever had. Garrett had kept her laughing throughout the meal, regaling her with stories of the three demon Dante brothers in their prime.

On the way home she and Jess hadn't talked much. He'd seemed preoccupied, and she'd been thinking of the things Garrett had revealed about Jess's past.

At her insistence he'd dropped her at the office so she could pick up her car. At *his* insistence he'd followed her home. Suggesting that he come in for a drink had been a natural result. Now she was having second thoughts.

If he pressed for an answer to his proposal, she wasn't sure she could bring herself to accept. She was equally uncertain whether or not she had the will to decline.

Outside the open window, the air was beginning to cool and the tree-lined street was settling for the night. Most of the old houses had been bought and reclaimed by young professionals who went to bed right after sunset and got up before dawn.

It was a great neighborhood in which to raise children. Safe, friendly, with good schools within walking distance. Ideal, in fact. She was one of the few single residents in the entire area.

She heard Jess coming a second before she sensed his presence. "How's the baby?" she asked, turning toward him.

"She's finally asleep. That's a direct quote from Kels."

"Has she been fussy?"

He rubbed the back of his neck, as though it pained him. His hair was mussed and his jaw shadowed and tense.

"I'm not sure. According to Kels, Cait was in bed and Ty was at a meeting, so I couldn't get corroborating testimony."

Hazel frowned. "Francey seemed fine yesterday, although Cait did seem a bit frazzled, now that I think about it."

"Yesterday?"

"I had some errands to run on my lunch hour and stopped by for a quick cup of coffee with Cait."

"Do that often, do you?"

He was watching her with a trial lawyer's shrewd gaze, but the lines around his mouth hinted at a far more human side that seemed to show up only when he was tired.

"On occasion, yes."

She carried the pot to the table and indicated that he should sit. "I hope you don't mind hanging out in my kitchen. Actually, it's my favorite place."

His gaze made a slow, thorough circuit of the room. "Nice and homey. The fish tank is an especially nice touch."

Hazel glanced fondly at her flea market find. "Isn't it! I love to watch them, especially the catfish. They're so ugly they're cute."

"Cute, huh?"

Jess reached for his coffee and discovered that it was some kind of weak-looking tea instead.

"Chamomile," she said when his gaze found hers. "It helps relieve tension."

Jess took a sip and decided that he would rather have had a drink. Scotch, bourbon, even some of that insipid white wine she liked so much.

At home, alone, he welcomed the easing of thought the booze gave him, even courted the illusion of relaxing. In Hazel's home, however, illusions were a danger he intended to avoid.

Even the few times when he'd had his arm around her and his mouth on hers, he hadn't let himself think past the physical needs they could satisfy for each other.

Jess leaned back and ordered his tight muscles to relax. Having to use one hand for everything put as much strain on his back as it did his arm. If he'd been alone, he would have allowed himself the luxury of massaging away some of the ache.

"Tell me about this Mrs. Weller," he prompted, stretching out his legs to ease the tautness in his lower back.

It was the right thing to say. Hazel's sudden smile seemed lit from within. "Oh, Jess, she's such a dear! Raised six kids of her own and then missed the last one so much she decided to take in other people's children to raise. Along the way, she got her license as a practical nurse. And," she added, leaning forward for emphasis, "she makes chocolate chip cookies to die for."

He was getting used to the sudden bursts of whimsy that seemed to overtake her at odd moments. Besides a tendency to draw a man in emotionally, they encouraged an intimacy that he'd done his best to avoid for a long time now.

"I see why the other parts of her résumé are important in a baby nurse," he said, "but why the cookies?"

"Isn't that obvious? Cookies are a very serious factor in molding a child's character." She seemed entirely serious. And, with the light shimmering over the soft material covering her breasts, damn near irresistible.

"How do you figure?"

"Think back. What do you remember most about your childhood?"

"The smell of the carbolic my mother used when I got banged up."

Her mouth twitched. "Besides that."

"Getting sent to the principal's office."

"Jess! Be serious." Her soft cry made him want to hustle her upstairs and undress her very slowly, something that he could no longer manage without making a fool of himself.

"I am being serious."

He took a sip of her foul-tasting tea, then relented. "Okay, okay, don't look at me like I'm breaking your heart. I seem to remember coming home from school and having milk and cookies before chores."

Her lips curved slowly as she closed in for the kill. "And what kind of cookies were they?"

He made her wait, mostly to see the soft look of anticipation turning her eyes to bronze.

"Chocolate chip."

"Aha, I rest my case."

He tasted the tea yet one more time, found absolutely nothing he liked about it and pushed it away.

"You don't like it?" she asked, pouting just enough to make his heart speed faster. With deliberate mental effort, he leveled it again.

"Not much, no. But I'm not much for tea of any kind."

Hazel saw something flicker in his eyes, like a desire for more than something else to drink. Her own desire grew more insistent. "Actually, I'm not all that crazy about tea, either, but it makes me feel virtuous when I drink it, so I do."

He shifted position, frowned, then shifted again until his shoulders were angled just right. Was he too large for the chair, or too restless to relax? she wondered.

"How do you feel when you drink coffee?" he asked, eyeing her from beneath black eyebrows.

"Guilty as sin." She sighed. "It's my second greatest vice, but I wouldn't dream of giving it up."

One corner of Jess's mouth lifted in a curve far short of a smile. He knew that he was letting this woman get to him in ways that broke all his rules, rules he'd made for survival. When he was with her, he couldn't seem to help himself.

"Second greatest vice?" he asked, raising his eyebrows.

"I'd better warn you now," she said, a teasing lilt hiding the slight breathiness in her voice. "I'm a hopeless chocoholic. I keep a secret hoard in my office and another by my bed. Not to mention the stash I have here in the kitchen, of course."

"Sounds hard core."

"Sad to say, it is."

She tasted her tea, then regarded him through the steam. "It's your turn. What's your biggest vice?"

Jess ran through the list, then decided on the one he'd been fighting the longest with the least success. "My temper."

"Bad, is it?"

"Used to be. Now I have a decent hold on it most of the time."

"And when you don't?"

"People tend to...scatter."

"Good way to keep them from getting too close, though, isn't it?"

Jess wasn't used to being challenged. Worse, he wasn't used to having his motives probed, his actions analyzed. He didn't want to be understood. In fact, he'd fought hard to maintain his privacy most of his life. Understanding led to control, something he would never willingly relinquish to anyone.

"Got any Scotch stashed in with that chocolate?"

Her eyes told him that she'd gotten his message and was deciding whether or not to back off. Giving her the option had been a mistake. It made her stronger and him more vulnerable.

"So much for the tea," Hazel said with a dramatic sigh. Leaving her chair, she walked to what he took to be the pantry, returning moments later brandishing a dusty bottle.

"Cherry Bounce. One of my 'parents' gave it to me for Christmas a few years back. It's homemade and, um, just the teensiest bit alcoholic."

"How teensy?" Jess felt compelled to ask as she used a towel to wipe off the dust.

"About sixty proof." Frowning with the exertion, she tried to open the cap. "Darn, it's stuck."

"Don't look at me," he muttered, more laconic than angry.

She laughed. "What do you do at home when you get a stubborn lid?" She turned on the hot tap and held the neck of the bottle under the faucet.

"I have this thing attached to the underside of one of the cabinets that acts as another hand."

"Very clever." Wrapping the cap with a wet towel, she gave a prodigious effort, then cried softly in triumph.

"Now for a proper glass."

Which turned out to be something delicate and expensive-looking, with an impossibly skinny stem and crystal so thin he was almost afraid to touch it.

"Is that better?" Hazel asked, watching him with a smile hovering over soft lips that were just waiting to curve.

The Cherry Bounce had the look of fine claret and a seductive taste that tempted a man to take chances and forget lessons learned.

Jess ran his tongue over the lingering taste of sweet cherries on his lips and fought down the urge to transfer that same taste from his mouth to hers.

"Much better."

Their eyes held a moment too long, and Hazel knew they were close to crossing some invisible line into physical intimacy. Once crossed, she, at least, would be committed. It was a decision she wasn't ready to make.

Jess sensed the moment she pulled back. Pulling back himself, he felt the loss more acutely than was perhaps wise.

"I understand you've been talking to Ms. FitzGerald on my behalf. That little errand you had yesterday." He found himself slipping into the cadence of the courtroom and realized that he felt more at ease with the familiar. The safe.

Surprise flickered in her eyes, but none of the guilt he'd half expected. "I told you that I would do what I could to help. Like you, I do try to keep my promises."

Jess ran his finger along the curve of the glass's slick stem, but his gaze remained focused on her face. On those eyes that seemed to change from green to gold with her mood.

"Did she tell you I had about as much chance of gaining sole custody of Francey as I have of growing another arm?"

"Yes, she told me."

"Did she also tell you that I'd have a much better chance if I were married? Say, to someone with impeccable standing in the community, someone eminently qualified to raise a child? Someone normal?"

Hazel heard the bitterness she had come to expect of him. This time there was an undercurrent of frustration that twisted her heart.

"She didn't use those words, but yes, that's essentially what she said. But then, if you remember, I did warn you that Lynn went strictly by the book."

Her trained eyes caught the quick press of his strong fingers against her wedding crystal. He had a strong mouth, she noticed. Uncompromising, even when he permitted himself the rare intimacy of a kiss.

"Bottom-line," he drawled with deceptive laziness, "it's up to you whether or not I can keep my promise to Silvia."

"That's not fair," she cried softly.

Jess responded with a shift of expression so subtle she nearly missed it—until a flurry of nerves filled her stomach.

"Was it fair when you all but accused me of being a selfish bastard for not instantly jumping at the chance to put myself through an emotional wringer again?"

"I didn't!"

"Sure you did. Told me to fight, remember?" He glanced at his drink, then shoved it aside and stood up. His expression was grim, his eyes hard. "I only know one way to do that, Hazel. Fight to win. If you don't like it, fine. But if you marry me, you'd better get used to it, because I don't intend to change."

Hazel opened her mouth, but no words came out. Swallowing, she tried again. "That sounds like an ultimatum. Follow your rules or get out of your way."

His jaw grew taut, and his skin paled beneath the dusting of stubble. "Perhaps it is an ultimatum," he said, his words clipped and his tone stiff. "Or maybe I'm just tired of waiting for you to make up your mind whether or not Francey's worth tying yourself to a guy like me for the next twenty years or so."

Too upset to risk saying more, Hazel turned around and headed for the door. "Finish your drink if you'd like. Finish the bottle if it'll make you feel better. I'm going to bed, and I'd appreciate it if you locked up when you leave."

He caught her just as she reached the darkened hallway. For an instant, as he spun her around to face him, she was sure that he intended to use force to hurt her this time instead of words. His fingers dug into her arm, then quickly gentled as he brought himself under rigid control.

"I told you I'm not a nice man," he grated, his voice hard and tight and forceful.

"Yes, you did. And it's my fault for not believing you," she said evenly. "I won't make that mistake again."

He dropped his hand from her arm and shoved it into his pocket. "Good night, O'Connor. Sleep well."

He left her standing by the door, her heart hammering in her chest and her stomach already growing queasy.

"I'm not home."

Hazel snuggled her face deeper into her pillow. Her first appointment was at ten. Sometime around four she'd reset her alarm for eight. It couldn't be that late.

The doorbell rang again, jarring her fully awake. Forcing her eyes open, she glared toward the door leading to the second-floor landing. Somewhere below was the old-fashioned bell that had announced visitors to this house for over a hundred years.

When she'd bought the place a decade ago, the bell had been one of many things that hadn't worked. Whatever had possessed her to have it repaired? she wondered now.

The bell chimed again and kept on chiming. Someone had mashed a thumb against the button, someone who was about to get an earful.

"That's it," she muttered. "I'm ripping out the wires." Still more asleep than awake, she slipped from the warm blankets and groped for her bathrobe.

"Will you stop that noise? I'm coming!" she shouted into the din.

In spite of her self-taught skill as a carpenter, the stairs still creaked no matter how light the tread. The thick runner protected her feet from the cold floor, but not even the inside shutters could block out the brilliant morning sun.

"Okay, okay!" she muttered, jerking open the door.

Hazel had expected a salesman or a religious zealot. Instead she found Jess standing there with Francey tucked awkwardly but securely against his shoulder.

He was dressed in somber blue pinstripes and a white shirt, open at the throat. His tie had been shoved in his breast pocket, and his hair desperately needed brushing.

"Cait has the flu."

"I'm sorry about that, but I'm sure she's in good hands."

Hazel was discovering that a nearly sleepless night did wonders for a person's sales resistance but very little for her poker face.

Jess scowled. Apparently his mood matched hers perfectly. "Call her if you don't believe me. Although I have to warn you, she promised to take herself to bed as soon as I left."

Her hair flopped in her eyes. Impatiently she pushed it back. "I believe you," she said without warmth. "I just don't understand why you're here."

"Mrs. Weller, that's why. That perfectly wonderful baker of cookies and baby nurse."

Hazel allowed a quick wave of her hand. "Two doors down on the left. The house with the roses in front."

He closed his eyes for an instant. When he opened them again the ambivalence seething in the dark depths tugged at her just as surely as if he'd uttered an abject plea. She hardened her heart, telling herself not to let this man get close enough to hurt her again.

"I could use a little help here, O'Connor."

"Why? Because you're a helpless cripple?"

He winced. "No, damn it. Because I'm due in court at ten, and Judge Brevard doesn't take kindly to granting recesses so the defense attorney can change a diaper."

He had a point. Not much of one, but a point nonetheless.

"Oh, all right," she muttered, stepping back. "Come in while I give Mrs. Weller a call. The poor dear is probably still asleep."

He stepped across the threshold like a man going to the gallows, bringing with him the tang of soap and a hint of morning fog.

Hazel closed the door and turned, only to find herself looking at Francey's sleepy eyes peeking over Jess's squared shoulder.

"Well, good morning, punkin'," she cooed. "Did you get jerked out of your nice warm crib at the crack of dawn too?"

Francey hiccuped, then closed her eyes again. Someone had wrapped the baby papoose-fashion in one of the blankets she and Cait had purchased only a few days before. Probably Cait, Hazel surmised, resisting the urge to take Francey into her arms for a quick cuddle. The sooner she distanced herself, the better.

"Seven-fifteen isn't exactly dawn," Jess muttered, turning to face her. She refused to be moved by the lines of fatigue in his face and the shadows under his eyes.

"It is when a person doesn't intend to get up until eight." She stalked down the hall toward the den, pointedly refusing to issue an invitation to follow.

"Don't you have appointments this morning?" His voice, morning deep and lashed with irritation, was close. Invitation or not, Jess was right behind her.

"Yes, starting at ten." She turned when she reached her desk and gave him a cool look. "So you see, we both have obligations this morning," she said as she paged through her book for her neighbor's number.

Jess watched in strained silence for a moment before crossing in front of her to reach the big recliner where she usually curled up for one of her marathon reads.

Instead of sitting, however, he gently lowered Francey to the seat, prompting a few squeaks of protest from the baby before she once again settled into sleep.

Pretty soon he wouldn't be able to carry her that way, Hazel realized as she lifted the phone and punched out Mrs. Weller's number, and then reminded herself that it was none of her business what Jess could or couldn't do. He'd made that very clear last night.

"So how about it, Dante? Do we have a deal?"

Belatedly, Jess realized that he'd lost track of the pretrial negotiations that he himself had initiated with the assistant D.A.

"Put it in writing," he said, "And I'll discuss it with my client."

"Writing, hell. You and I have never needed to be that formal before."

"That's the best I can do, Fred. Take it or leave it."

D.A. Fred Smith crumpled his soda can and tossed it at the trash barrel under the courthouse oak tree. "What's with you today, anyway, Dante? You look like hell, and a guy could light a match on that mood of yours."

Jess swallowed the last of his coffee and sent his cup to join his colleague's crushed can. "Too much bad coffee and not enough sleep, I guess."

"Maybe you need a vacation."

"Maybe." Or maybe he needed to get his mind back on his work and off a bullheaded, big-hearted, impossible woman who'd managed to push herself into his life in spite of all his efforts to keep her out.

"Ten minutes until court resumes. You coming?"

Jess glanced up to find his favorite adversary watching him curiously. "In a minute."

"Right. See you in court." Fred hesitated, then added gruffly, "And, Dante, if you need someone to talk to, I've been a few places and seen a few things in my time. Maybe I could help."

Jess was on the verge of telling Smith what he could do with his help when he found himself awkwardly thanking the man instead.

Damn that woman, he thought, watching Fred walk toward the courthouse. Now she even had him going soft in the head. All because she'd dragged a lot of things out of him that he'd successfully buried for a long time and made him look at each and every one with different eyes.

He hadn't liked what he'd seen. He just didn't know what to do about it.

Jess jabbed his thumb against the bell harder than necessary. Inside the old house three tones chimed in genteel succession.

His scowl pulled harder at the tired muscles of his face. Leave it to O'Connor to have a musical doorbell. His place had a no-nonsense buzzer that would wake the dead.

Jess jabbed his thumb on the button again and this time held it there long enough to play three choruses. Short of patience on the best of days, his long hours in court had left him with none.

Besides, he knew she was home. Her yuppie BMW was parked in front of a detached garage no bigger than a doll's house.

Jess glanced over his shoulder at the house belonging to Mrs. Weller. She had seemed a nice enough old lady. Capable, certainly. Sweet tempered, and thrilled to have an infant in her care again.

While he'd hauled in all the baby paraphernalia he'd been able to stuff in the Mercedes, Mrs. Weller and Hazel had coordinated their three schedules.

Mrs. Weller had a five o'clock doctor's appointment she couldn't break. He had an appointment with a new client right after court adjourned, and Hazel had an afternoon meeting.

He'd expected to make it back to Hazel's place before Mrs. Weller had to leave. He'd gotten involved with a call from the Hargrove County's prosecutor's office about the Yoder case, and by the time he'd left his office, the traffic had already snarled.

O'Connor was probably ticked at him for being late, and in all fairness, he couldn't blame her. Turning back, he caught sight of a quick purple blur beyond the frosted pane in the fancy door. The scowl was still on his face when Hazel swung open the door to admit him.

Sure enough, she was wearing a purple sweatshirt with a bunch of wildflowers embossed on the front and paint-spattered jeans that hugged her fanny like a man's hand. One shoulder was wet, and talcum powder smudged her chin.

Francey, bundled in a soft flannel gown and sucking noisily on her fist, was nestled against the shoulder that was dry. Hazel looked every bit as harried and frayed as any new mother he'd ever encountered.

"Sorry I'm late."

Impatiently, she blew her bangs from her eyes, but they flopped back instantly, neatly obscuring her vision.

"It's okay this time. My meeting was a short one, so I was able to make it back before Mrs. Weller had to leave."

"I stopped at Cait's and picked up some more of Francey's things," he told her, gesturing with a curt nod toward the two bags at his feet.

"Fine. You know where they go."

As he passed her, Jess couldn't help catching a whiff of her scent, a blend of baby powder and something far more provocative. He recognized the first stirring of desire, but nothing showed on his face.

"I'll put on the coffee," she said to his back as he headed up the stairs.

"I take mine black," he tossed over his shoulder.

"Yes, I know," he heard her say. "I have an excellent memory."

Jess walked into the kitchen a few minutes later to find Hazel seated at the table, sipping coffee, with Francey sitting nearby in her padded infant seat, sound asleep.

Hazel glanced up when he entered. "Your daughter tried to stay awake, but..." She shrugged. "As you can see, she didn't quite manage."

"Is she okay?" Jess's voice was pitched low, somewhere between a growl and a whisper.

"As far as I can tell."

He gave her a look that she was sure she reserved for unfriendly witnesses. "Sleeps a lot, doesn't she?"

"The book I bought says that's normal," she said tersely.

His gaze met hers, and she sensed surprise, quickly concealed. "I would have thought a kiddy shrink like you knew all there was to know about kids."

"No one knows that, Dante, just as I imagine there are things about the law you have, shall we say, yet to learn?"

Jess watched her lift her cup to her lips and drink the hot coffee with a certain gusto. She was furious with him, and he didn't blame her.

"What does the book say about an over-the-hill jerk who always seems to say the wrong thing when he's with a woman he admires?"

Her expression didn't change. "That particular book only covers the years up to eighteen."

"Then what?" he asked in his most persuasive tone. It didn't faze her.

"Then you're on your own. Behaviorally speaking, that is." Her tone consigned him to the fires of hell. Too bad she didn't know he'd put himself there sometime during the dark lonely hours of a sleepless night.

"Free to make stupid mistakes?" he asked.

She nodded. "And to learn from them."

His eyes lost none of their directness, but Hazel sensed a gathering of shadows in the depths. "How do you know for sure if the things you've learned are the right things?"

Hazel managed a careless shrug, but the sensual tug she felt whenever Jess came near was still there, still powerful. And just as dangerous.

"Perhaps by learning to trust your feelings more—if you haven't shoved them so far down you don't even know what, or where, they are."

He was very still, very focused, as though he were taking in her words with great care, leading her to marvel at his power of concentration.

"Maybe some feelings are easier to read than others."

"Undoubtedly. We all develop selective blindness as we get older."

"And wiser?"

"Not always."

Jess hesitated, then took the same seat he'd had the night before. His coffee was waiting, and he took a quick sip. It was strong and hot.

"No tea this evening?"

Instead of smiling, she simply shrugged. "I got the message the first time."

Jess stifled a sigh. His patience had just run out—along with the rope he'd planned to give her. "O'Connor—"

The kitchen phone rang, startling them both. Frowning, Hazel got up to answer it.

"Dr. O'Connor...oh, hi, Mrs. Weller. What did the doctor say?"

As she listened, Hazel's gaze suddenly filled with concern. "Of course you have to...certainly...yes, I understand perfectly...no, that's not a problem, really. And don't worry. Everything will be fine." She hung up after promising to call Mrs. Weller the next day.

"The doctor found an irregular heartbeat that has him worried enough to order her to go into the hospital tomorrow for tests," she said, returning slowly to the table. "She expects to be in two days, maybe three."

"Ah hell," Jess muttered with heartfelt frustration.

"My sentiments exactly."

Jess woke to find himself flat on his stomach with his arm dangling over the side of the bed. It was hot in the room, even with the window wide open, and he was sweating.

Still groggy, he rolled to his back, then realized that he'd worn his T-shirt to bed, something he did so seldom that he couldn't at first figure out why.

It was only when he started to reach for the aspirin he kept in a drawer by his bed that he remembered. He was in Hazel's guest room, trying with only limited success to get a decent night's sleep.

Slipping his hand under the pillow, he stared upward, listening to the sound of his own breathing in the darkness. He was used to sleeping alone. He was used to waking up alone. He'd done both for so long that he'd all but convinced himself he liked it best that way.

Now... He expelled a long, uneasy breath.

How old did a man have to get before he stopped making stupid mistakes? he wondered. Or maybe it wasn't possible for him to live that long.

This one was a real prizewinner, no doubt about it. Agreeing to spend the night in Hazel's house because he wasn't due in court tomorrow and she had early appointments. As though he couldn't get himself across town in plenty of time to handle the 6:00 a.m. feeding.

Gritting his teeth, Jess turned to his side and stared at the hazy outline of the door he'd closed firmly behind him a few minutes after he'd moved the portable crib from this room to Hazel's.

Since she'd volunteered to handle the middle-of-the-night feeding, it seemed logical that she have the baby close to her.

It hadn't occurred to him that he might want to check on Francey now and then, just to make sure she was all right. Or that he might find himself too restless to sleep and feel an urge to prowl.

Rolling onto his back, he kicked off the sheet and sat up. Maybe a cold beer would help. O'Connor had some in her refrigerator. He'd seen them when he'd helped her clean up after the supper she'd made them both following Mrs. Weller's call.

He slipped into his trousers quietly, then clicked open the door and walked barefoot into the hall. He was just closing the door behind him when he heard Francey wail.

It sounded exactly like a small animal caught in a trap. Without thinking he bolted down the hall and into the master bedroom.

Hazel was bending over the crib when he entered and looked up in alarm. "Jess! You scared the bejabbers out of me."

"What's wrong?" he said with a scowl.

"It's two o'clock. She's hungry."

She bent over again, and her pale blue nightie slipped up to mid-thigh, giving Jess a very nice view of her legs. This time desire didn't stir politely. It hit with the force of a spasm, making him very glad he'd pulled on his trousers over his shorts.

"Right on schedule, aren't you lamb?" Hazel cooed, then clucked her tongue. "And very, very messy for such a proper little lady."

Jess groaned. It was ridiculous to be embarrassed because he and O'Connor were in the same room with a naked baby. A female baby. And then he realized it would have been worse if Francey had been a boy.

"Since Daddy's up, let's give him a choice, okay with you, Francey?"

The baby screwed up her face, took in a lungful of air and cried even harder. Hazel laughed softly and reached for the infant wipes. "You're right. Maybe it would be safer if *I* told him."

"Why do I think I'm not going to like this?" Jess muttered.

"Don't worry. The choices aren't that tough." Hazel glanced over her shoulder, her sleepy gaze finding his again. Her hair was tousled, and one cheek was pink where she'd slept on it. Without lipstick, her mouth was pale and far too tempting for a man balanced precariously on a very thin ledge.

"You can finish changing her, or you can fix her bottle," she said, her tone perfectly serious.

Jess raked back his hair with his hand and swore a silent oath never to barge into a woman's bedroom without knocking again, no matter what the provocation.

"I'll fix her bottle." He escaped before he was tempted to do something he would regret.

Chapter 12

Hazel was feeding the baby on the bed, propped up against the headboard with Francey snuggled in her arms. Jess was slouched in her chintz chair, his shirt a wide white swath against the patterned upholstery.

One leg was braced on the floor, the other stretched over the chair's padded arm, serving as a resting place for the beer bottle he'd propped against his thigh. His feet were bare.

"I can't believe she really likes that stuff." Taking a satisfying pull on the long-necked bottle, he watched Francey working equally hard on hers. Hazel found his casualness disarming. The subtle sexual signals he was unwittingly sending out were even more so.

"Maybe it's not as bad as it looks."

"It's worse than it looks," he declared, wiping his mouth with the back of his hand.

Hazel indicated her skepticism with a slight smile. "How do you know? Did you ever taste it?"

"Yeah, I've tasted it." He was overcome by a yawn, before adding wryly, "How do you think I found out if it was too hot or not?"

She seemed to find that intriguing, or so the sudden spark in her eyes wanted him to believe. "I wondered how you had managed," she said, adjusting the angle of the baby's bottle before looking up again. "But I have to admit that was one, um, option I never considered."

"Care to share any of those other options you came up with?"

Hazel changed position so that the elbow supporting the baby's head was resting on the pile of pillows she'd constructed. "Oops, sorry, sweetie," she murmured, slipping the nipple back into the baby's greedy little mouth.

Francey opened and closed her tiny hands as she tried to hang on to the bottle. Hazel wondered how those little fingers would feel grasping her breast.

"First I thought you might be able to determine the temperature by pressing your wrist against the bottle," she continued belatedly and a bit hurriedly. "But that didn't seem like a real accurate measure."

"Not to mention painful."

"So then I tried to imagine what I would do and came up with my, um, best . . . guess."

His eyebrows rose slowly, giving his face a younger man's unbloodied innocence. "Which was?"

Hazel cleared her throat. "To use your belly."

His gaze dropped involuntarily to the fabric-covered washboard plane of his midriff.

"I'm not sure I'm following you, O'Connor."

"The skin of your belly," she said somewhat more tartly than she'd intended. "It's almost as sensitive as your wrist and in your case more, um, accessible."

His mouth moved, pushing shallow indentations into his lean cheeks, but his tone was totally serious. "In my case it's also hairier."

"I wouldn't know."

Diligently, she checked the amount of formula remaining in the small bottle. It was nearly gone, and Francey's eyes were just about closed.

"Care to check it out?" Jess's voice was smooth as new cream and just as warm. "My belly, I mean."

"No thanks." She could picture him without his shirt far too readily. Hairy belly or not, his chest would be magnificently formed, with spare lines and hardened muscle.

Compensation, she reminded herself, but her thoughts kept straying toward an altogether different kind of dynamic.

"Maybe you're right," he said, his voice subtly changed from gruffly provocative to distinctly cool. "I'm hardly a beautiful woman's pinup."

Her head came up quickly. "And I'm hardly a beautiful woman," she returned, striving to mimic his coolness. At the same time Francey spat out the nipple and started to fuss.

By the time Hazel had the baby pressed against her shoulder for the burp that the uncomfortable little girl needed to get out, Jess was on his feet.

"If you're done with that, I'll take it down and wash it out," he said, indicating the nearly empty nursing bottle. "I'm going down to get another beer anyway."

"We're all done, aren't we, sweetie?" she murmured, rubbing Francey's back. The baby's head wobbled slightly, then rested against Hazel's shoulder in absolute trust.

"How about you?" he asked, holding up his empty beer bottle. "Want one?" The glint in his eyes told her that he expected her to refuse.

"Sure," she said with just a hint of a devilish grin. "I'd love a beer."

She was almost sure his eyes were smiling as he held the beer bottle with two fingers and scooped up the nursing bottle with the other three. Glass clinked against glass as he carried them out of the room.

Hazel waited until she heard the creaking of the stairs before she carefully slipped from the bed and carried Francey to the crib.

"Know what, Francey love? Your daddy's a very complicated man," she murmured to the little girl as she set about changing her again.

"He'd like everyone to think he's all muscle and brain and no heart, no . . . feelings. But to tell you the truth, I think he runs on his emotions even more than I do. Which is just one of the reasons why I'm afraid I just might be hopelessly in love with him."

Francey gurgled, then yawned hugely and closed her eyes. "Don't worry, I don't intend to let him know. Nothing could be more of a mistake with Jess Dante than that," Hazel crooned softly as she turned the baby to her tummy and pulled the light blanket over her.

Francey squirmed and wiggled until her diapered bottom was in the air and her cheek was resting against the soft sheet. Another big yawn and she was settled for another few hours, at least.

"Sleep well, my dearest," Hazel whispered, pressing a kiss to the baby's head. "I love you."

Fighting an unexpected rush of tears, she lifted her shoulders in a deep sigh, then headed for the adjoining bathroom to wash her hands.

She was drying them when she heard what sounded like a light rap of glass against wood. "I'm in here," she murmured, hastily throwing the towel over the bar.

Returning to the bedroom, she found Jess waiting politely by the door, two bottles of beer held securely in his fingers. Framed by the doorway, his hip cocked and his shoulders back, he looked like a very large, very sleepy male with an attitude problem.

"Why so formal?" she asked, taking one of the beers.

"It's your house, and your bedroom."

"That didn't stop you earlier." Turning, she walked slowly back to her bed and sat down.

"I heard the baby." He leaned his bad shoulder against the jamb and lifted the bottle to his mouth for a long swallow before adding, "I thought she needed help."

Was that how he showed his deepest feelings? she wondered. With actions instead of words? Was that the reason Garrett had so many reservations about his character? Because he kept those feelings so fiercely hidden?

"Since we're both awake, it might be a good time to discuss the arrangements for the weekend," she suggested, tasting the beer she hadn't really wanted.

"Fine with me." He contemplated the sweating bottle. "You're the expert. What do you suggest?"

Hazel took another quick sip and tried to remember the last time she'd had a beer in the middle of the night, then decided that there had never *been* a last time.

"First off, I don't think we should move her around too much, which means she should stay here until you can make permanent arrangements for child care." She glanced up inquiringly.

"I was sort of counting on Mrs. Weller."

Jess stood where he was, deliberately too far away to see the dark circles of her nipples through the light-colored material of her gown, but his imagination was busy filling in the blanks.

He had a fair share of experience with women, a good imagination and an unlimited supply of nights spent alone, more than enough to have formed an impression of the size and shape of her breasts. Instantly his thoughts were graphically X-rated.

"So was I, but we won't know much before Monday at the earliest." Pausing, she frowned. "Poor dear. She was so worried that we would blame her. Kept saying that she hated to let us...you...down when it was plain you needed her."

"She's right about that."

He needed more than Mrs. Weller could begin to imagine. Starting with a swift kick in the butt for standing there like the village idiot, mooning over the prettiest girl in the county when he should be doing his darnedest to slip between those sexy, flowered sheets with her.

"Francey and I have an appointment with Ms. Fitz-Gerald tomorrow at three," he said before grabbing another long swallow. The beer was perfectly chilled, just the way he liked it—on a hot day in summer, that is.

"I'm free after two, if you'd like to leave Francey here with me."

"Be cutting it pretty tight by the time you made it across town to here, and then I drove all the way back to Fitz-Gerald's office."

"That's true, especially if the traffic is bad."

Lost in thought, Hazel raised the bottle slowly toward her lips. His own relaxed at the thought of kissing her again.

Like a driver testing a new ride, he would start slowly, letting her warm to the feel of his mouth on hers. And then, when he felt her anxieties easing, he would apply more pressure, just enough to get a sense of how she liked her kisses best.

Slow and dry, maybe. Or hard and moist. He wouldn't use his tongue, not right away. Not until he knew for sure that she would accept that kind of intimacy from him.

Suddenly Jess realized that the room had gotten considerably hotter and finished off the beer in two long swallows.

"I could meet you there, and then take Francey home with me," Hazel said, claiming his full attention.

"Or the two of you could wait for me there, and we could have dinner someplace afterward, so you wouldn't have to cook."

Her frown turned the corners of her lips down almost as provocatively as a smile. "I don't know, Jess." Her eyes met his. "I think Francey's too young for that."

He shrugged. "You're the expert."

"Will you please stop saying that!" she exclaimed emphatically, but softly, so as not to disturb Francey. "I am not an expert on babies. Far from it."

"You know more than I do."

Straightening, he walked to the small desk and dropped his empty bottle into the wastebasket to one side, more because he needed to move than from any urge toward compulsive neatness. His own place was clean, thanks to bossy Mrs. Rodriquez who came in once a week. It was far from neat.

"I'll lend you my books on infant behavior, if you'd like," Hazel said, following his every movement with those wide green eyes of hers. "It shouldn't take you long before you know as much as I do."

"There's a difference between knowing and doing."

He hesitated, then sat down on the edge of her bed. Even though he'd left plenty of room between them, he was close enough to catch a subtle whiff of perfume.

He didn't want to like it. He didn't want to like her. And most of all he didn't want to like being here in her bedroom with her and the baby.

It felt too much like the kind of life he'd forsworn when Gayla had walked out and taken a big chunk of his self-esteem with her.

But reality was pushing him hard at the moment. He wanted Francey, and every legal instinct he'd developed over the years told him that he didn't have a chance without a suitable wife standing by his side.

"O'Connor, I'm not much for playing psychological games," he said more brusquely than he'd intended.

She looked puzzled. "Are you saying we're playing a game?"

Jess stared at the fluffy rug covering the hardwood floor. "Gayla and I were married so fast I never learned how to court a woman. If that's what you need, I'm not your man."

Hazel wondered if he knew how bleak his voice sounded or how tense he appeared to her right now, sitting so rigid and unmoving, as though, inexplicable as it seemed, he was in some way afraid of her.

It moved her to touch the big hand pressed so tightly to his thigh. To tell him how much she wanted to love him and how desperately he needed to be loved. But Jess had been too badly wounded to believe mere words.

"I've been courted," she told him in a low voice. "Flowers every day, romantic candlelight dinners, champagne. I have to admit that I loved it."

His mouth flattened. "Most women do, I hear."

"Ron and I had been married almost two years when I lost our baby. She was full-term, perfect in every way, and we named her Gloria. The doctors simply couldn't make her breathe, even with all the high-tech equipment they had at their disposal. An act of God, one of the nurses said before they took my baby away."

His gaze came to her slowly, as though he were afraid to intrude. "Sounds rough," he said gruffly. "In fact, if I'd known I'm not sure I would have asked your help in this case."

She acknowledged his sympathy with a nod. "I haven't told many people about that part of my life. Cait knows, and my mother and father. And of course Ron's parents. They've been very sweet to me over the years."

His eyes narrowed. "You forgot to mention your husband."

She drew a long, not quite steady breath before leaning forward to set her beer bottle on the nightstand.

"Ron's been dead for eleven years."

"I see." Questions darkened his eyes, questions she had a feeling he wouldn't ask. Because he was a private person, he allowed everyone else that same courtesy.

"In the hospital, after we finally realized that our baby was gone, I fell apart. Screaming hysterics, black depression, blaming God and the doctors and even Ron, because he hadn't wanted the baby. Through it all, Ron was a rock. Calm, supportive, understanding."

"Sounds like a good guy to have on your side." Jess glanced away, when she really wanted him to move closer, to hold her close.

"He was, except I didn't want understanding. I wanted him to hurt as much as I did. And to show it in the same way. I wanted emotion from him, I wanted to see his pain, his fury—all the things I was feeling. When he wouldn't— or couldn't—give me those things, I accused him of not caring. Of... of being secretly glad our baby had died.''

Hazel had to pause to catch her breath. She wasn't sure she should go on, then found herself plunging ahead as though some kind of inner dam had just cracked.

''He didn't show up to take me home from the hospital when he was supposed to. I waited as long as I could, then took a taxi. When I walked into our apartment, I found him in the baby's room, slumped over the crib. He'd... shot himself.'' She drew another breath, then attempted a rueful smile. ''To this day, the smell of fresh paint makes me sick to my stomach.''

Jess flattened his palm on his thigh and looked at the veins crisscrossing the back of his hand. ''With me, it's rubbing alcohol,'' he said without looking at her. ''Every time I smell it it's like I'm flat on my back in the hospital again, swearing at God and mad at the world—and myself.''

Hazel was careful not to show even a hint of pity. ''It's strange how the senses can trigger emotions.''

His mouth quirked. ''Not so much strange as a damned nuisance. Some things are better off buried.''

''But that's the problem, isn't it?'' she cried softly. ''Burying things, I mean. They're still there, waiting to catch you with your guard down, no matter how far down you shove them or how busy you keep yourself.''

Jess eyed her curiously. ''Isn't that your job? Exorcising ghosts?''

''In a way, yes.''

''So how come you haven't exorcised this one?''

''Actually, I did, although it took me almost two years before I didn't start every day in tears.'' She managed a chuckle. ''And then I woke up one morning bored with grieving for what might have been and tired of feeling sorry for myself. That's when I decided to devote my practice to children.''

He allowed a faint smile. "Sounds logical."

"It is, but that doesn't mean I've forgiven myself for what I did." Hazel dropped her gaze. "I said terrible things to Ron, things he didn't deserve." She let him see the whispers of pain she still carried in her eyes. "He loved me so much."

He looked uncomfortable, the way he always did whenever anyone mentioned love. "If he loved you so much, how come he set it up so you'd be sure to find the mess?"

Hazel gasped softly. "That's a terrible thing to say."

He shrugged. "Maybe, but he had to have known what it would do to you to find him like that. Seems to me he wanted you to feel guilty."

She shook her head. "He was a sensitive man. Gentle. I should have known how much he was suffering. I should have been there for him."

"Why? He wasn't there for you. In my book that makes him a quitter."

"But he wasn't! I just told you how supportive he was. How caring."

He shook his head. "If he really cared, he would have hung in there for you, no matter how much he was hurting."

She started to protest, then realized that he had a point, one she really didn't want to face just yet. Instead, as was her habit, she turned her thoughts away from herself and onto him.

"Did you ever consider suicide?" she asked matter-of-factly.

He seemed to stop breathing for a moment before he nodded. "Hell, yes. More than once, actually."

"When your wife left?"

His face tightened. "Something like that, yeah."

"What stopped you?"

One side of his mouth lifted. "I didn't want to go out a loser, which is what I would have been if I'd bailed out when things got rocky."

Hazel looked deep into his eyes and saw a man of such courage and implacable strength that it stunned her. Jess was a winner and always would be. He had faced his pain and worked through it, was still working through it in his own way—just as Neil and Jimmy and her other patients were doing. Just as she had been doing for a lot of years.

She blinked as anger overwhelmed her. Jess was right. She had loved Ron too much to have left him in such a nightmarish way—no matter how much she'd been hurting.

"I...never thought of Ron as a loser," she admitted with painful honesty. "Or a quitter, for that matter, which in a way, he...was."

Unexpectedly Jess took her hand. His fingers were reassuringly strong, his palm warm and comforting against hers. It was an uncomplicated gesture of comfort, one she suspected he hadn't planned.

"You didn't put that gun to your husband's head and pull the trigger, and I'm not sure you could have stopped him, no matter what you said or didn't say. Take my advice and remember that whenever you start feeling guilty."

"I...thank you for that. It helps." The guilt was still there, but strangely, it was less barbed somehow, as though she'd taken a big step toward forgiving herself.

Jess glanced down at their entwined hands. "For the record, I'm sorry about your daughter."

"I am, too."

"No wonder Francey got to you."

"I would be lying if I said she didn't bring back memories of my own daughter, but she's in no way a substitute for Gloria."

"But she could be."

Hazel shook her head. "No. Francey is Francey, a perfect little person in her own right. And," she added softly, "your daughter."

Jess bunched his eyebrows over his nose and slowly shook his head. "I can't let myself believe that, O'Connor. The odds are too long against it."

Hazel didn't try to convince him otherwise. What he was saying was true. Still, there was always hope.

"What happens if Lynn FitzGerald recommends against your adopting Francey?"

Emotion flashed in his eyes and was as quickly mastered. "She becomes a ward of the court until 'suitable' parents can be found."

"That might take months. In the meantime, Francey will be absorbing all the wrong signals."

"Bonding wise." His mouth quirked, but not with humor.

"Yes, bonding wise."

"Which is why I think you should apply."

Hazel absorbed his words slowly, carefully. "Adopt her myself, you mean?"

"You'd have a great shot at it, and in a way..." Pausing, he drew a deep breath, as though the words came hard. "In a way there would still be a connection to Silvia and what she wanted."

His fingers pressed hers ever so slightly, or maybe she was just imagining the increased tension in his touch. Just as she was imagining the whisper of pain in the deep brown eyes watching her so steadily.

"Does that mean you're withdrawing your marriage proposal?"

One side of his mouth jerked, as though he'd been struck with something hard. "After last night, I figured you were going to turn me down."

She drew a deep breath, let it out. "I was...upset."

"And now?"

"Perhaps I've reconsidered."

His eyes, so dark, so deeply shadowed, searched hers. "Why?" he demanded in a low rough tone.

"Because you're decent and fair and...um, extremely interesting." And so sexy my teeth grind together and my skin gets hot when I just think about making love with you.

"Interesting." His tone was thoughtful, as though he were searching for hidden meanings.

"Mmm, I might mention that I also find you annoyingly good-looking—when you're not glaring at me, that is."

Half turning toward him, she rested the hand he wasn't holding against his cheek. The sandpaper stubble was strangely provocative, and so was the quick vulnerable slant to his mouth before he controlled it.

"When?" His voice was hoarse.

"When what?"

"When will you marry me?"

If she hadn't known better, she would have sworn Jess was as smitten with her as she was with him.

"How about a week from Saturday?"

His smile started slowly, then curved with a certain shyness until it took over his eyes and softened the stern lines of his face.

"Works for me."

"We'll have it here, in my rose garden." She traced the beguiling crease in one cheek with her fingertip, surprised and pleased that he didn't immediately draw back, as she'd half expected.

"Wherever."

The texture of his skin was pleasing beneath the sensitive pads of her fingers. "I'll have Cait as my attendant. And a cake, of course."

"By all means," he said dryly.

"The reception will be small, but oh so elegant." Her smile wobbled. "I hope."

He brought his hand up to cover hers, as though she'd pushed him beyond his ability to withstand even that small intimacy. Turning it slowly, he pressed a kiss into her palm, arousing sensations that spread until her body seemed to be warming and tensing at the same time.

"And, um, I'll need a new dress." Her breath was coming in little jerks, and her mind was reeling as he used his thumb to nudge her chin higher.

"Whatever you want," he said, his mouth hovering. His breath was warm and flavored with hops.

Hazel's lashes lowered until her vision narrowed to the firm, aggressive lips that so rarely smiled and yet kissed with such exquisite tenderness.

"You'll want to invite your brother and his daughter." Her suddenly rapid breathing gave her voice a whispery quality.

"Yes, ma'am." His mouth moved a fraction closer. Hazel's heart flip-flopped, and her lips trembled with a need to be touching his. When he still hesitated, she leaned forward and brushed his mouth lightly.

Jess inhaled violently, and his already speeding heart went crazy, thudding piston-hard against his ribs.

He wasn't going to ask her if she knew what she was doing or why she was doing it. At the moment he didn't care.

It had been a lifetime since a woman had kissed him first with more than sisterly affection. A lifetime since he'd wanted more.

Closing his eyes, he took her mouth with the eagerness of a kid. She strained toward him, her hands going around his neck eagerly.

He teased her with his tongue, and her lips parted with a hunger that rocked him. There was no coyness to be overcome, no hesitancy to be broken down with empty promises of love that neither really believed.

Something took off racing inside him, like a sprint gone out of control. Unnerved, Jess drew back, assessing his own reaction, struggling to keep his own needs in perspective. Acting on impulse was something a man with his physical limitations learned very quickly to avoid.

What if, at the last minute, she recoiled from him? What if she cringed when he thrust into her the way Gayla had?

But the room was quiet and so dimly lit that the corners seemed to blur, as though nothing was real. He felt safe here, cocooned. And tempted to throw away all the lessons he'd learned about himself and the way others saw him.

He drew back slowly until her hands slipped from his neck to his shoulders. Unable to completely break the connection between them, he waited. Hazel opened her eyes slowly, still dazed.

"I'll draw up the papers tomorrow."

"Papers?" she murmured.

"The prenuptial agreement."

Comprehension came into her eyes gradually, turning them from a soft blurry gold to a more rational, sane hazel.

"Oh, yes, I almost forgot."

Withdrawing her hands, she folded them in her lap and slowly drew her shoulders back until they were very straight. It was only then that her gaze came to his, the lingering drowsiness slowly slipping away.

"At least we've solved one problem. Tomorrow we can both see Lynn FitzGerald and tell her we're engaged."

"Would you like a ring? Gayla had a diamond, but if you'd like something different—"

"A plain gold band will be fine. After all, we both know this isn't a conventional marriage."

Her voice was very calm, her expression composed, but Jess found himself tensing the way he invariably did in court when he sensed that a witness was hiding some crucial piece of evidence.

He got to his feet slowly. An effective advocate knew when to press and when to retreat. "I'd better let you get some sleep."

"You, too," she said with a friendly enough smile. "You have the morning shift, remember?"

Nodding, he glanced toward the crib and the sleeping baby. "Uh, if you're not awake—"

"I will be," she said, slipping her feet under the covers and pulling them up to her waist. "And don't worry about knocking. *Mi casa es su casa.*"

But not her bed, Jess thought as he left.

Chapter 13

Jess lifted his chin, allowing Tyler to finish tying the tie given to him by Cait as a wedding present. It felt like a noose.

"We should have flown to Vegas," he grumbled when Ty snapped down the starched collar and pronounced him presentable.

Garrett turned from the window. "Too late now, J.D. Pollard just walked up the drive. At least, he looks like a judge—gray hair, a hanging look in his eyes, bullwhip in hand."

Jess wiggled the knot of his tie until the pressure on his gullet eased. Ty had already buttoned his shirt cuff for him, something he had to do with his teeth—if he did it at all. "Very funny, Garrett."

"No sweat, buddy," Tyler chimed in. "Ten minutes, a few words, and we can get down to the serious partying."

Jess shot his friend a disgruntled look. He should have insisted on a nice quiet ceremony in Pollard's office, no matter how disappointed Hazel might have been.

"Nice suit," Garrett tossed off, clearly enjoying his discomfort. "Is it new?"

Jess scowled at the sober gray flannel. It was his lucky suit, the one he wore on the first day of any trial. "No, is yours?"

"I hope to shout," Garrett said as he picked up the suit coat he'd carried in with him and shoved his long arms into the sleeves. "Andi would skin me alive before she'd let me disgrace her favorite uncle by wearing jeans and an old jacket like I'd planned."

Jess muttered an obscenity that set his brother to chuckling. Scowling, Jess glanced at his watch one more time. Hazel was upstairs with Cait and the baby. He hadn't seen her yet.

Even though Mrs. Weller had been given a clean bill of health, he'd continued to stay at Hazel's house, sleeping in the guest room, helping her as much as he could with the baby and other chores around the house.

He'd done it to be more convincing to Ms. FitzGerald. That was the excuse he'd used when Hazel had questioned him. To make sure his skittish bride didn't have a sudden change of heart was more to the point.

But Hazel had insisted that he sleep at his own house the night before the wedding. Some superstitions were just too strong to break, she'd told him with a surprisingly hesitant smile.

He'd figured she was having the same prewedding jitters that had him walking the floors at odd hours. Getting tangled up with a guy a lot of people still shunned was a big commitment for any woman.

"Uh-oh. Almost forgot these. Cait would have killed me." Ty opened the florist's box on the desk and took out three white carnations. After tossing one to Garrett, he pinned one to Jess's lapel and one to his own.

"Too bad you can't get away for a honeymoon."

Jess resisted the urge to run his finger around the constricting edge of his starched collar. "No time."

"Take my advice, make time. Getting a marriage off to the right start is more important than schedules."

"Maybe later, when this trial's over."

Garrett consulted his watch. "Last chance, buddy," he said, clapping Jess on the shoulder.

Jess's mouth went dry, and adrenaline rushed through his veins, but his shrug conveyed indifference.

"Might as well get it over with," he said as he strode hellbent for the door.

Behind his back, Garrett and Tyler exchanged looks. There was no need for words. Both men had known Jess before and after his accident. In his own way, each had suffered with him through his early struggles to conquer the ordinary day-to-day intricacies of living. Each had seen the changes in him, both good and bad.

Now, as they followed him into the garden, both wished for the best. Because they knew Jess, both expected the worst.

"Oh, the baby!"

Stricken with guilt, Hazel stepped back from the top of the stairs, only to have Cait squeeze her arm. "Don't worry. Kelsey's already taken Francey downstairs, remember?"

Hazel shook her head. The delicate tiara of white daisies bunching her hair into a semblance of order wobbled precariously.

"So help me, Cait, I'll be lucky if I can remember my name."

"Just don't forget Jess's. Let him take care of remembering yours."

Hazel managed a smile, but inside, her emotions were swooping and diving like crazy. It had been that way since the night she'd accepted Jess's proposal.

Eight days of doubts and hopes, anticipation and dread during which she and Jess had gotten their blood tests and marriage license, filled out reams of paperwork necessary to begin adoption proceedings, and bit by bit moved most of his things to her house.

In a few minutes she would become Mrs. Jess Dante. And, according to Lynn FitzGerald's repeated assurances, well on her way to becoming Francey's legal mother.

Hazel bit her lip, then remembered that she'd just applied fresh lipstick, replacing the previous coat she'd gnawed off earlier.

"Are you sure he's going to be there? In front of the judge, I mean?"

"Yes, he'll be there, looking gorgeous, I might add, in a conservative gray suit that does terrific things for those big shoulders of his. And for once his tie isn't all that bad. In fact, it's almost staid—well, for Jess anyway." Cait grinned. "I know, because I gave it to him."

Hazel knew that Cait was trying to distract her from the full-blown anxiety attack that had been hovering since she'd stepped out of her comfy robe and into her new dress twenty minutes earlier.

It was just a simple silk dress, a nice plain ivory. No big deal, except she'd never noticed before how provocative silk felt against her skin when she moved. Like the whisper-soft touch of a man's fingers mapping the body of the woman he loved.

"Don't look so scared," Cait said softly. "It'll all work out."

Hazel wanted to believe her. But Cait hadn't seen the agreement Jess had drawn up between them. Like a partnership contract, he'd addressed every possible aspect of their relationship, everything laid out in terse legalese. Which of them was to pay which bills, who was to assume what responsibilities for Francey's health care and schooling, who was to have control of the trust fund Jess had set up, how custody would be accorded in case of a divorce.

She'd read it, signed it and stuck it back in the envelope—after she'd taped together several particularly cold-blooded pages that she'd at first ripped to shreds.

Remembering the dry, emotionless words she'd all but memorized, Hazel drew a shaky breath. "Help me, Cait.

Why do I suddenly feel as though I'm about to walk off a cliff?''

"Bride's syndrome," Cait said blithely. "All brides feel that way right before they walk down the aisle. Or, in this case, across the patio."

"You didn't."

"Oh yes I did. You were just too busy ordering everyone around to notice."

Hazel lifted her chin. "I didn't—"

"The caterer, the minister, the organist." Cait ticked off each one on her fingers. "Even Jess, who, as I recall, was the only calm one in the church that day."

"Jess is always calm."

"True, but calm doesn't necessarily mean unfeeling," Cait said, reading her mind.

"Nice try, Caitie, but—"

The deep rumble of masculine laughter interrupted her train of thought. Jess was down there somewhere, his copy of their agreement tucked away someplace, his dark eyes hiding everything but his solidly entrenched distrust of women.

"Oh, Lord!" she exclaimed, her pulse spiking furiously. "Maybe we should rethink this."

"There's only one thing that matters," Cait told her, suddenly dead serious. "You love the man and you want to be his wife."

"Do I, Cait? Or am I in love with a man who doesn't exist, except in my mind?"

Cait drew a long breath. "Think of Francey, then. And maybe another baby. Your baby and Jess's."

Hazel's mouth went dry. "I don't even know if Jess wants more children." Her hands clutched Cait's. "This is happening too soon. I need time—"

"Hey, I've got an antsy groom down here," Tyler called from the bottom of the stairs. "And a superior court judge who's sure it's about to rain any second now."

Hazel and Cait exchanged looks. "We'll be right there," Cait called down. "Give us five minutes and then tell Kels to put on the music."

"Five minutes, right," Tyler confirmed before disappearing from view.

Cait gave Hazel a quick hug. "Here we go. And for the record, you're a beautiful, beautiful bride."

Hazel swallowed, then swallowed again. Her face felt hot, but she was freezing cold inside.

"I'm probably the only forty-year-old bride in the history of the modern world who's never slept with the groom before the ceremony," she muttered, taking a deep breath.

Cait laughed. "Makes for a better wedding night."

Hazel glanced behind her at the corner of the bed visible through the open bedroom door.

"Hold that thought," she murmured as she started down the stairs.

"Weatherman says rain," Garrett observed, cocking a worried glance toward the rain-fat strato-cumulus clouds piling up to the west. "Too bad, too. This wedding of yours was settin' up to be a nice party."

Kels and Jesse had been on the patio to greet Jess when he'd come outside, sitting on picnic benches turned into makeshift pews and decorated with ribbons and flowers. Francey was there, too, perched in her baby carrier between Kelsey and his niece, Andrea.

Catching his eyes, Andi raised clasped hands over her head and flashed him a grin so wide her braces shone in spite of the building overcast.

Nearby, Henry Pollard cleared his throat, looking as judicially somber standing under the flowery arch as he did on the bench.

Garrett was hovering like an old-maid aunt, no doubt worried that the groom was about to bolt. Tyler had stationed himself by the patio doors, probably worried about the same thing.

In spite of the music and the flowers and the general excitement, Jess couldn't help remembering that this was the second time in his life when he would make sacred promises to a woman.

To love and to cherish. In sickness and in health. Words someone somewhere had written down for others to recite.

When Gayla had walked out on those vows, he'd come close to quitting. He was honest enough to admit he would have, too, if Ty McClane hadn't kicked his sorry ass. Damn near killed him getting the booze out of him, then made him take a good long look in the mirror.

The guy staring back at him had been a bum, a real gold-plated, self-pitying, booze-soaked jerk. Gray skin roughened by a week's worth of whiskers, eyes so bloodshot they were pink. A burned-out, washed-up loser, the kind who used to hang around Gasoline Alley looking for handouts. Just thinking about that guy made his gut knot and his face burn.

Seeing that same face stare at him from the front page of one of the tabloids hadn't helped his job prospects—or his self-esteem.

It had been a long road back. Starting college at twenty-eight had been an exercise in patience, but it had given him a reason for getting out of bed every morning. Law school had been tougher for him than any race, but surviving, getting decent grades, winning the respect of his professors and fellow students, had helped him learn to accept the man he had to be instead of the man he'd been.

Winning his first case had been a milepost. He still remembered the rush he'd gotten. He had a feeling he'd crossed some kind of line at that moment. Not the one with a checkered flag, but almost as good.

Still, he'd lived alone because, if he was sometimes frustrated or inept or occasionally bitter, no one knew it but him. If he failed at something, no one else had to suffer the consequences or the indignities. In a few minutes all that would change. In a few minutes he would be a husband and a father, responsible for two other lives.

Who was he kidding? He was still a selfish bastard, still thinking of himself. He'd been lying awake nights in a sweat because, damn it, he had no idea how to make Hazel O'Connor love him. None.

Jess had just consulted his watch again when a flash of movement to his left caught his eye. Tyler was opening the French doors leading to Hazel's den.

Cait came first, giving her husband a quick kiss full on the mouth as she passed. And then Tyler was extending his hand for Hazel, who offered him a radiant smile as she stepped into the growing gloom.

Her hair was a halo of light and sheen as though the meager sunlight filtering through the overcast had gathered in one spot.

As she took Tyler's arm to walk toward him, he had trouble breathing, trouble focusing on anything but Hazel.

Henry Pollard cleared his throat, his seamed face relaxing into a fatherly smile the likes of which Jess had never gotten from him in the courtroom.

With a surprisingly nervous smile, she stopped at Jess's side, facing the judge. Her scent teased his nostrils, and her arm brushed his. The spray of white orchids he'd remembered to send at the last minute trembled.

Hazel heard the hushed conversation cease abruptly, making the rich music from Kelsey's prized boom box ripple like suddenly unleashed emotion over the small backyard.

She took a steadying breath, aware that everyone but Jess was looking at her. Kelsey and Andrea wore nearly identical expressions of bemusement, Jesse fidgeted, unused to the strictures of his first suit, and Francey was busily attempting to devour her fist.

"Shall we begin?" the judge asked kindly, a twinkle softening his shrewd eyes. Hazel decided she liked the man Jess had chosen. She nodded, her gaze going unerringly to Jess. He was watching her now, his black eyebrows shadowing eyes that reflected the flat surface of the overcast sky.

"Last chance," she murmured. The smile she'd meant to be casual ended up wobbling. Just being close to him scrambled her senses and warmed her from the inside out.

"For you, too," he said, his voice low and surprisingly husky. Hazel found herself staring into his eyes, trying to see past the smooth slate to the scarred, wounded soul it protected.

So now here inside was the man willing to rearrange his life to keep an unspoken promise to a dying woman, the man she wanted so desperately to love. Still, there was no guarantee Jess would let her see that man again.

"I'm ready if you are," she whispered.

"Okay, let's do it."

He held out his hand, palm up, the invitation obvious. Shaking inside, she rested her palm on his and was surprised that the fingers curling possessively over hers weren't quite steady.

Judge Pollard began to read from the slim book in his hand, his precise voice infusing the timeless words with a grandeur and sincerity that touched Hazel deeply. Her own responses were quiet and a bit tremulous. Jess, too, seemed caught by the moment, his voice thick, his grip firm.

When the judge called for the ring, Jess had to release her hand to accept the band from Tyler, and Hazel missed the warmth of his skin and the reassuring pressure of his hard fingers.

The ring slid halfway, then stuck. Jess muttered something under his breath about the wrong size, which made her smile.

"When I told you my ring size, I forgot that abject panic makes your hands swell," she said as he wiggled the band over her knuckle.

"Doesn't do much for a guy's coordination, either," he muttered, lifting his gaze to hers. To her surprise, there was a glint of amusement in his eyes instead of the frustration she'd expected. Before she could respond, he'd taken her hand again and signaled the judge to continue.

Several minutes later the judge pronounced them husband and wife and it was over. Almost.

"Hurry up, Dante," Pollard added with a pleased grin. "Kiss that beautiful bride of yours before those clouds up there unload on us."

"Yessir, Your Honor."

Jess tugged on her hand, drawing her closer. His mouth angled over hers, giving her time to do nothing more than close her eyes before his lips pressed hers in a kiss that went on and on until she lost track of the wind swirling her skirt and the embarrassed teenaged giggling behind them.

Like petals on a rosebud, sensations unfolded one after the other, leaving her bemused and dazed by the time Jess finally dragged his mouth from hers. She was still swaying when she was spun around and enfolded in Tyler's strong arms.

"Keep it up, kiddo, you're definitely on the right track," he whispered close to her ear while Garrett and the judge took turns shaking Jess's hand and pounding him on the back.

Someone snapped a picture, temporarily blinding her. Laughing, she let herself be squeezed one more time against Tyler's solid chest before Cait claimed her for a hug.

"See how easy that was?"

"Where's Francey?" Hazel asked, taking back the bouquet Cait had been holding for her.

"Don't worry, Jess has her."

Hazel saw him then, sitting on the bench, holding Francey in the crook of his arm. His dark head was bent as though he were saying something very important only to her.

Sudden emotion banded Hazel's chest and blurred her eyes. Her husband, she thought. And their daughter.

"Auntie Hazel, you really did it."

Swiping a hand over her wet lashes, Hazel returned Kelsey's exuberant hug. "I sure did," she managed to get out before Jesse barreled into her legs, claiming a hug for himself.

"Hurry up and cut the cake, Auntie Hazel," he urged. "I'm hungry."

Hazel laughed. "In a few minutes, Jesse Bear. In the meantime, why don't you help yourself to some juice from the fridge? You know where it is."

"Okay." Jesse made a beeline toward the patio door. Turning, Hazel nearly collided with the judge.

"My very best wishes, Mrs. Dante."

"Thank you, Your Honor. And thank you so much for agreeing to preside. Jess admires you very much, and I know it meant a lot to him to have you here."

"You've got yourself a good man," the judge said in a low voice. "Just don't let him bully you into thinking there's no heart under that hard crust, because there is. I've seen it, and so, I suspect, have you."

Hazel managed a grateful look and a nod before Jess's brother claimed her for a quick kiss on the mouth.

"Welcome to the family, such as it is," he said, his grin jubilant.

"Thank you," she murmured, wiping a smudge of lipstick from his lips.

"And this is Andi," Garrett said, dropping an affectionate arm over his daughter's shoulder. The resemblance between father and daughter was marked, and Hazel noted some of Jess in the teenager, as well.

Around the eyes, mainly, which were the same changeable mix of brown and black, and in the inky thickness of her wavy hair. In spite of the braces on her teeth and her angular height, Jess's niece was definitely swan material.

"Hello, Andi," Hazel murmured, offering her hand, because she sensed a suggestion of shyness in the girl's demeanor. "And thank you for coming."

"I never had an aunt before," the girl said, blushing as she touched her hand to Hazel's. "Uncle Jess was divorced when I was just a baby."

"Then this is a big day for all of us," Hazel said with a smile she didn't have to force. "You're gaining an aunt and three cousins, and I'm getting a whole other family."

"Three cousins?"

"Sure. Francey and Kelsey and Jesse."

"Hey, that's right," Andi said, looking a tad over-whelmed. Her father chuckled before pointing her toward the McClane clan. "Better break the news to them gently."

"Oh, Dad, don't be a dork!" she exclaimed, but she went off anyway.

The wind swirled, catching Hazel's skirt. At the same time she found herself caught around the waist and held tight against a solid male body.

Looking up, she found her husband of only a few min-utes looking down at her, his face more relaxed than he'd been since the day he'd picked her up at her office for the trip to Pleasanton.

He smelled like expensive wool and soap, and looked in-credibly handsome, and yet she couldn't help wondering what was really behind the enigmatic eyes and the very masculine planes of his face.

Anyone watching would be convinced that he was a man crazy in love with his bride. But Hazel reminded herself that a successful trial attorney was also part actor.

"Hi," she said softly, and then realized that she was staring at him like one of those moonstruck courtroom groupies Tyler had teased him about more than once. "Uh, where's the baby?"

"Cait took her inside." He jerked his chin at the sky, and she noticed the way his eyes took on the same turbulent texture of the clouds. "Wind's picking up. Temperature's dropping."

"Is it? I didn't notice." Not when she was securely shel-tered in the heat of his body.

"No wonder." His expression turned teasing as he pulled her closer. "You're such a hit, I was beginning to wonder if I was ever going to get near you again."

The thought of his coming nearer still sent a shiver through her. "How about some cake?" she murmured.

His eyebrows rose. "Chocolate?"

"Of course," she said archly. "What else?"

The look she gave him was pure imp with just enough spice to rile his blood but good. Intended or not, it was an invitation he could no more resist than he could stop breathing.

Jess bent his head and took her mouth, his tongue plunging between lips she'd parted in surprise, lips that she was suddenly allowing to soften and cling.

She tasted like the wind, but she made him think of hot summer sunshine and a young man who'd been high on life and eager to chase a dream.

Her hands wound around his neck, and he forgot he'd given her the choice of whether or not to invite him into her bed. With her warmth seeping into him and her small hands kneading the bow-taut tendons of his neck, keeping his word didn't quite matter as much as it should.

Not when he was feeling the softness of her breasts against his shirt and tasting the sweetness of desire on the soft lips moving so responsively under his.

He revered logic, but not when his blood was heating and his body hardening. He rigorously kept his promises, but that didn't stop him from imagining her naked and quivering and desperate with desire, her smooth, pale skin on fire for him.

Wanting, needing—those were the things driving him, things he'd worked long and hard to contain. As punishing as any track, as frustrating as any obstacle he'd faced.

Feeling her move, feeling her yield, suddenly made this real, and he dragged his mouth from hers. She made a small sound like a whimper, and then her eyes were fluttering open.

"My goodness," she murmured, her voice shaky and her lips swollen and pink.

Before Jess could apologize, he heard the sound of cheering. Jerking his gaze toward the sound, he saw a ring of beaming faces aimed their way.

As soon as his eyes met his brother's, Garrett grinned like the tormenting devil he'd been as a kid and broke into loud applause.

"Not bad for the practice lap," he shouted. "But don't you think you'd better wait for the green flag to drop before you start the race?"

Chapter 14

Blurry taillights faded into the fog, leaving the street in front of Hazel's house empty. The McClanes had been the last of the guests to leave, and they'd taken Francey with them.

Hazel swung the door closed and hoped Jess didn't notice the trembling of her hands or hear the pounding of her heart.

"It was nice of Cait and Ty to take Francey, wasn't it?" She snapped off the porch light and made certain the door was locked before turning to face Jess, who was busy removing his tie. His jacket was already draped over one of the chairs in the dining room.

Since they'd been caught kissing on the patio, his mood had gotten steadily worse. And the more his brother had teased him, the more withdrawn he'd become. Like a grizzly facing winter and a long, lonely hibernation.

Jess looped the loosely knotted tie over the newel post, then used his hand to smooth his hair. "Yeah, well, Ty's got this burr up...this notion that we need a honeymoon."

"Of course, you explained why that was...unnecessary."

"I gave it a shot, yeah, but the man's gone soft in the head since he talked Cait into marrying him. Thinks every marriage is a match made in heaven like his."

"Which, of course, ours isn't," Hazel said, smiling at her husband of four hours.

"Damn right it isn't."

"Still, I've been thinking that it wouldn't do for too many people to know the truth about our, er, agreement. Because of Francey, I mean. Especially if things don't work out and we divorce. We wouldn't want her to think that it was her fault, would we?"

"No."

His mouth flattened. He didn't look like a man who needed pampering and petting and enough tenderness to fill a house, but she'd felt all of those needs and more in his kiss. And that, simply and in a nutshell, was why she'd asked Cait to take Francey for the night.

She'd never seduced a man before, and she had a feeling he was going to need most of her concentration—and all of her nerve.

"Make yourself at home," she said, extending a hand toward the parlor. "I need to check on the caterer."

"Problems?"

"No, everything went very smoothly. Everyone seemed to have a good time."

Particularly his good-for-nothing brother, Jess thought sourly as he watched her breeze past him on her way to the kitchen.

Garrett had hung around Hazel as if he was the groom and couldn't wait for the guests to leave so he could hustle her upstairs. Over fifty and he was still a horny bastard.

Ticked at his brother and ticked at himself, he stalked into the living room and switched on a couple of lights at random.

Nudging back the lacy curtain, he looked out at the deserted street. It wasn't late, barely seven, but the thickening fog hid the sunset and lent an air of isolation to the old house.

"Isn't it a great night? All cozy and mysterious."

Jess glanced over his shoulder, a scowl fighting with a hot, sinking feeling in his belly. She'd exchanged the silky dress that he'd been taking off her in his mind all afternoon for a shimmering wisp of a nightie that had his hormones cooking on high and his imagination going crazy.

"I thought you were checking on the caterers," he said when he could trust his voice again.

"I was. They're paid off, tipped generously and on their way."

She came toward him slowly, her gown swirling around the ripe curves he'd been doing his best to ignore all day. In a desperate effort to keep his sanity, Jess fastened his attention on the glasses in her hand and told himself that a man could survive anything if he kept himself under control.

"What's that, champagne?"

"Mmm. I asked the caterer to leave an extra bottle. I thought a toast to launch our...partnership might be appropriate. Only I just now realized I hadn't given much thought to the toast itself."

She handed him a glass, then raised her own, her eyes focusing on his expectantly. "Any suggestions?"

Jess felt slightly off kilter, as though he'd found himself in the middle of a race where he didn't know the rules and wasn't sure he could keep himself under control long enough to find out.

"To Francisca Silvia O'Connor Dante," he said, his voice unexpectedly rough.

Her mouth trembled slightly as she smiled. "And to Silvia," she added softly. "I hope she's finally found the peace she deserved."

They drank together and in silence.

Lowering her glass, Hazel stood motionless, her expression pensive. "Do you think she knows we're married?" she asked quietly, as though wondering aloud.

Jess shrugged. "If you're asking me if I believe in heaven, the answer is no. When you're dead, you're dead. Period."

A sad-angel smile played over her face. "I think she knows, and I think she's grateful."

Jess wanted to tell her that thinking like that belonged in fairy tales and bad movies. Instead, he simply shrugged and changed the subject.

"I got a call from a deputy D.A. in Hargrove. He thinks they have enough against Yoder to take it to the grand jury, but only one count."

"Cleve Junior?"

Jess nodded. The details still made him sick, and he decided to spare her an exact repetition. "Seems Yoder caught the boy speaking Spanish to some of his friends and found out Silvia had been the one to teach him, even though Yoder had expressly forbidden her ever to speak Spanish again."

"What a horrible man!" Hazel shuddered as though suddenly chilled, and Jess frowned.

"Cold?"

"No, disgusted."

She stared into her glass for a moment before lifting it to her lips again. Jess watched her throat work as she swallowed, severely testing his determination to give them both time to get used to each other before he worked on that invitation to her bedroom.

He thought about the case notes piled high on his desk and the depositions he had scheduled for the next few weeks. It didn't help.

She had a slender neck, delicate bone structure and a generous mouth that didn't quite fit the rest of her small face.

Too bad, too, he thought, because she would have been a stunningly beautiful woman if it hadn't been for that one flaw, then found himself remembering the way her mouth had softened under his.

"It was a nice wedding, wasn't it?"

"Sure." Nice and short, which was all he remembered about it—until Henry Pollard had given him the okay to kiss his bride. That he remembered in vivid, and very disturbing, detail.

Jess had barely touched his champagne. Now he found himself pouring a good half of it down his throat.

"I liked Judge Pollard." Hazel settled herself in the corner of the love seat, her legs curled comfortably and her eyes half-closed. "He seems like a sweet man."

Sweet? Hanging Henry Pollard? "About as sweet as a rattler."

"He told me right before he left that he and his wife had been married for forty years before she died last year."

One thin strap had slipped from her shoulders, revealing the generous curve of her breast. Jess kept his gaze on her face, but his thoughts were on that patch of smooth creamy skin, and his mouth went dry.

Jess drained his glass in one swallow and suddenly wanted more. Shooting to his feet, he excused himself brusquely.

"Where are you going?" Hazel asked, her alarm far too blatant to be ignored.

"To get good and drunk and do my damnedest to figure out what the hell I'm going to do about this damn mess I got myself into this time." Furious, he headed for the kitchen and the magnum of champagne he hoped to hell he would find there.

Hazel stomped into her room and slammed the door. Her cheeks were burning, and her stomach was far from steady.

"I knew it was a stupid idea," she muttered. "Stupid, stupid, stupid."

She wasn't cut out to be a femme fatale. One good look in the mirror should have told her that.

Avoiding the mirror over the dresser, she crossed to the bed and perched on the edge. Okay, so she'd made a fool of herself, but it wouldn't kill her. She'd survived worse agonies with only a few permanent scars, and she would survive this.

And okay, this was just one night. The first night of her marriage. There would be other nights. Jess wasn't made of stone, although he wanted to think he was.

He could guard his words and ration his smiles, even disconnect his emotions. But, like it or not, Dante was a very lusty, very passionate man under all that hard-hewn reserve. A man who'd convinced himself he had no use for love.

Wrong, wrong, wrong, she stormed silently, flopping backward and turning her head to keep the tears pooling in her eyes from falling. Jess needed loving so badly it hurt her to think how much.

Hazel groaned and closed her eyes. Maybe a cold shower would help or a walk in the fog. Something, anything...

"Where do you keep your aspirin?" Jess was standing by the door, his hand propped against the jamb and a prodigious frown on his face.

Heart in her throat, she stared at him. His jaw was tight, his shirt flapping outside his trousers, and his feet were bare.

"In the medicine chest in my bathroom, and for the record, you scared the bejabbers out of me."

"You're the one who told me not to knock, remember?" he all but growled. *"Mi casa es su casa."*

He had to pass the bed to get to the bathroom, and Hazel watched every step until he disappeared, her heart racing and her breathing rushed.

He didn't look drunk. Not even tipsy. He did, however, look all male and extremely put out about something.

A shivery tension beyond her control coiled and uncoiled inside her. She was still sitting perfectly still when he reappeared, the aspirin bottle in his hand, impatience in his face.

"I can use my teeth or you can pry this sucker open," he grated. "Your choice."

Hazel blinked, then understood. The childproof cap would be impossible to manage one-handed. Stowing her sympathy for another day, she held out her hand. It was her room and her aspirin.

"I'll do it. Teeth marks can be so unsightly."

Surprise drove some of the black frustration from his eyes. "I hate to tell you this, O'Connor, but you'd better get used to them," he said as he handed over the aspirin bottle.

"That or follow me around whenever I'm on the premises."

On the premises, but not at home. Hazel wondered if his choice of words was deliberate, and then decided that it was. As Jess had once told her, he made his living with words.

"How many do you want?" she asked when the cap popped free.

"A couple should do it."

She shook out two tablets and dropped them into his cupped palm. "Do you have a headache?"

"Yeah, a real bitch." He tossed the tablets into his mouth and swallowed without chewing.

"Too much champagne?" she asked sweetly.

"Not enough to eat."

"Well, whose fault was that? The table was practically sagging from all the food the caterer set out."

He gave her a pained look. "I didn't say there wasn't food," he said in his cool attorney's voice. "I said I didn't eat any."

"Oh." She bunched her eyebrows and sought an explanation in his face. "Why ever not?"

"Because I was too busy trying to figure out how come a guy smart enough to get through law school was dumb enough to think he could live in the same house with you and not take you to bed."

Hazel blinked. "And did you? Figure it out, I mean?"

He shook his head. "I tried, but I always ended up thinking about you parading around with nothing under that slinky nightie but perfume and kept losing my train of thought."

Hazel tilted her head in order to see him better. His eyes weren't as shadowed now. Nor were they indifferent.

"If my nightie bothers you so much, I could change into something else."

He took a lock of hair between his fingers. "True, or you could take it off entirely."

He let his fingers brush her throat, and Hazel's pulse went crazy. "A possibility, I agree. I'll give it some thought."

The pads of his fingers played with the wisps of hair at the nape of her neck. She shivered, her head going to one side involuntarily, like a kitten being stroked.

"How about a suggestion from . . . a friend?"

He flattened his hand and skimmed the palm along the curve of her bare shoulder. Encountering the gossamer strap holding the gown's bodice, his fingers hesitated, then slipped beneath the slender scrap of satin.

"A bit . . . inappropriate for such an intimate decision, don't you think?" It was impossible to keep the ragged shiver of pleasure from her voice.

"Your husband, then?"

Slowly, deftly, he slipped the strap free of her shoulder. Instead of releasing her, however, his big hand molded to the curve of her upper arm, holding her captive as he bent his head and pressed a kiss to the warm flesh just above the swell of her breast.

Hazel fought to suppress the moan already forming in her throat. "I . . . you seem to have made up your mind already."

"Any objections?" His breath warmed her skin as he spoke, and she detected a flush along the hard ridge of his cheekbone.

"I can't think of a one so far."

She thought she heard him chuckle, and then she felt the slow flick of his tongue against her skin. This time she couldn't keep herself from gasping.

As though her response was all he'd been waiting for, Jess pulled her to her feet, and his mouth crashed down on hers.

Desperate, almost angry at first, his mouth gentled quickly, cajoling a response instead of demanding, teasing instead of taking.

Hazel gave herself into his care, willing to go wherever he would take her. Winding her arms around his neck, she arched as high as she could, eager to feel as much of his body against hers as possible.

Relaxing his mouth, he caressed her lips with the tip of his tongue, causing them to tremble. His palm pressed against her back, his fingers firm and warm, the pads rough against her skin.

And then he was slipping the other strap free of her shoulder while his mouth skipped with shivery slowness to her ear. His tongue stroked and darted. His teeth gently nipped her earlobe, drawing a long slow moan from her parted lips.

Heat rushed through her body, and her knees were unsteady. Needing to hold on, her fingers clutched at his shirt and encountered the hard slab of his belly.

Slowly he drew back enough to allow the bodice of her gown to slip past her breasts. Satin brushed skin, and her nipples shivered erect and at the same time, sent warm little needles of sensation into the swelling flesh of her breasts.

Jess inhaled fiercely, and his eyes narrowed as though he were enduring intense pain. Slowly he raised his head until his gaze locked with hers.

"Any complaints?" she whispered tremulously.

His eyes shone with a sudden fire. "Not a one."

"Good." She leaned forward until her breasts were pressing against his chest and her mouth was fitted to the hollow of his throat.

His skin was smooth under her lips and exuded a potent heat scented faintly with soap. His shirt collar brushed her ear as she used her tongue on him this time, exploring the vulnerable triangle where a hard, heavy pulse was beating visibly. He groaned, his breath shuddering.

"Just let me hold you a minute," he murmured, his arm tightening until she was held fast against him, unable to move.

Hazel murmured a protest, then realized that he, too, was standing motionless, his body swollen and rigid behind the fly of his trousers.

That he was fully aroused and very close to climax was more than evident in the tiny ripples cascading down his body and the desperate rhythm of his breathing.

Dropping his head, he pressed his face to her neck, his cheek hot and damp and lightly roughened by a day's growth of whiskers.

Closing her eyes, Hazel rested her head against his deep chest and held herself unmoving, her own breathing far from controlled and her body warming and softening, preparing to welcome his.

His heart thudded furiously, audible beneath his cotton shirt, and tension strained the muscles of his arm and shoulders.

Caught in his embrace, she felt safe and cherished and wonderfully delicate—all the things a bride wanted to feel on the first night of her new life with the man she loved.

Drenched by his heat, she felt as though she would never again be cold, never again be lonely or sad or despairing.

Lifting his head, he murmured her name. Still smiling, she opened her eyes and slowly raised her gaze to his. Instead of speaking, he simply looked at her, his eyes smoldering between the thick black lashes.

His embrace eased, and he stepped back, using his hand to draw hers away from his mutilated shoulder. Unsure of his intentions, she let her other hand fall away.

She murmured his name, her lips curving in a smile to tell him without words that she understood. If this was all he could give her now, it was enough.

Something changed in his face, in his eyes, and then he kissed her again, a long draining, arousing kiss that left her trembling when it ended. Instead of releasing her as she expected, he skimmed his palm the length of her arm. Gravity finished what his fingers had begun, and the slippery gown slid to the floor.

He said nothing, but the swift intake of his breath and the molten look in his eyes told her that to him, at this moment, she was beautiful and desirable and all the things she wanted to be just for him.

Slowly, his eyes holding hers, he flattened his hand against her neck, his fingers resting on the wildly fluttering pulse just below the skin.

"Don't be afraid," he murmured, his voice husky. "Not of me."

"I'm not," she whispered and felt him tremble. Using her index finger she traced his mouth, feeling the tension and strength of him even there.

His hand moved lower until his wrist was nestled between her breasts. Spreading his fingers wider, he lightly ran his hand over both breasts, stroking gently until her nipples were quivering.

Crying out, she reached out blindly, her hands fumbling with the buckle of his belt. Haste made her clumsy, but soon his trousers joined her gown at their feet.

He kicked them away, then stood silent, waiting, allowing her to take the same visual liberties he'd taken earlier.

Surprised and touched, Hazel noted the plain white boxer shorts, the thick muscular thighs furred with soft-looking black hair, the long powerful legs. Most of all she noticed the blatant, aggressive, magnificent arousal.

Her gaze flew to his, only to find his eyebrows drawn and his eyes unreadable. Did he think she would be frightened? she wondered. Embarrassed? The subtle hint of vulnerability touched her almost as much as it beguiled her.

"Did I do that?" she murmured, amusement and desire blending to make her voice thick and her tone breathy.

"'Fraid so. Do you mind?"

Hazel shook her head. "Not unless you're saving it all for yourself."

He froze, then choked off a laugh. "I think I'm in deep trouble here."

"Absolutely," Hazel murmured, her hands going to the top button of his shirt.

"Not this time, okay?" he said in a surprisingly hesitant tone, capturing her hand with his.

Hazel wanted to tell him that it was all right to bare his body to her. That she wouldn't find him ugly or pathetic or deformed, things that she sensed he'd heard or felt or sensed from women before. But she found herself strangely hesitant to make such a promise.

"My bed or yours?" she whispered instead, her voice shivery with desire and thick with anticipation.

Instead of answering her, he released her hand, leaned past her and jerked back the spread. Still without speaking, his gaze hard and searching on hers, he slipped two fingers beneath the band of his shorts and slid them off.

When his arm circled her shoulders, urging her to the mattress, she went eagerly, willingly.

Her hands clutched his shoulders and she lifted her mouth to meet his as he loomed over her, his body slowly easing full-length until they were lying side by side, his right side pressed to the mattress.

His hand roamed freely, exploring, caressing, until she was moaning and moving and desperate for him.

He murmured compliments, kissed her face and her neck and each breast, his mouth lingering and moist over each nipple until she arched upward, out of control.

His hand moved lower, stroking her belly, her thighs, his fingers talented and deft, driving her mad.

She cried his name over and over, frantic to feel him slip inside her, her love for him so intense that she felt she might burst with it.

When he tested her readiness to receive him with the gentlest of probing touches, she whimpered helplessly. And when he replaced his hard fingers with his even harder arousal, she arched backward in pleasure and hunger.

For such a big man he was incredibly tender, restraining his own hunger while making sure that she could take all of him without pain before he began to move. Slowly, caressingly, his gaze fixed on her face, his muscular forearm taking most of his weight, leaving her free to move with him.

Pleasure built upon pleasure, her mind and body merging until she felt as though she were soaring weightless and free.

And then she was tumbling, hot shivers gathering, gathering, until she was sobbing out his name.

He groaned, his body moving faster, deeper, until he, too, cried out, a long hoarse explosion of sound muffled by soft flesh as he buried his face between her breasts. His breath was hot, his chest heaving as tremors shook him.

"I'm too heavy," he murmured.

"Never."

"Does that mean I can stay like this for a while?" His tone was wry, relaxed.

Hazel hugged him again, feeling so full of love she thought she might burst. "Just try to get away," she growled softly.

She felt him smile against her hot damp flesh. "Yes, ma'am."

"That's better," she murmured, kissing the top of his head.

"How about that?" he muttered, his voice drowsy. "Married one day and already henpecked."

A lump formed in her throat. "Any complaints?" she asked softly.

But Jess didn't answer. Her brand-new husband was asleep.

Chapter 15

Sunlight assaulting his closed eyelids told Jess it was morning. Averting his face, he encountered a mass of soft, perfumed hair and a warm shoulder.

Hazel was draped over him like a milk-sated, fast-asleep mama cat, her cheek pillowed on his bad shoulder, her hair a bright slash against his white shirt.

Drawing a deep breath and holding it, he inched sideways on the pillow until he could see her face. Her skin was translucent in the soft morning light, her lips rosy and still slightly swollen.

He hadn't kissed a woman in years the way he'd kissed her. And damn her, she'd kissed him back like a wild woman.

The brilliant Ph.D. whose haughty stare and crisp professionalism had reduced Assistant District Attorney Jackson Lamont to a shell during Tyler's second trial was full of fun and fire in bed.

And the lady shrink who wore classic suits and sensible blouses during office hours turned into a voluptuous temptress in slinky satin after dark.

Very slinky satin, as he seemed to recall, that was now a forlorn puddle in the middle of her bedroom floor. Which meant that under the yellow flowered sheet and the bright green blanket, his wild lady lover was as bare as the day she was born.

The warm flesh-and-blood reality of her had been beyond even his ability to fantasize. Her skin had been uniformly pale, with no tan lines, no imperfections, her nipples dark and tempting. He could still feel their gravelly roughness against his tongue, still taste the tang of her skin.

Jess groaned silently, already far too aroused for his peace of mind. Not to mention the strain on his already sore, out-of-practice body.

At least everything still worked the way it was supposed to, he thought, slowly pushing his hand through the mess her fingers had made of his hair. From the slow heat settling between his legs and the quicker surges of pulsing blood, his body was already preparing for a repeat performance.

Even he didn't have the ego to believe he was better than average in the sack, especially now, with the restrictions his handicap put on him.

But damn, she'd come apart when he'd touched her. And she'd been wet and ready for him, something that not even a great actress could fake.

He'd known what sexual desire had felt like in physical terms since the age of ten, when he had fallen asleep reading in the foaling barn and woken up listening to the sounds of Garrett and Evelyn Marquette getting it on in one of the empty stalls.

But this need he had for Hazel O'Connor was more than physical, and that was what scared him. At the moment, however, he was having trouble keeping his mind on much else.

Lying perfectly still, he pictured himself walking into a half-frozen pond in the dead of winter. When that failed to distract him, he started to inch away.

She opened her eyes and reached for him before she was fully awake. "No, don't go," she murmured, her voice drowsy and her mouth sulky. "I like sleeping with you."

Just like that, he wanted her again. "On top of me, you mean," he said, kissing the tip of her nose.

Instantly there was a smile in her sleepy cat's eyes and a hint of last night's temptress in the curve of her lips. "You're such an aggressive sleeper," she murmured. "There didn't seem to be any other way."

Jess froze. "Aggressive?" he asked cautiously. He hadn't lashed out in his sleep for a long time. At least, he didn't think he had.

"Hmm. Hogging the covers, pushing me around, all but crushing me. I think the first thing on our agenda today is shopping for a king-size bed."

Jess felt emotion swell his chest, but he managed to mask it with a groan. "No way," he said, turning suddenly so that they were face-to-face. "This one suits me just fine."

"Are you sure, because—"

He covered her mouth with his and slid easily, effortlessly into her again.

When Hazel woke again, she was tangled in the sheets and hugging Jess's pillow.

It was way past the time she usually climbed out of bed on Sunday morning. The neighbors would wonder why she hadn't collected her Sunday paper. Or maybe they wouldn't, she decided, remembering yesterday's ceremony.

Allowing herself a smile, she turned onto her back and stretched. Her body felt heavy and fluid, as though she were moving in slow motion, and she was definitely sore where she'd felt such pleasure only a few hours earlier.

The sun was high, washing the room with yellow light. As she moved, her ring caught a sunbeam, flashing a brilliant gold.

Her smile grew dreamy.

Her new husband was a tempestuous, demanding lover, treating her more like the seductress she'd secretly yearned to become rather than the modest, self-effacing lady her mother had tried so hard to rear.

He'd been as eager as a boy, scarcely containing himself while making sure that she was satisfied first, and then he'd been a demanding and noisy and out of control savage.

"And you, Hazel Louise O'Connor Dante, loved every single, dangerous, glorious minute," she whispered and then wondered how soon she could entice Jess into doing it all again. Tonight, for sure, she told herself as she left their marriage bed and headed for the shower.

Fifteen minutes later she was wrapped in a warm terry cloth robe, rubbing her hair furiously with a towel, when she sensed she wasn't alone. Jess was standing on the threshold between the two rooms.

He'd been up long enough to have shaved and showered and pulled on jeans and yet another disreputable T-shirt. This one was a very faded orange, with the logo of a famous oil treatment company emblazoned on the front, and it had apparently shrunk as it had faded, because it was molded like a second skin across his massive chest.

"Tell me there's coffee made."

"There's coffee. There's also a problem."

Hazel frowned. She'd been so busy admiring the fit of his shirt that she'd failed to notice the strained look on his face. "What kind of problem?"

"Cait called while you were in the shower and—"

"Has something happened to Francey? It has, hasn't it? I see it in your face." She clutched his arm with frantic fingers.

"Take it easy, honey. It's just a minor ear infection. Ty's already phoned the pharmacy near their place for antibiotics."

"What does that mean?"

Jess saw the real fear in her eyes and cursed himself for not softening the truth. "It means that she's in good hands and there's no reason for you to panic."

"This is not panic. This is guilt. Panic comes next."

She snatched the towel from her hair, which flopped into her eyes. Impatiently she brushed it back, already picturing Francey burning up with fever and screaming in pain.

"Babies get sick. Why should you feel guilty?" Jess watched her impassively, looking far too calm. She wanted him to be worried and nervous and generally scared to death, as she was.

"This is all my fault," she muttered in the direction of his chin. "I never should have asked Cait to take her."

"I thought Cait insisted?" His silky tone stopped her for a beat, long enough to find her way blocked.

"She did. I just had to ask her first," she murmured. "And don't look at me like I just called you a dirty name. This is as much your fault as mine."

"Care to explain that?"

She grabbed the towel she'd just discarded and whomped it over the shower door. Turning, she eyed him with a mixture of panic and impatience. "You were being noble. I had to do something."

His mouth twitched. "Noble? Me?"

"Yes, you," she said, poking him hard in the chest with an index finger. "For some reason you'd gotten it into your head that we were going to have a platonic marriage."

"You didn't put up an argument."

"I've seen you in the courtroom, remember? You darn near demolished that supercilious prosecutor when he tried to argue with you."

"That was business."

"And this?"

"Definitely pleasure," he drawled, his mouth relaxing into the tentative half smile she adored.

"So what's the point of arguing?"

"Can't think of one."

Hooking her neck with his hand, he hauled her against him and kissed her. He tasted of toothpaste, and his mouth was hot.

He drew back too soon. "For the record, I've always known what I wanted. I just wasn't sure about you." The heated look in his eyes made her warm all over. The rumble of truth in his voice made her smile.

"And now?" she asked, bemused. Could she possibly have read him wrong all these years?

"Now I'd better get out of here so you can get some clothes on. Otherwise Francey will be ready for college before we pick her up."

Hovering like a sleepy guardian angel, Hazel laid the backs of her fingers against Francey's forehead. Watching from the doorway of the half-completed nursery, Jess wondered if she knew how adorable she looked with her hair mussed and her lower lip trapped between her teeth.

"She's still burning up," she whispered, raising anxious eyes to his. Two days and a night of worry had paled her skin and shadowed her eyes.

His own concern had been just as sharp, even after he'd grilled Ty for twenty solid minutes on everything from symptoms to warning signs of complications to possible side effects from the antibiotic drops they were to give her every four hours. Now, however, from every indication he could detect, Francey was on the mend.

"O'Connor, you just took her temperature twenty minutes ago. Ninety-nine point eight hardly qualifies as 'burning up.'"

She shot him an impatient look. The only time she'd settled for more than a half-hour since they'd brought the baby home from the McClanes was when she was trying to get Francey to take her bottle. Now it was close to midnight, and Hazel was still fretting.

"Yes, but that thermometer could be wrong."

"Not three times in a row."

Jess knew that she was annoyed with him. He also knew that she was going to wear herself out worrying if she didn't get some rest.

Last night, the second night of their marriage, they'd taken turns sleeping so that one of them had always been with the baby.

"How do you know about thermometers? You're a lawyer, not a doctor."

Jess joined her next to the crib. Francey was dressed in a thin shirt and a diaper and covered with a light blanket. Exactly what Ty had advised.

"Would it help if I ran down to that all-night drugstore on the corner and bought a couple more baby thermometers?"

"If you wouldn't mind—" Relief gave way to a sudden suspicion. "What do you mean, a couple?"

"I figured you could get an average that way." Jess was careful to keep a straight face. Trying to distract a worried mother hen flapping over her chick was tougher than winning a favorable ruling from Henry Pollard.

"That's not funny, Dante," she whispered, her eyes warning that she would brain anyone who dared to make light of her daughter's first illness. "She's in pain. I know, because I had an ear infection when I was in the fourth grade, and it was a nightmare."

"Trust me, O'Connor. If Francey was hurting, she wouldn't be sleeping."

"You'd be sleeping, too, if you'd cried for two solid hours."

"She was crying because every time she moved, you jumped out of bed to check on her and woke her up."

Jess slid his fingers along the rumpled lapel of her very sensible, very ordinary, impossibly sexy bathrobe. He figured he would roast in hell for a long time because he was busy wanting to make love to her while she was so worried. He also figured it would be worth it.

"I didn't."

"Yes, O'Connor, you did."

"It's just that she's so little, and I keep thinking I should be doing more." Her lashes trembled, more from fatigue, he decided, than anger. If anyone ever had needed eight hours of oblivion, she did.

"The best thing you can do right now is get some sleep."

"Oh no, I couldn't possibly! Not until her temperature is down to normal again." Craning her neck, she tried to peer around his big chest at the sleeping baby.

"Bedtime, Mommy," he ordered.

"Just let me check one more time."

"I'll do it—after I make sure you're tucked in nice and tight." He slid his hand to her shoulder and turned her gently but firmly toward the bedroom. They made it to the bed before she had another go at rebelling.

"Jess, wait, you said you'd get another thermometer."

"In the morning."

"But—"

"No more buts, O'Connor."

He grabbed a handful of lapel and pulled her toward him. Angling his mouth over hers, he smothered the protest still brewing in her eyes with the only method he hadn't already tried.

As soon as his mouth touched hers, the desire that had been on slow boil all day spilled over. Now that he knew how responsive she was and how sweet it felt to be inside her, he was having the devil's own time convincing himself to take things slow and easy the way he had to take most things in his life.

Pulling his mouth from hers, he managed his version of a teasing smile. "Lights out in five minutes."

She was using his shoulders for support, and her eyes were soft and anxious, tugging at him hard. She was one tough, self-sufficient career woman, all right. Except when it came to those she loved. And then she was a bundle of nerves and tension.

"Jess, she's going to be okay, isn't she? Ty didn't tell you anything you're keeping from me?"

"I don't know how many ways I can say the same thing. She has a minor ear infection, nothing serious."

He rested his hand in the warm spot of her neck, where the hair was thickest. Beneath his palm her small bones seemed painfully fragile, too easily crushed. He wanted to slay dragons and climb mountains and build moats to keep her safe. Instead, he had to settle for massaging her taut muscles and distracting her from her terrors.

Her mouth wobbled, then decided on a small, fey smile. "I'm being silly, right? A run-of-the-mill neurotic first-time mother. A typical textbook case."

His mouth brushed through her hair to find her forehead, and he breathed in her fragrance. Just being with her, finding himself surrounded by the whimsy and color and light of her house, was bringing his senses to life again.

"I don't know about textbooks, but there's nothing typical about you."

Hazel absorbed his words, but it was the beginning of a genuine smile in his eyes that held her. He wasn't in love with her, but that didn't mean he didn't find her interesting. With a man as controlled as Jess had made himself, perhaps that was as far as he was able to stretch his feelings. She told herself that it was enough.

"Should I be insulted or pleased?"

"What do you think?"

"Hmm, I'm not sure." She tilted her back so that she could see his face. Some of the lines had smoothed away, but his eyes were still hooded, more from worry, she decided, than wariness.

For more than two days he'd been as patient and understanding as a saint. He'd warmed bottles and helped her sponge Francey's hot little body and run through his entire vocabulary of soothing phrases—all without once showing a hint of his famous impatience.

Slowly, giving him plenty of time to guess her motives, she lifted her hand to his face and traced the aggressive curve of his mouth. His lips firmed under her touch, then slowly, imperceptibly, relaxed.

Hazel hid her pleasure behind a slow, teasing grin. "Something tells me you're too easily bored to be happy with a conventional wife."

"What is this, married less than a week and already you're psychoanalyzing me?" She sensed that he was absorbing her words, testing her mood, like a crafty trial attorney at his best.

"Wrong school. I'm partial to Jung, not Freud."

"Yeah, well, it's all mumbo jumbo to me."

"And you don't believe any of it, do you, tough guy?" She drew his head down and brushed his mouth with hers.

"Behave yourself, woman. You need rest, remember?"

"Hmm."

Her tongue feathered his lower lip with the lightest of pressure. If tension had a taste, it would have a masculine tang, like his mouth.

"Lights out in five minutes," she repeated softly. "For you, too, Daddy."

His eyes narrowed and grew intense. "O'Connor, I'm working hard at being self-sacrificing," he grated in a low rumble that she felt as well as heard. "You're not helping."

"Am I supposed to?"

She nuzzled his chin with her forehead, and Jess wondered if a guy could get high on the fragrance of a woman's hair.

He skimmed his palm down the curve of her spine and felt her tremble. His hand lingered at the small of her back, pressing her closer.

He brought his mouth to hers with as much restraint as he could handle. When her lips parted and her arms lifted to his neck, he fought to remember that she needed rest more than she needed kissing.

"O'Connor..."

He discovered that he didn't have the words, only the desperate hunger. Her face was tilted toward him, her mouth pouting for his and her eyes a shimmering gold reflection of his needs.

His hand was unsteady as it worked on the sash cinching her robe. It was even more unsteady when he slipped it inside the soft material to find soft warm skin.

"You feel so good," he murmured. "Unbelievably good."

"Mmm, so do you."

Flattening his palm against her abdomen, he rubbed gently, seductively, until she moaned softly.

"I ... could make you pregnant. Neither of us took precautions last night."

She drew back, her gaze fixed intently on his. "I want to have your baby," she murmured. "Now, as soon as possible, before it's impossible for me."

Jess closed his eyes, still unwilling to let her see the depth of the emotion he was feeling. "I'd like that," he breathed against her throat. "Thank you."

"I love you, Jess," she whispered. "I think I've loved you for a long time."

He groaned, too overcome to speak. Instead, he used his mouth to kiss every inch of her he could reach. When he encountered the roll of her lapel, he nudged it aside and lowered his mouth to her breast. At the same time his hand slipped the robe free of her shoulder.

Gravity carried it to the floor, with a little help from her. Using his tongue, he lashed the small brown nipple into hardness, then transferred his attention to the other. Her hands kneaded his shoulders, tugged at his shirt.

He circled her waist with his arm, then lifted her gently onto the bed. Her hands freed the snap of his jeans, slid down the zipper, found hot distended flesh.

A groan shook him, and he pulled away. Before she could protest, he reached past her to snap off the light, plunging the room into darkness relieved only by the faint glow of the night-light across the hall.

"Jess?" Her voice was anxious, tinged with desire.

"Right here, honey," he murmured, shedding the last of his clothes. His chest felt vulnerably naked, his skin hot.

The bed dipped, and then she felt the heat of him. He was lying on his right side again, as though to keep it hidden, caressing her breasts with his hand. At the same time her fingers sought to know him, the hard contours of bone and sinew, the steely leanness of muscle, the slightly rough texture of his skin.

He trembled under even that gentle exploration, the reaction of a man unused to being touched for too long.
Moving closer, she kissed his mouth, then slipped her tongue
along his lower lip.

Her hand kneaded his upper arm, his shoulder, feeling the
solid strength of him. The warmth. The tension.

She wanted to tell him that he would always be perfect to
her, but she didn't dare, so she tried to show him with her
mouth and her hands.

Pushing him flat, she lowered her head to his chest and
teased his nipples with her tongue as he'd teased hers. His
chest was wide and hard under the soft furring of hair, his
midriff flat, his skin resilient.

Her fingers moved lower, encountering an increase in
heat, a change in texture. A rough groan shuddered from his
throat before his hand trapped hers.

"God, honey, you're killing me," he grated hoarsely, his
breathing coming in short, desperate bursts that lifted his
big chest and fluttered her hair.

"I need to feel you inside me," she murmured. "Please,
Jess—"

He turned them both in one fluid motion, then plunged
into her with another. Hazel cried out, clutching at him as
the pleasure rolled through her.

Jess waited, so ready it hurt him not to move. Still he
waited, until the first urgency passed for both of them, and
then he began to move, absorbing every soft sigh, exulting
in every gasp, glorying in the slick heat enveloping him.

She arched upward, eager for more, desperate as he'd
been desperate for so long, needing as he'd needed. Gritting his teeth, he let her take over the rhythm, let her make
his body hers, surrendering control.

And then, at the moment when her body began to tremble and her fingers were clenching hardest, he took over
again, thrusting faster and faster until she cried out and
raked his shoulders with her nails.

Only then did he give in to his own rhythm, his own
needs. And as he did, he prayed that he'd given her the child
she'd asked him for.

* * *

Hazel woke slowly, her body deliciously heavy, her emotions humming. It wasn't quite morning, but the deepest part of night had slipped into a pearly dawn.

Lifting her lashes slowly, she saw the hazy outline of a man's chest half-covered by the sheet. It rose and fell evenly, deeply, and she smiled with lazy smugness.

Enjoying the first flutters of excitement, she slowly raised her lashes, following the long, lean contours of his chest to the massive shoulders.

And froze, her breath catching like a small painful gasp in her throat. His shoulder was one raw, puckered scar, the ugly redness tendriling like octopus legs all the way down his side.

The pain he must have suffered, she thought. The agony endured. Tears filled her eyes, and her teeth clamped her lower lip to stop its trembling.

Raising her gaze, she encountered the blackest, hardest, most pain-filled eyes she'd ever seen. Jess was awake, and from the look in his eyes, he'd seen every nuance of horror that must have crossed her face.

"Jess..." she whispered, her voice catching. "It's not what you think."

Jess didn't hear the words or feel her reaching for him. He'd been through this before. Ice inside and out, his brain numb with hurt he would never be able to articulate, he made himself move.

Like a robot under remote control, he left the bed, picked up the clothes he'd shed with such haste only a few hours before and walked into the bathroom, locking the door behind him.

Chapter 16

Hazel shifted Francey to her left shoulder and closed the door to Jess's office behind them. As the door clicked, an immaculately groomed woman about her age looked up from her keyboard and smiled.

"Good afternoon, ma'am. May I help you?"

"I hope so." She returned the woman's courteous smile with one of her own. "I don't have an appointment, but I was hoping I could see Mr. Dante for a few minutes. I'm . . . his wife, Hazel."

The woman brightened, banishing all formality from her expression as she rose to circle the desk, her hand extended eagerly. "Mrs. Dante, how very nice to meet you at last. I'm Ardiss Henderson, Jess's paralegal. We've spoken on the phone."

Shaking the woman's hand, Hazel hid her nervousness behind a cheery grin. "Of course. A pleasure to meet you at last."

"So this is Francisca," Ms. Henderson exclaimed softly. "Jess said that she was the prettiest baby he'd ever seen, and I agree."

Hazel smiled down at the baby. Fists flailing, Francey stared up at her with intense blue eyes. The day was a typical August scorcher, and Hazel had dressed the baby in one of the thin cotton dresses she'd bought at the mall.

"That's not what he says when he's changing her messy diapers."

"Now *that* is a concept—Dangerous Dante changing a diaper."

Hazel kept her smile firmly in place. "Actually, he's been working so many long hours recently that he hasn't had a chance to change all that many."

Ms. Henderson's expression sobered. "So what else is new?"

"Okay if I go on in?" Hazel murmured.

Ms. Henderson glanced toward her desk, where the red light on the phone console had just blinked on.

"Please do—only I'd advise you to be careful about making any sudden moves. You just might get your head handed to you if you do."

Hazel frowned. "He's in a bad mood?"

"Oh no. Bad is normal these days. We're talking impossible today." Ms. Henderson returned to her desk and sat down. "Like a bear with a sore paw. A very large, very unpredictable bear. To tell you the truth, I haven't seen him so preoccupied since the McClane retrial."

"Must be an important case."

The other woman looked at her oddly. "That's just it. The jury brought in an acquittal day before yesterday, against everyone's expectations—including Jess's. He should be on top of the world." She shrugged, then looked embarrassed. "But, of course, you know all of that better than I do."

Hazel gave her an all-purpose smile, the one she used with patients when she didn't know what to say. "Actually, I hadn't heard. We're both so busy, and then there's the baby."

Ms. Henderson looked suddenly very uncomfortable. "Of course."

Hazel rapped once with her free hand, then slowly eased open the door. Jess was seated behind a large mahogany desk with the phone clamped between his right shoulder and his ear, writing furiously on a yellow legal pad.

He glanced up at the interruption, a scowl on his face changing instantly to remote coolness that shut her out as effectively as any door.

"Hell, yes, I'll testify," he growled into the receiver, but his gaze followed her progress as she and the baby came toward him.

"Yeah, well, I saw those bruises on both kids, and they didn't get them playing with the dog."

Hazel hesitated, then slipped into one of the two leather chairs pulled conveniently close to the desk, shifting Francey to her lap at the same time. A quick check reassured her that the little lamb was now fast asleep again.

"Yeah, all right, I'll hold."

Jess dropped his pen and leaned back. He was wearing a long-sleeved yellow and brown plaid shirt with the cuff rolled, something that she'd discovered he did with all his shirts before he put them on, and jeans worn almost white in spots. A bright orange knit tie, still knotted, was looped over the shade of his brass desk lamp.

"Welcome to my office." His mouth took on the cynical, half-mocking look she'd come to detest. "If I'd known you were coming I would have tidied up."

"If you'd known I was coming you would have been somewhere else, the way you've been for the past three weeks."

Dusty color stained his cheeks, but he didn't bother contradicting her. "I figured that was best for both of us."

"Another unilateral decision, like the one you made to move back into the guest room?"

Before he could reply, the person on the other end of the phone began speaking again.

While she waited, Hazel gave the large space a slow, thorough inspection. One theory of human behavior had it that the surroundings a person chose reflected his or her true personality. In this case it seemed bang on. Who else but Jess would have chosen impermeable brick walls, impossible to reach ceilings and scarred hardwood floors?

She was studying the landscapes on the wall when he hung up. "Sorry to keep you waiting," he said, looking anything but.

"No problem. In case I forgot to mention it during the few times we've talked recently, I'm taking this week off."

"You didn't forget."

Jess swiveled his chair to the left and reached for the bottle of Scotch and the water glass he kept in the bottom drawer of his desk.

Opening the bottle with one hand, pouring, recapping the bottle—those things he'd learned easily enough. Just as he'd learned to drive a car and get himself dressed and fed. Forgetting was something he hadn't learned.

"What did the doctor say?"

"Our little girl is blooming. Weighs over seven pounds now, and everything else checks out. He wants to see her again in three weeks for her first shots."

He grimaced. "Sounds painful."

"Sometimes a little pain is necessary," she murmured.

Jess finished his drink and thought about pouring another. Bad idea, Dante, he reminded himself. He had a tendency to talk too much about the wrong things when he'd had a few.

Carefully replacing the bottle and glass, he slammed the drawer closed again. "Yoder's preliminary hearing is scheduled for the nineteenth of this month. I intend to attend."

Two weeks from now, Hazel calculated. A lifetime, these days. "Perhaps I should, as well."

The hard wedge of his shoulders moved a fraction, the only reaction he permitted himself. "If you'd like, although there's no practical need."

Sometimes needs *weren't* practical or logical, but that didn't make them any less real. Hazel glanced down at the sleeping baby. She was so small, so utterly perfect. Hazel was dying inside, thinking about having to give her up if she couldn't make this marriage work.

"Jess, do you want a divorce?"

"No, do you?" The coldness in his tone brought her head up quickly. He'd been polite but distant since the morning she'd gotten her first look at his scars.

Since then he had rebuffed all her attempts to break through the wall he'd put between them. Telling herself that she understood, that she couldn't really judge him unless she'd lived in his skin, seen the stares, felt the humiliation of sometimes having to ask perfect strangers for help, she had no right to be impatient with him. Or angry. Or, heaven help her, so ready to brain the man that she was sometimes shaking with the restraint she'd put on herself.

"I'll give you one more month," she said, her voice ominously soft. "Do whatever you have to do to convince yourself that I'm a terrible, insensitive, unloving jerk, just because I reacted to the evidence of pain I can't begin to imagine. Hide away in the guest room all you want, sleep alone if that's easier. For another thirty days, you have my permission to feel sorry for yourself twenty-four hours a day if that makes you happy."

A muscle jumped in his cheek, and his eyes seared hers. "And after that, then what?"

Holding Francey carefully, she eased forward to the edge of her chair, then stood up and gathered her purse and diaper bag.

"After that, you have two choices. One, you can file for divorce. Or two, you can stop acting like a spoiled, self-centered, selfish brat and start acting like a man who's worthy of being loved, honored and cherished. In short, like the man I thought I'd married."

His face was white, his eyes seething. He didn't move. "I'll take it under advisement," he said, his voice winter silk.

"You do that."

Hazel steadied Francey on one shoulder, slipped the diaper bag and her purse onto the other and walked to the door with her head high and her heart pounding.

She paused with her hand on the knob and turned to face him again. "If you need to figure out how a man is supposed to act when he gets knocked down, ask Neil Kenyon. If you're very humble, he just might take pity on you and show you what real courage is all about."

She didn't slam the door, but she thought about it.

The old brick building emptied early on Fridays. The young and not-so-young professionals who usually thronged the hallways now gathered in Old Sacramento's plentiful bars and restaurants instead, sharing drinks and lies and generally having a good time.

Ardiss had left early in order to drop off some papers at the courthouse before she headed home. Jess had the office to himself, something he usually relished.

But not tonight.

Tonight the empty building only made him realize how solitary his life had become over the years. When he walked into one of the popular spots along the street outside, he was almost always there on business. And when his business was over, no one invited him for a friendly drink.

It was his own fault, no doubt about it. He'd consciously cultivated a reputation as a bad-tempered tough guy because, in the beginning, it had been easier that way. Better to be disliked than pitied, he'd told himself. It hadn't taken him long to realize that he was both.

Before he'd met Hazel, he hadn't known how lonely he'd been in his self-imposed isolation, or how much he wanted to change that.

Yeah, Dante, you changed it, all right. Not only does she think you're a freak, but now she thinks you're a coward.

Who was he kidding? That was exactly what he was.

Because he was alone, with no one to see, he let his shoulders slump and his guard relax. The ache in his shoulder never completely eased, although rubbing it sometimes helped. Closing his eyes, Jess dug his fingers into the scarred pad of sutured flesh where his arm had once been.

He'd worked hard learning to live his life as a cripple. Now he realized that he'd done too good a job.

Hazel spooned a small amount of rice cereal into Francey's eager little mouth, then waited for it to come right back out again. Coordinating her tongue and her appetite was a skill her little angel had yet to master.

It was Saturday morning and drizzling, forcing Jess to postpone his scheduled ride with Tyler. She'd expected him to head for the office as soon as he'd finished his morning coffee. Instead, he had headed for the den, muttering about calls he needed to make.

"She doesn't look too happy."

Hazel glanced up to find Jess watching her from the door, his empty coffee mug in hand. He had dressed for riding in boots, jeans and a pale blue western shirt. He'd recently shaved, and his hair was longer than it had been at their wedding, brushing his collar softly in the back and feathering over his ears.

Her heart thumped, and her skin warmed. He hadn't touched her since that terrible morning, but that didn't mean she'd been able to shut off her mind or her body.

The sex drive was part of the package a person brought into the world. Nature's way. A proven matter of chemistry. Necessary to continue life. All those things she knew and accepted, even on occasion found herself explaining to a patient or a parent.

Somehow none of that mattered when she thought about Jess. Not when her body was too warm and her skin was too tight and her mouth was going dry just thinking of his big hand skimming her breasts, her belly, lower.

"She's not very partial to cereal yet," she murmured as she cleaned the overflow from the baby's chin. Glancing at the mess on the baby's bib and on her own shirt, she managed a small smile. "In the meantime, I'm thinking of covering myself and her and the kitchen with plastic."

Jess crossed to the table and put his cup near his usual place before bringing the pot from the counter to refill her cup and his.

"This isn't bad," he said as he settled into his chair and stretched his legs. "You should have seen me when I was learning to eat left-handed. Damn near starved to death before I got so I was eating my dinner instead of wearing it."

Hazel glanced up to find a rueful grin slanting his lips. He wasn't quite as remote, but he wasn't tearing down any walls, either. "Looks like you survived."

"It was a near thing, though. I was skin and bones by the time I got the hang of it."

Hazel managed a wary smile. Since she'd told him off in his office, they had forged an uneasy truce. But Hazel had few illusions. Unless Jess learned to trust her wholeheartedly, to accept whatever feelings he raised in her without turning cold if they didn't suit him, their marriage was over.

Hazel wiped the baby's face with a soft washcloth, then scooped up the last of the cereal for one more try.

"Here we go, precious, one more yummy bite for Mommy," she cooed, smiling for all she was worth.

Clearly unimpressed, Francey turned her head to the side and let out a warning squall. Hastily Hazel put aside the spoon and set about extricating Francey from her infant seat.

"Stubborn little cuss," Jess commented dryly, watching her in that brooding way she'd come to expect.

"Not as stubborn as her daddy," Hazel muttered, settling Francey comfortably in the crook of one arm and reaching for the bottle of formula she'd prepared earlier.

"Her daddy's trying. Doesn't he get points for that?"

Hazel glanced up to find his gaze roaming her face intently, as though he'd set his mind on memorizing every line and curve.

"This isn't a race, Jess. If this marriage folds, neither one of us wins. Worst of all, Francey will end up the biggest loser."

His jaw was tight as he took a swallow of coffee, his gaze focused on the rain steaming the windows. Tense silence filled the kitchen, broken only by the steady patter of rain on the patio tiles and the baby's eager suckling.

Minutes later, apparently full now, Francey was busily trying to spit out the nipple she'd been so eager to take earlier.

"Okay, I get the message," Hazel said softly. She put the bottle on the table, then used the damp cloth to wipe the tiny milk-sated mouth before transferring the baby to her shoulder.

"Give Mommy a nice big burp now," Hazel soothed, rubbing gentle circles on the baby's back. Right on cue Francey belched, and Hazel laughed.

"What a good girl you are," she cooed, kissing the top of the silky head.

"I'll take her," Jess said gruffly. "Drink your coffee. You look like you could use it."

Hazel settled the baby in the crook of Jess's arm. As she did, her fingers brushed his thigh, and he flinched.

"Sorry about that. Believe me, it wasn't intentional." She was too tired at the moment to care about anyone or anything but the baby and her patients, in that order.

Hazel grabbed her cup with both hands and drank until the cup was half-empty. "There," she murmured with a heavy sigh. "Do I look better now?"

Glancing up, she saw pain flash in his eyes. For her? she wondered. Or himself?

"O'Connor, I can't watch everything I say," he said with heavy impatience.

"Why not? You expect me to watch everything I say and do."

He scowled. "That's different."

"The heck it is." Hazel got to her feet, intending to take Francey upstairs. Instead she found herself clamping her hand over her mouth and running for the downstairs powder room.

Slamming the door behind her, she bent over the toilet and quickly and noisily got rid of everything in her stomach.

"O'Connor?"

She wiped her mouth with a towel, closed the lid on the toilet and sat down, willing the nausea to disappear. "I'll be out in a minute."

"What's wrong? Do you need help?"

"No. Just see to Francey, okay?"

But he didn't go. Instead, he opened the door and stuck his head in. His mouth was hard, his eyes filled with worry. For some odd reason the realization that he was worried about her only made things worse.

"Where's Francey?" she asked peevishly.

"In her seat." He came closer, filling the small room, crowding her with his raw masculinity. "Are you all right?"

"Fine. Wonderful, now that I've tossed my cookies."

One side of his mouth moved, making her wonder if he were thinking about that night in the bar. "What is it, a touch of the flu?"

Hazel wanted to cry. Instead she settled for a short nervous laugh. "No, a touch of pregnancy."

His eyes went blank, and his jaw turned white. "You're expecting a baby?"

"So my doctor tells me."

She had it then, the emotion she'd wanted from him for so long. Only instead of happiness or joy in his eyes, she saw raw, unbound anguish. Jess didn't want the baby.

Hazel got to her feet slowly, brushed past the hand he held out to her and walked into the kitchen to get her daughter.

Upstairs, she changed Francey's diaper, tucked her in for a nap, and walked calmly to her own room and shut the door.

Then she cried.

When the rain tailed off around four, Jess headed for the ranch, leaving both Hazel and Francey sleeping.

He'd told himself Sting needed exercise. When he found himself walking past the pasture where the gelding was grazing, however, he realized that he'd headed for the ranch in the way that a wounded animal heads for its lair.

He found Garrett in the barn, mucking out one of the stalls. As soon as Jess crossed the threshold from light into gloom, Garret looked up from the manure he was shoveling and grinned. "Hey, look what the cat dragged in!"

Jess knew Garrett had heard his car when he'd driven in. He also knew that his big brother wouldn't ask him why he'd driven all the way from Sacramento to Placerville without notice.

"I had a day off. Thought I'd take a look around. Make sure you're doing right by the place."

Garrett snorted. "How would you know? You're a white-collar worker these days. No more bucking hay and shoveling manure for you."

"Us educated types leave that to you country boys."

"You educated types are full of this stuff I've been shoveling."

Putting aside his shovel, Garrett removed his hat and wiped his damp forehead with the back of his hand before resettling the old Stetson.

Then, since he was taking a break anyway, Garrett refilled his mug from the thermos, then lifted his eyebrows. "Coffee?"

Jess shook his head. "I'm trying to cut down."

Garrett slugged down half a cup with relish, then sipped the rest more slowly. "Did you hear? Madonna took first. Andi's walking on air."

"I thought teenage girls were supposed to be addicted to boys, not horse breeding."

"I expect that'll come sooner or later. Right now I'm grateful she's still horse-crazy like her mom." Pain filled his face for a brief span before he grinned. "So how's my favorite sister-in-law?"

It occurred to Jess that he'd come out here because he knew sooner or later Garrett would get around to talking about Hazel. He might even give him the advice he was too proud to beg for. Lord knew he needed it.

"She's expecting a baby."

Garrett looked stunned, then tossed aside his coffee in favor of pounding Jess on the back with gusto. "Congratulations, buddy. I'm proud of you!"

Jess had trouble keeping himself under control. The idea of Hazel carrying his baby had his gut in a knot. Not because he didn't want to be a father, but because he wasn't sure he had what it took to be a husband, let alone the father of two.

"Don't be. I'll be lucky if she lets me stay around long enough to help with the delivery."

"You blew it, huh?"

"Yeah, big-time."

Garrett reached above his head to pull the chain on the bulb looped over a rafter. Behind them, one of the horses nickered nervously, leading the other three to shift in their stalls.

Neither brother broke the silence as they walked to the big barn doors and secured them from the outside. Flexing his shoulders, Garrett stared up at the gray sky, while Jess let his gaze roam over the familiar rise and fall of the surrounding mountains.

"Want to talk about it?" Garrett asked without looking at him.

"Not much to tell." Jess kept his eyes on the jagged peaks. "She claims I've been acting like a spoiled brat, so wrapped up in my own problems that I mistook natural empathy for pity."

"When you took your shirt off?" Jess had never been much good at fooling his brother. Maybe that was why they'd grown up squabbling over just about everything.

"Yeah. I guess I overreacted, lost my temper and generally made an ass of myself."

Garrett shook his head. "Pop always said you were one-part mule and the other part pride. Looks like he was right."

Jess shoved his fist into his pocket and walked to the corral fence. "Big, tough trial attorney, a rep for being mean in the clinches, and I fold up because the woman I admire most in the world couldn't handle the scars the way I thought she should."

"Let it go, Jess." Garrett's tone was suddenly dead serious. "It's ancient history."

"Not so ancient, Garrett. When I left the house, my wife was in her bedroom crying her eyes out. I wanted to hold her, to beg her to give me another chance, on my knees if I had to. But I couldn't."

"Why the hell not?"

Jess stared into his brother's frustrated, pain-filled eyes and saw himself. "Because, damn it, she's locked me out."

Chapter 17

Hazel was working upstairs, at the small desk in her bedroom, so that she could hear Francey if she fussed. It was late, past her usual bedtime, and she was tired.

Lowering her head, she massaged the dull throb at the base of her neck. Between the morning sickness and her seesawing emotions, she was worn out.

Yawning, she slipped her feet into her shoes and stood up. As she did, the phone shrilled, startling her.

"Hello?"

"Let me speak to Dante." It was a cold voice. Male without a doubt. One that seemed oddly familiar.

"Who is this?"

The caller answered with a particularly harsh sound. A growl? A laugh? Whatever it was, it made chills run over skin.

"Heard you two got married. Kept the kid, too."

Recognition came in a rush, and Hazel drew a sharp breath. "Is there something in particular you want, Mr. Yoder?"

"You bet your life there's somethin' *in particular* I want, lady. Dante's ass, that's what, whipped but good, until he knows better'n to interfere where he's got no damned business."

"The safety and welfare of Silvia's children *are* his business, Mr. Yoder. And mine."

Hazel hung up, then sat staring at the phone, seething and sick to her stomach. Jess. She had to call Jess. Only she didn't know where he was. Maybe Ty would know.

She was reaching for the phone when it rang again. She snatched it up before the second ring. "Look you—"

"Take my advice, lady. Never hang up on a man who's trying to decide whether to kill you or just leave you scarred for life."

This time he was the one to hang up first.

It was almost ten by the time Jess turned off the freeway and headed toward Hazel's neighborhood. His shoulders ached, and his back was sore from helping Garrett with the stalls.

The hard physical exertion had banished some of the tension. It hadn't helped his mood. If anything, it had only made it worse.

The porch was dark, the facade of the big old house cold and forbidding save for a light showing upstairs in her bedroom.

Jess parked on the street instead of pulling into the driveway the way he usually did. In case she was sleeping, he told himself. But the truth was, he needed time to marshal the arguments to convince her to forgive him and start over.

He let himself in with his key, snapped on the hall light and headed slowly up the stairs. Too late he remembered the bad step, wincing at the loud screech.

He would wake Hazel for sure, but maybe it was better this way. He'd just made up his mind to plead his case now, while he still had the nerve, when he heard a shout from above, followed by a thud.

He'd just grabbed the banister and started his sprint when Cleve Yoder appeared at the top of the stairs, dragging Hazel after him by her hair. In his other hand he held a policeman's heavy flashlight like a truncheon.

Jess stopped short, held by the fear in Hazel's eyes. Yoder's dung-colored eyes were silvered by a maniacal gleam, and he was smiling.

"Come on up here, Dante," he commanded with a sneer. "Me'n your missus here and Silvia's brat have been waiting for you to get home."

"Let her go," Jess said quietly, holding up his hand to show that he was no threat. Hazel murmured his name, then cried out as Yoder tightened his grip.

"Are you all right?" Jess asked her urgently.

"Yes," she managed to answer quietly before Yoder's hand tightened again.

"Enough, Yoder. It's me you want to hurt, not her."

Yoder grinned, his gaze focused on Jess's eyes. "Did that bitch wife of mine ever tell you some of the methods I used to keep her in line? For instance, I got real good with this here flashlight. Might even call me an artist, like."

Jess tasted real fear for the first time in his life. "If you hurt my wife or the baby, I'll kill you."

Yoder's disdain was palpable. "I hear you've been a busy boy," he taunted, his mouth hooking to one side in a sneer. "Making folks down in my neck of the woods real nervous-like. Trying to get 'em to take away my boys permanent. All but got 'em convinced, according to that shyster lawyer I hired. Think that greaser sister of Silvia's and that pansy husband of hers know better'n me what's good for my own flesh and blood."

Jess saw a fresh bruise blooming on Hazel's cheek, and he knew what Silvia had felt all those years. Killing was too good for an animal like Yoder.

"I'm not the one who gave Cleve and Johnny those bruises," Jess said with an icy calm he was far from feeling.

Yoder tossed off his words with a grunt. "Hell, they don't mind, same as I didn't mind when my old man hit me. A good beating now and then toughens a boy, makes him into a man."

"What kind of a man hits a woman?" Hazel exclaimed, her tone disdainful in spite of the fear in her eyes.

"More of a man than you got." Yoder's gaze slid sideways, his pleasure in taunting them as obvious in his face as a malignant sore.

"Tell me somethin', Miz Dante. Crippled like he is, don't it make your flesh crawl when he touches you?"

Hazel's eyes flashed. At the same time, her elbow shot sideways into Yoder's gut. Air flew from his lungs, and he recoiled.

Seeing his chance, Jess launched himself at Yoder's knees. They crashed to the floor together, and Jess felt something crunch when he landed on the flashlight.

He had no time to take stock, however, because Yoder was already struggling free of his one-armed tackle, using his fists like battering rams.

Dodging blows as best he could, Jess managed to roll, then connected with a solid hook to Yoder's jaw. Like petrified wood, there was no give to the man.

Jess's advantage was in the quick reflexes that had saved his life more than once. Sidestepping another blow, he spun around, then connected with an uppercut to the belly and a knee in the groin. With a hoarse grunt Yoder folded, hitting the floor like a lumpy sack of meal, out for the count.

Out of breath, Jess sat down on the top step and waited for his head to stop swimming. Hazel sat next to him, her trembling hands moving over his face, wiping away the blood from a cut on his lip he didn't remember receiving.

"Are you all right?" she demanded. "What hurts?"

"My pride," he grated, then turned his face upward to inspect the damage to her face. Her eyes were shadowed and brimming with the tears he'd caused, her cheek swollen, but other than that she seemed okay. And so lovely he wanted to wrap her in that satin nightie of hers and keep her all to himself for the next hundred years.

Instead, he asked gruffly, "What about you? Are you okay? Francey?"

"Both of us are fine." She shot a disgusted look at Yoder's pasty face. "He said he was going to kidnap the boys and take them to Mexico—after he'd made sure we would...remember him."

Jess ground his teeth. "How'd he get in here?"

Her eyes flashed, warning him not to push her too hard. "I heard someone on the porch. I thought it was you, so I opened the door."

"Naturally you didn't check."

Her mouth pouted. "I was worried. Ty didn't know where you were, so I called Garrett. He said you'd left hours ago."

"I was driving some of the roads I used to know as a kid. Sometimes it helps me sort things out."

"And did it?" Talc and perfume swirled through his senses until he was filled with her.

"It helped—until I got a ticket for going fifty miles over the limit. Then all I could think about was the money it was gonna cost me."

She inhaled slowly, raggedly, giving him a mind-shattering glimpse of the shadow separating her breasts. "Jess Dante, if...you...ever do something that stupid again," she said in a rush, "I swear I'll steal the keys and throw them away."

Emotions he couldn't begin to sort out pounded in his head. All he knew for sure was that he was going to fight to win her back, and when he was done, she would know what it felt like to be wooed.

"Don't worry," he muttered. "With another baby on the way, I can't afford too many hundred dollar fines just to figure out a few things I should have known all along."

He lifted his hand and lightly touched the bruise. At the same time pain seared him so strongly that he nearly cried out, and he rested her head on his shoulder.

"I'm sorry," he said, his voice thick. "Everything you said about me is true. I'm spoiled and selfish and a damned hypocrite."

"Hypocrite?"

"Damn straight! Just before the cop pulled me over, I realized I wasn't much better than Ron, bailing out on you because I'd gotten my feelings hurt."

Her hand circled his wrist and pressed his hand more firmly to her face. "I shouldn't have said those things. I can't begin to imagine how it feels. Not for you or for Neil or my other patients with physical disabilities."

Jess studied her eyes. They were shimmering with a depth of emotion that should have scared him. Instead, knowing that he had inspired that emotion had him humbly vowing to do his best never to hurt her again.

"Don't spoil it, honey. Admitting I'm wrong is not something I do all that often." His voice was quiet, an uncomplicated statement of fact.

"Neither do I, actually." She smiled. "Perhaps we both could stand to change a few things. Like our sleeping arrangements, for starters." Her mouth wobbled. "I miss fighting you for the covers. And I miss waking up with your arm around me."

Jess found his eyes misting and emotion swelling in his chest until he had trouble drawing breath. "I guess I could handle that—eventually."

Her eyebrows flew up. "Eventually?"

"Not the sleeping part," he assured her hastily. "The waking up with my arm around you."

Her eyebrows flew down again and then drew into an ominous line. "Jess Dante, if you start that feeling sorry bit again—"

He stopped the tirade he sensed was coming with a kiss. Her lips responded so eagerly, so intensely, that he had trouble dragging his mouth from hers.

"Now, don't be upset," he said with a slight hitch in his tone. "And don't yell, okay? But much as I really, really don't want to, there's something important I have to tell you. But first, keep this in mind, okay?''

This time he kissed her with all the fire he'd held back for so long, his tongue tasting, his mouth searching and clinging until they were both starved for air.

"Oh my," she murmured, her eyes soft and sensuous and just a bit dazed. "Now I remember why I love you."

Jess had to swallow twice before he could find his voice. "And I love you," he ground out. "But you're going to have to wait awhile before I can show you how much the way I'd like to."

She blinked. "If you're talking about Yoder, I'll call the police right now and have him hauled off to jail where he belongs."

Jess grinned. "Good plan, honey, and I suggest you get to it before he wakes up, but there's another small problem."

"You mean Francey?"

"No, not directly, although we should drop her off at the McClanes's on our way to the hospital. Once the police have taken Yoder off our hands, that is."

She drew an audible breath. "The hospital?"

Jess felt his face flame, and his mood edge toward dangerous. "Remember that last uppercut that put Yoder down for the count?" he asked gruffly.

"Hmm, magnificent, my hero," she teased, but her eyes were somber.

"Yeah, well, your hero broke his wrist delivering it."

"Oh no!" she squeaked in dismay. "Oh, Jess. What should I do? How can I help?"

Jess felt himself stiffening, all the old pain returning. And then he looked into his wife's eyes. It wasn't pity he was seeing there. He knew now he never would.

"For starters, you can promise not to divorce me when I'm driving you up walls while the damn thing heals."

Her smile was the most beautiful he'd ever seen. "I promise."

"Even when I'm yelling at you and kicking down doors and generally making an ass of myself?"

Hazel heard the rough vulnerability and saw the bleak concern in his deep dark eyes. "Nope, not even then."

So happy she could laugh and cry and shout all at once, she very gently cradled his hand in her lap and kissed the square chin that was starting to take on a pugnacious stubbornness she had a feeling she'd better get used to.

"Besides," she whispered when he closed his eyes on what she sensed was a moment of deep relief, "remember what you told Neil. I'm crazy for your body, so I'm pretty much committed to taking everything that comes with it."

"For better or worse?"

"Hmm, till death us do part."

Epilogue

The sun was warm on her tummy and wonderfully soft on her face. It was turning out to be a perfect spring Sunday in Sacramento.

The Yoder boys had left a few hours earlier after a week's visit, and Jess had issued strict orders that she wasn't to lift a hand the rest of the day. Playing mother to four had been fun—and exhausting.

Much as she'd loved having them and the noisy confusion they invariably brought with them on their frequent visits, she was happy to have Jess and Francey to herself again.

It wouldn't be long before another member of the family would be making his appearance. Smiling to herself, she mentally ticked off the days.

Sixteen days and counting until Garrett Tyler Dante would be in her arms instead of trying to kick his way through her belly.

"Here we go, ice water for Mama Buddha."

Opening her eyes, she saw Jess smiling down at her, Francey perched securely on his hip, holding a Sesame Street cup in her chubby hands.

"Wah-wah," she said with a pleased grin that showed off six pearly teeth and another on its way.

"Thank you, punkin'," Hazel murmured, taking the cup carefully. Because Francey's dark eyes were fixed expectantly on her face, Hazel took a long, thirsty swallow, smacked her lips and expelled a pleased sigh. "Hmm, good," she murmured.

"Goo'," Francey repeated, and Hazel beamed. After much logical discussion and objective soul-searching, both she and Jess had proclaimed their daughter a genius.

Of course, the McClanes and the Dantes and even Mrs. Weller had agreed. In addition, they had bestowed sainthood on Hazel, for putting up with a teething baby and a grumpy, bad-tempered, generally hateful husband at the same time.

As promised, he'd been impossible, especially when Hazel or Mrs. Weller, or sometimes Garrett, had had to feed him. There had been occasions when Garrett had resorted to anatomically graphic words Hazel hadn't even dreamed existed.

Mrs. Weller had threatened to quit at least once a week. One morning, pushed to her limit by Jess's bad temper, she'd even hit him square in the face with the red satin pillow he liked so much, ordering him to keep his mouth shut for the rest of the day or he'd be eating that same pillow.

Hazel hadn't dared laugh, but later she'd given Mrs Weller her most profuse thanks.

"So, little mama, how are we feeling today?" he asked in that whiskey smooth voice she loved—especially when they were alone in their bedroom with the door closed and the lights low.

"Mellow," she murmured, watching through half-closed eyes as Jess set Francey carefully on her heavily padded bottom and handed her the bottle of juice he'd stashed in the back pocket of his cutoff jeans.

"Mellow, huh?" he drawled, sprawling next to Hazel on the fresh-cut grass and pressing his ear to her belly. "And how are you doing, slugger?" he murmured to the baby, caressing the swell of her tummy with the gentlest of touches.

He smelled of sun-block and the honest sweat he'd worked up cutting the grass. Sunlight tangled in his hair, turning it a tempting mix of black and silver that automatically drew her fingers to the soft thickness.

"Slugger's getting anxious," Hazel said with a laugh. "Just like his father with a cast on his arm, he can't seem to settle in one position very long."

Jess raised his head and fused his dark, intense gaze with hers. "Hey, c'mon, admit it. I wasn't that bad."

Hazel snorted. "You were absolutely the most aggravating, most infuriating person—man, woman, or child—that I've *ever* encountered."

How a man as big and tough as Jess could manage to look boyishly chastened and impossibly sexy at the same time, Hazel didn't know. She just knew she was more in love with him with every day that passed.

"Didn't I have any redeeming qualities?" he coaxed with one of his heart-stopping half smiles.

Hazel pursed her lips, then watched his eyes heat. "I have to admit you did develop some very...innovative techniques in bed to compensate for not being able to use your hand."

He looked smugly pleased. "Compensation does have its rewards."

"I'll say it does," she murmured. "And you, my husband, are a true master."

Turning her head, she nuzzled her face against his sun-warmed bare skin for a moment before very tenderly, very lovingly kissing the puckered flesh he was no longer hesitant to expose.

Jess didn't even flinch. He was too busy kissing her back.

* * * * *

**And now for
something completely different
from Silhouette....**

Every once in a while, Silhouette brings you a
book that is truly unique and innovative, taking
you into the world of paranormal happenings.
And now these stories will carry our special
"Spellbound" flash, letting you know that you're
in for a truly exciting reading experience!

In October, look for *McLain's Law* (IM #528)
by Kylie Brant

Lieutenant Detective Connor McLain believes
only in what he can see—until Michele Easton's
haunting visions help him solve a case...and her
love opens his heart!

McLain's Law is also the Intimate Moments
"Premiere" title, introducing you to a debut
author, sure to be the star of tomorrow!

Available in October...only from
Silhouette Intimate Moments

Take 4 bestselling love stories FREE

Plus get a FREE surprise gift!

Special Limited-time Offer

Mail to Silhouette Reader Service™

3010 Walden Avenue
P.O. Box 1867
Buffalo, N.Y. 14269-1867

YES! Please send me 4 free Silhouette Intimate Moments® novels and my free surprise gift. Then send me 6 brand-new novels every month, which I will receive months before they appear in bookstores. Bill me at the low price of $2.71 each plus 25¢ delivery and applicable sales tax, if any.° That's the complete price and—compared to the cover prices of $3.50 each—quite a bargain! I understand that accepting the books and gift places me under no obligation ever to buy any books. I can always return a shipment and cancel at any time. Even if I never buy another book from Silhouette, the 4 free books and the surprise gift are mine to keep forever.

245 BPA AJH9

Name	(PLEASE PRINT)	
Address	Apt. No.	
City	State	Zip

This offer is limited to one order per household and not valid to present Silhouette Intimate Moments® subscribers. °Terms and prices are subject to change without notice. Sales tax applicable in N.Y.

UMOM-93R

©1990 Harlequin Enterprises Limited

TAKE A WALK ON THE
DARK SIDE OF LOVE WITH

October is the shivery season, when chill winds blow and shadows walk the night. Come along with us into a haunting world where love and danger go hand in hand, where passions will thrill you and dangers will chill you. Silhouette's second annual collection from the dark side of love brings you three perfectly haunting tales from three of our most bewitching authors:

Kathleen Korbel

Carla Cassidy

Lori Herter

Haunting a store near you this October.

Only from 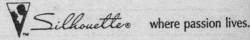 where passion lives.

ROMANTIC TRADITIONS

Paula Detmer Riggs kicks off
ROMANTIC TRADITIONS this month with
ONCE UPON A WEDDING (IM #524), which
features a fresh spin on the marriage-of-
convenience motif. Jesse Dante married
Hazel O'Connor to help an orphaned baby,
underestimating the powers of passion and
parenthood....

Coming to stores in January will be bestselling
author Marilyn Pappano's FINALLY A FATHER
(IM #542), spotlighting the time-honored secret-
baby story line. Quin Ellis had lied about her
daughter's real parentage for over nine years.
But Mac McEwen's return to town signaled an
end to her secret.

In April, expect an innovative look at the
amnesia plot line in Carla Cassidy's
TRY TO REMEMBER.

And ROMANTIC TRADITIONS doesn't stop there! In
months to come we'll be bringing you more
classic plot lines told the Intimate Moments way.
So, if you're the romantic type who appreciates
tradition with a twist, come experience
ROMANTIC TRADITIONS—only in

SIMRT2

INTIMATE MOMENTS®
Silhouette®

SILHOUETTE.... Where Passion Lives

Don't miss these Silhouette favorites by some of our most popular authors!
And now, you can receive a discount by ordering two or more titles!

Silhouette Desire®

#05751	THE MAN WITH THE MIDNIGHT EYES BJ James	$2.89	☐
#05763	THE COWBOY Cait London	$2.89	☐
#05774	TENNESSEE WALTZ Jackie Merritt	$2.89	☐
#05779	THE RANCHER AND THE RUNAWAY BRIDE Joan Johnston	$2.89	☐

Silhouette Intimate Moments®

#07417	WOLF AND THE ANGEL Kathleen Creighton	$3.29	☐
#07480	DIAMOND WILLOW Kathleen Eagle	$3.39	☐
#07486	MEMORIES OF LAURA Marilyn Pappano	$3.39	☐
#07493	QUINN EISLEY'S WAR Patricia Gardner Evans	$3.39	☐

Silhouette Shadows®

#27003	STRANGER IN THE MIST Lee Karr	$3.50	☐
#27007	FLASHBACK Terri Herrington	$3.50	☐
#27009	BREAK THE NIGHT Anne Stuart	$3.50	☐
#27012	DARK ENCHANTMENT Jane Toombs	$3.50	☐

Silhouette Special Edition®

#09754	THERE AND NOW Linda Lael Miller	$3.39	☐
#09770	FATHER: UNKNOWN Andrea Edwards	$3.39	☐
#09791	THE CAT THAT LIVED ON PARK AVENUE Tracy Sinclair	$3.39	☐
#09811	HE'S THE RICH BOY Lisa Jackson	$3.39	☐

Silhouette Romance®

#08893	LETTERS FROM HOME Toni Collins	$2.69	☐
#08915	NEW YEAR'S BABY Stella Bagwell	$2.69	☐
#08927	THE PURSUIT OF HAPPINESS Anne Peters	$2.69	☐
#08952	INSTANT FATHER Lucy Gordon	$2.75	☐

	AMOUNT	$ _____
DEDUCT:	10% DISCOUNT FOR 2+ BOOKS	$ _____
	POSTAGE & HANDLING	$ _____
	($1.00 for one book, 50¢ for each additional)	
	APPLICABLE TAXES*	$ _____
	TOTAL PAYABLE	$ _____
	(check or money order—please do not send cash)	

To order, complete this form and send it, along with a check or money order for the total above, payable to Silhouette Books, to: *In the U.S.*: 3010 Walden Avenue, P.O. Box 9077, Buffalo, NY 14269-9077; *In Canada*: P.O. Box 636, Fort Erie, Ontario, L2A 5X3.

Name: _____

Address: _____ City: _____

State/Prov.: _____ Zip/Postal Code: _____

*New York residents remit applicable sales taxes.
Canadian residents remit applicable GST and provincial taxes.

SBACK-OD

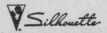